A GAME THAT TWO COULD PLAY

Leah was startled, then shocked, then enraged, when her fiancé left the ballroom with the ravishing Elaine Chandler. She had not imagined that Anthony would dare flaunt his mistress before her on the eve of their betrothal.

At that moment Marcus Halvert, the Earl of Rotherfield, appeared at her side. If Anthony was the most notorious lord in London, Rotherfield was the most feared—yet Leah found his dark good looks strangely and unsettlingly magnetic.

If Leah turned to this man to gain revenge and recompense for Anthony's infuriating insult, who could blame her . . . or save her . . . ?

"Ms. Mills demonstrates an incredible range of talent . . . quickwitted humor and panache . . . and electrifying passion that enhances the Regency format . . . such virtuosity makes her a treasure trove of superlative writing."

—*Romantic Times*

Anita Mills lives in Kansas City, Missouri, with her husband, four children, sister, and seven cats in a restored turn-of-the-century house. A former English and history teacher, she has turned a lifelong passion for both into a writing career.

SIGNET REGENCY ROMANCE

COMING IN JANUARY 1989

Emma Lange
Brighton Intrigue

Jane Ashford
Meddlesome Miranda

Mary Jo Putney
The Controversial Countess

DUEL OF HEARTS

ANITA MILLS

A SIGNET BOOK
NEW AMERICAN LIBRARY

NAL BOOKS ARE AVAILABLE AT QUANTITY DISCOUNTS WHEN USED TO PROMOTE PRODUCTS OR SERVICES. FOR INFORMATION PLEASE WRITE TO PREMIUM MARKETING DIVISION, NEW AMERICAN LIBRARY, 1633 BROADWAY, NEW YORK, NEW YORK 10019.

SIGNET TRADEMARK REG. U.S. PAT. OFF. AND FOREIGN COUNTRIES
REGISTERED TRADEMARK—MARCA REGISTRADA
HECHO EN CHICAGO, U.S.A.

SIGNET, SIGNET CLASSIC, MENTOR, ONYX, PLUME, MERIDIAN and NAL BOOKS are published by NAL PENGUIN INC., 1633 Broadway, New York, New York 10019

First Printing, December, 1988

1 2 3 4 5 6 7 8 9

PRINTED IN THE UNITED STATES OF AMERICA

1

Having just been set down in front of Hookham's lending library in busy Bond Street, Leah Cole breathed the fresh, unseasonably warm air deeply before turning to her companion. "I cannot credit the weather—'tis lovely." Directing the abigail's gaze toward the boxes of flowers that lined the street, she murmured, "I own the crocuses give promise of spring already, and I am glad of it. I hate the dreariness of winter."

"Watch out!"

Leah scarce had time to look up before she froze. The street was crowded with carriages, curricles, and all manner of conveyances, and a young buck, impatient with the delay, was attempting to shoot the gap between a carriage and the curb, with disastrous results. He'd lost control of his horses when the wheel of his smart curricle had jumped the curb, glanced off a lamppost, and careened wildly. Now his ribbons trailed on the ground and the two-seater skimmed along the walkway toward them. Beside Leah, Annie screamed.

At almost the same instant Leah realized her peril, someone came from nowhere, barreled into her, and carried her to the ground. Both she and her abigail rolled to the pavement in a tangle of arms and legs as the curricle wheel passed over the edge of Annie's pelisse. Leah closed her eyes just before she felt the rattle of the axle inches from her head. She heard the crash, the sudden stillness, and then running footsteps and excited chatter. Gingerly she opened her eyes to discover they had survived.

She was pinned to the ground beneath the weight of a man, and she looked up into the brightest blue eyes she'd ever seen. And they were set in the face of an incredibly handsome man. Despite the fact that he was lying on her, she felt her heart beating rapidly, as much from the sight of him as from their narrow escape. Beside her, Annie lay motionless.

"I believe the danger is past," Leah murmured, coming to her senses and struggling beneath him. "And you are on my person."

Tony Barsett stared down into the most arresting pair of gray eyes he had ever seen, and as he too collected himself, he realized the young female beneath him was a beauty. She had lost her chipstraw hat when he had hit her, and it dangled loosely from grosgrain ties that miraculously still clung beneath her chin. Her hair, a glorious honey blond, tumbled in a profusion of curls that escaped from what had been a twisted coil at the back of her head. And her voice was pleasantly husky, the kind that always intrigued a man.

Reluctantly he rolled away and struggled to his feet. Leaning over to assist her, he asked quickly, "Are you hurt? Do you think you have injured anything?"

"Only my dignity," she assured him, smiling. "But Annie . . ." She turned to her abigail, who sat up in a daze. Quickly fumbling in the reticule that dangled from the older woman's wrist, Leah found the vinaigrette, uncapped it, and waved it beneath her nose. The strong fumes seemed to revive the woman. "Poor Annie," Leah clucked sympathetically, "you are unused to such excitement. But you are all right now."

"Oh, miss—I thought we was killed!"

"There's no harm to anything but our clothes. Here . . ." Before Anthony Barsett could intervene, she'd lifted her companion and was busily engaged in brushing her off.

"My pelisse is quite ruined!" the woman wailed, noting for the first time where the curricle wheel had torn it.

"But you are alive. Indeed, our thanks to . . . ?" The girl turned to their rescuer and extended her hand in an almost businesslike gesture. "We are grateful, sir."

"Lyndon—Viscount Lyndon." Even later, Tony was to

wonder how it was that he'd used his title rather than his name. Perhaps it was because he wanted to impress her.

"And I am Leah Cole."

Behind them, the youthful driver of the curricle was still disentangling himself from the wreckage where his vehicle had hit another iron lamppost and overturned. A crowd formed around him, its members evenly divided between loud censure and concern for his well-being. A tall gentleman, distinguished by a cold arrogance that set itself against his handsomeness, stepped down from the carriage that had been sideswiped to start the whole unfortunate affair, and walked toward them.

"Are there any injuries?" he inquired politely, his black eyes taking in the three pedestrians.

"Hallo, Marcus," Tony acknowledged curtly.

"Lyndon." Turning to Leah Cole, the newcomer unbent enough to introduce himself. "I am Rotherfield."

"Leah Cole."

For a moment the earl's interest was whetted by her lack of recognition and then his eyes were veiled. "The young fool scraped my carriage, but there's little enough harm done, I suppose. If any of you needs to be taken up, I shall be happy to oblige."

"No . . . no." Leah met his black eyes squarely, unaware that even the men of his acquaintance avoided them. "My driver will be back directly, sir, for we were but set down to borrow some books." Turning back to Tony, she murmured, "But perhaps Lord Lyndon . . ."

"I was walking, Miss Cole." He'd been watching her, noting her openness with Rotherfield, and a certain suspicion took root in his mind. He stared at her frankly now, his own eyes raking her with jaded experience, taking in the expensive gown she wore, lingering on her pleasing figure, noting her full breasts above her narrow waist, and traveling upward with a knowing smile. Leah Cole was as fine a fancy piece as he'd ever seen.

"Tell me, Lord Lyndon," she asked with sudden coldness, "do you always inspect the females you meet?"

"Only the pretty ones."

"I say, but I am sorry." The redheaded driver, having managed to right his curricle and disentangle his horses, came forward to apologize. Noting the irate expression on the abigail's face and the coldness of the others, his face flushed. "Cow-handed of me, I know. Name's Hawkins—Christopher Hawkins, but I am called Kit."

"Ought to be clapped up!" the older woman fumed at him. "Streets of Lunnon ain't safe with you on 'em—just look what you have done!" she demanded, holding up the tattered corner of her pelisse.

"Well, I thought I could handle 'em—could have, too, but for . . ." He stopped, aware now of Rotherfield. "That is—"

"Precisely," the earl cut in succinctly.

The boy's blush deepened, but with the characteristic self-centeredness of youth, he turned to Anthony Barsett. "How bad do you think it is? I mean, can it be mended, do you think?" he asked anxiously. "It ain't mine, you know—borrowed it from m'uncle, but he don't know it yet." Heaving a heavy sigh, he looked at the pavement for a moment. "Daresay he will now."

"Axle's broken," Rotherfield observed dispassionately, sending another wave of color to the boy's face.

But Tony wasn't attending. His eyes never left Leah Cole as he speculated on his chances. She was turned out as smartly as he'd ever seen one, but if she had been wearing rags, it would have made no difference. Those smoky eyes of hers, that hair, and that voice were enough to turn any man's head. Almost as if she had read his thoughts, she stepped back.

"Come, Annie," she ordered her companion. "As we are scarce presentable, I think we should forgo Hookham's today." Without looking up at Tony again, she nodded. "Again I must thank you for your prompt assistance, my lord. Good day, gentlemen."

"Perhaps I could call on you tomorrow to assure myself you are unhurt?" Tony asked, unwilling to let the delectable Leah go.

Her brief smile revealed the edges of fine, even teeth, but did not warm the smoky eyes. "That will be unnecessary, my lord."

For the first time in his life, Tony had received a set-down from a female, and he did not like it. In his experience, women from the lowest to the highest ranks cast out lures to him, loved him, and forgave him anything. And certainly he'd never been turned aside so definitely. Usually, at the worst of it, they said "maybe." Recovering, he bent to retrieve his beaver-brimmed hat and set it at a rakish angle on his head. "Well, I daresay we shall meet again, Miss Cole."

She appeared to consider the matter and then shook her head. "I should not think it likely, sir." To Rotherfield she extended her hand. "Your offer of a lift was appreciated, my lord. And, Mr. Hawkins, I pray your uncle does not deal too harshly with you."

The three of them stared after her as the two women walked to the corner. A carriage pulled into view and liveried footmen jumped down to assist them. Even from the distance of fifty or sixty feet, Tony could see the coach was sumptuously furnished inside.

"Gawd!" Hawkins breathed. " 'Tis the most expensive thing I have ever seen."

"She is that," Tony agreed.

"Looked like a royal carriage without the crest, didn't it?"

"What? Oh, the coach." Still staring after her, Tony shook his head. "Well, it was not, I assure you. It probably belongs to a nabob," he guessed aloud.

"I have never seen the girl before," Rotherfield murmured beside them.

"Who do you think pays her bills?" Tony asked.

"Why, her father, I should think." Kit Hawkins looked from one to the other of them, and reddened anew at the sardonic gleam in the Earl of Rotherfield's black eyes.

"Hawkins, you are a green one." Tony grinned. "No. I know every eligible female on the Marriage Mart these five years past, and Leah Cole is not one of them. 'Tis as plain as the sun shines that she is a Cyprian of the first rank."

The elegant carriage disappeared around a corner several blocks down the street before Rotherfield murmured softly, "I wonder . . ."

"But wouldn't you have seen her somewhere then?"

"Not necessarily. A dress like that probably cost close

to fifty guineas,'' Tony hazarded knowingly. ''Ten to one, 'tis an old man who keeps her, and that sort never parades 'em about—afraid a young buck'll outbid 'em.'' Reaching to straighten the boy's hat on his head, he confided cheerfully, ''Within the space of a month, Kit Hawkins, that exquisite bit of fluff will be under my protection.''

2

Despite the fact that his coat and trousers were quite ruined, Anthony Barsett presented himself at Davenham House, prepared for the worst from his great-aunt. Although there was a bond of some affection between them, he resented her interest in his affairs. A *grande dame* of the *ton* for as long as he could remember, the dowager duchess had bestirred herself to exert her considerable influence to see him well-established amongst that select group, and she had managed the task well. But she would not leave it at that and continued to meddle in his affairs well past his majority, so much so that she was forever advancing candidates eager to become the next Viscountess Lyndon. And her continuous harping on the subject was fast straining his affection for her into irritation.

" 'Tis about time that you deign to visit an old woman," she greeted him sourly. "But then 'tis to be supposed that your other interests must keep you well-occupied." Her black eyes took in his ruined coat with a disdainful sniff. "In my day, Anthony, a gentleman did not pay morning calls dressed as a ruffian."

He surveyed the old woman with exasperation as he crossed the room toward her. "Well, now I have come, Aunt Hester, despite a very near carriage wreck, and you find me all ears to hear the peal you would read me." His fine blue eyes met hers steadily. "That is why you have summoned me, is it not?"

Hester Barsett Havinghurst, dowager Duchess of Davenham, rose imperiously from her thronelike chair, her gnarled and bony fingers gripping the chased-silver handle of her walking cane so tightly that the protuberant veins rose like dark cords across the back of her skeletal hand. Supporting herself with the stick, she reached to retrieve a folded newspaper from a chairside table. Her thin lips drawn tight with disapproval, her voice strong in contrast to her small, bent frame, she lifted the paper and waved it in his direction.

"This, Tony—'tis of this I would speak!"

Beneath his perfectly contrived blond Brutus, his brow furrowed and then lightened as he took the offending copy. "Oh that," he murmured, suppressing a grin at how well he'd read her intent. " 'Tis old news."

"Old news! A fortune gone this week or last—'tis all the same, is it not?" Her birdlike black eyes flashed as she poked the back of the paper with a bony finger. " 'Tis true enough, from all I have heard of it, Anthony—you have whistled the Lyndon fortune down the wind! Shipping! *Shipping*!" She shuddered with loathing at the word. "I know not how I shall bear it, Tony! 'Twas more than enough for you to engage in trade—the first of our name ever! Four hundred years of Barsetts, and not a one reduced to such . . . such straits! I *told* you no good would come of such nonsense, did I not? But would you listen to an old woman? Of course you would not!"

"Aunt Hester—"

"Do not try to turn me up sweet, Anthony! If you think I mean to bring you about after you have steered your barque into chancy water, I assure you that I do not! No—you'll not lose one farthing of my fortune with your schemes. Trade! Humph!"

His amusement faded in the face of her tirade, and the muscles in his jaw worked to control his anger at being called to book like a small schoolboy. "I assure you I have no such intent, Aunt Hester," he managed through clenched teeth. "My affairs are my own, and I intend to come about on my own."

"How much did you lose?" she demanded, cutting to the heart of the matter. "I had it of Thornhill 'twas fifty thousand pounds, but he cannot have the right of that, for you never had that much at the outset."

"I lost enough, but I am not done up," he snapped irritably. "No matter what you may have heard, my pockets are not to let yet—and so you may tell your gossips."

"Tony . . . Tony. What am I ever to do with you? You take no advice, you refuse my aid—"

"I was not aware that you had offered aid—quite the contrary, in fact," he bit off precisely. "As for advice, I have had a surfeit of it. I am no longer in leading strings, you know."

She knew she'd gone too far, that she'd angered him more than she'd intended. Nodding, she softened the tone of her voice. "All right then—how much did you lose? Perhaps I was overhasty, Tony. I'd not see the last Barsett in Newgate, no matter what the cost, and well you know it."

"I have no wish to discuss it. The ship went down, taking all hands and all goods with it, and that is the end of the matter. I am not without resources despite the loss, Aunt Hester."

"I see." She sighed heavily, indicating that she neither saw at all nor believed what he said. "Very well, I will allow that you are a man grown, Anthony, and as such, you are not bound to follow my advice. You must forgive an old woman's desire to see the last of her blood settled and well-established."

"Aha! And now we get to the true matter at hand, do we not? All right then—which long-toothed female is it that you would foist on me this time?"

"You would not be the first to mend your fortunes by marriage, Anthony," she reminded him stiffly. "But I have long since left off meddling in that basket of yarn, I assure you. My fondest wish is merely that you should find a girl with sufficient character to curb your excesses." Her black eyes were serious as she looked at him. "Do you think me unaware of how 'tis you amuse yourself? Do you think I cannot hear the gossip also? Well, I do, and I cannot like it. Opera dancers and gaming hells cannot bring you the satisfaction of a wife and an heir, despite what you seem to think. I fear that you will become naught but a confirmed rakehell, unable to settle down with one girl."

Her anger dissipated, she reached for the bell-pull and

nodded toward a damask couch. "You will stay for a glass of sherry, will you not? It helps the aches in my bones, you know, and I'd not drink it alone. Thankfully, Bucky's gone to visit a step-cousin or some such creature today, else I'd have to listen to her tell me spirits ain't the thing for a female."

A smile played at the corners of his mouth and his brilliant blue eyes warmed. "You know, Aunt Hester, I think I preferred it when you were angry with me. Now 'twould seem you think to shame me into doing my duty to my name." Nonetheless, he dropped his tall frame onto the couch and lounged easily against the well-padded back.

"And what of that?" she demanded, gesturing to a footman to pull her chair closer to where her great-nephew sat. "Do you think I wish to be in my dotage ere I see the name I was born with carried on? If I do not remind you of your duty on occasion, I fear I shall be in my grave first."

"I have never seen a female I could live with, Aunt," he answered, taking the glass offered him. "And I've no wish to wed any of the insipid misses paraded past me. There are no more Hester Barsetts to be had, else I'd have had one," he added affectionately.

"There's girls aplenty, Tony. Why, Maria Cosgrove told me that she'd never seen so many Incomparables as are out this year. And as for that farradiddle about me, well, be done with you. I ain't the sort to be turned up sweet by nonsense."

"You want to hear about the girls out this year?" he asked wickedly. "I went to the Marchbanks chit's come out to look 'em over, and do you wish to know what I found? They are so afraid of not taking that they have no thoughts of their own, Aunt Hester! The first one would not even allow as it was hot in the place until she discovered if I thought it so. Do you think I want to spend my life having my opinions prated back to me? 'Tis no wonder that full half the *ton* keeps mistresses!"

"Well, they cannot all be like that, Tony. Maria's—"

"Ah, the Cosgrove chit! She does not even read so

much as a scandal sheet—and God forbid she should look at a book!"

"Bluestockings are unfashionable," the old woman reminded him.

"I accept that, but do you know what the chit said to me? I asked if she liked the classics, and she stared blankly through three full measures of the dance before she said, 'Oh, I collect you mean my dress—yes, 'tis fashioned after the Empress Josephine's favorite one.' "

"Well, at least you are looking."

"No. Renfield persuaded me to go to the Marchbanks thing so that he could dangle after one of Lord Larchmont's spotted girls, but nothing came of it when he discovered she did not know a bay from a chestnut."

"Perhaps you should try Almack's. I have heard—"

"Thank you, but at least the Marchbankses offered a creditable supper at their little affair. Almack's, on the other hand, has absolutely nothing but stale cakes and weak lemonade to recommend it."

"Well, you will have to do something if you are to come about," she reasoned. "Don't suppose you have thought to go to Bath to look over the heiresses?"

"I have no desire for a provincial bride."

"All right," she conceded. "I wash my hands of the matter. But if you should ever happen to discover the chit you'd have, I hope you have sense enough to come up to scratch. And 'tis hoped also that she has money."

He set his glass down and reached across to cover her bony fingers with his own. "Do not worry about me, Aunt Hester. I promise you that I am not without resources. And if I ever discover a female who does not bore me beyond belief within a fortnight, I will wed her."

She looked down at his strong, warm hand before answering. "I hope I live long enough to meet her, Tony."

3

Having delivered her still-irate abigail to the solicitous ministrations of Mrs. Crome, the Coles' elderly housekeeper, Leah Cole was in the process of stripping her kid gloves from her hands while still in the wide marble-floored foyer when she noted the door ajar to her father's study. A quick glance at the ornate clock on the mantel of the entry fireplace revealed it to be but a few minutes past three o'clock, a highly suspect time for Jeptha Cole to be at home. But then he'd been a trifle pulled lately, something he chose to deny vehemently when taxed with it. He worked hard to earn her bread, he'd retorted, and was therefore entitled to be tired on occasion. She knew instinctively he was hiding something beneath that gruff exterior he affected, and it worried her.

"Papa?" she inquired tentatively as she pushed the door wider. "Is anything amiss?"

"Here now," he growled from the depths of his large leather chair, "can a man not take his ease one afternoon without having to answer for it? Damme, Leah, but if you think to coddle me, you are wide of the mark, girl!" His expression softened almost immediately even if his voice did not. "Do not be standing there with that injured look—it won't fadge, for one thing—and come tell your papa what you have been doing." As she moved forward, he patted a chair beside him, nodding. "That's the ticket, my love."

"Do not be thinking to fob me off by changing the subject, Papa," she murmured, leaning to plant a kiss on his balding head. "My day is like any other, unlike yours, for you are so seldom at home before 'tis dark."

"Cannot a man come home to see his dearest treasure?" he demanded.

"Since you are known to terrorize every female in this house but me, Papa, I collect you are attempting to turn me up sweet. It will not happen, you know," she added with a wry twist to her mouth. "I have not forgotten that just this morning I was the bane of your life."

"Never said it."

"You did. And if you will not send for Dr. Fournier, I shall."

"Damned Frenchie!" he snorted.

"Well, he *did* improve your gout," she reminded him.

"And starved me to death to do it! No mutton or pork or beef, he says! Humph! A man cannot live on birds, I tell you, Leah," he muttered with feeling. "And he took away my port."

"Not entirely, Papa."

"One glass—only this full." Indicating less than two inches with his thumb and forefinger, he shook his head. "Scarce enough to wet m' throat, and not enough to bother with."

"Fiddle. Do not think I do not know you have been cheating on it." She confronted him with a glint of amusement in her gray eyes, adding, "Your secret is out, I fear, for when I offered poor Mr. Crofton a glass, he nearly choked on it. It was but colored water, Papa."

"I suppose you found the other."

"And poured it out."

"Managing female," he growled.

"Now, do you send for Dr. Fournier, or do I?"

He eyed her with disfavor for a moment and then looked away. "I have already consulted him, if you must pry," he admitted grudgingly.

She stared for a moment, scarcely crediting her ears, for she could not remember his ever willingly seeking out a physician. His gout had taken him to such a pass that he could scarce support his ample frame with a cane to walk, and yet it had fallen to her to summon a doctor, and it had taken threats and tears to make him civil to the little Frenchman. Hiding her shock as best she could, she managed, "And?"

"And he told me to rest an hour or two each afternoon, if you must know everything. I ain't as young as I once was. There—you have the tale now, so leave me be on the matter." His eyes suddenly noted the dirt on her walking dress and the tear in the skirt. "Seems to me, miss, that it should be me taking you to task—what the devil happened to you?"

"A young paperskull thought himself a great whip and lost control of his horses," she answered blithely. "Had it not been for the handsome but somewhat odious Lord Lyndon, Annie and I should have been run down on the street—an ignominious end for two females gone to look for a novel, don't you think?"

"Your levity ill becomes you," he grumbled testily, and then his manner changed abruptly. "Lyndon? Lyndon—where have I heard the name before?" he mused. "Young fellow?"

"Yes, and he is possessed of the most abominable manners, if the truth were told, Papa. Just when I was about to thank him profusely for saving our lives, he . . . well, there is no delicate way to put it, I suppose—he *inspected* me! He looked at me as though I were some sort of Cyprian!"

"Daresay you mistook the matter then," her father said. "Can't have—you don't look like one. Not that I know any," he added hastily, "but I know there ain't a man living as would mistake you for one of them—there ain't."

"But he did. He was positively bold, Papa," she said indignantly. "Most men when you meet them look at your face first, but not Lord Lyndon."

"Lyndon." He rubbed his chin thoughtfully and tried to place the name. "Viscount Lyndon, you say?"

"To be precise, I did not mention it, but yes, I believe he said he was a viscount."

"Ah, I remember now—poor fellow lost his fortune last week when the *Windward* sank, as I heard it. Old family, too—a pity. Well, if he was behavin' peculiar-like, who could blame him, I ask you? Mind's still probably befuddled by the loss."

"He did not appear befuddled in the least," she retorted. "His manners were offensive."

"But you were civil to him?"

"Of course I was civil to him! I was all that was polite."

"Related to the Davenham dukes, I think."

"I should not doubt it—he appeared arrogant enough to be related to Prinny himself."

But Jeptha Cole was no longer listening as he continued to muse aloud, "Aye, the fellow tried his hand at cargo speculation, as I remember, and was in a fair way to turning a handsome profit until this. Can't be a bad lad if he's got a good head on his shoulders. What'd you say he looked like?"

"Actually, I did not really note him," she said, hoping to end the discussion.

"Thought you said he was handsome," he persisted.

"Well, I suppose he is, but his manner of looking at me can only be described as offensive in the extreme."

"He cannot be above twenty-five or so, I'd think."

"Papa, I have no wish to discuss Lord Lyndon."

"Tut—can't a man be curious when his daughter tells him she met a fine buck of the *ton*? It ain't as if you was still a chit in the schoolroom, after all."

"Papa . . ." she said warningly. "If you want the truth of it, I also met the Earl of Rotherfield, and he did not look at me in such a way. Indeed, I liked him the better of the two," she added, knowing full well she would probably never see either of them again.

"Rotherfield!" he snorted. "Now I know you do not know what you are about, for even I know he ain't good *ton*, missy!" For a moment he appeared distracted, and then his expression brightened. "Oh, as you was saying, you went to Hookham's. Yes, yes, well . . . uh, anything else of note happen to you today?" he asked, trying to keep his voice casual.

"Nothing."

"Madame Cecile come today?"

"Yes, though I cannot think how you managed it," she admitted. "After all, 'tis her busiest season, and I can scarce be a credit to her."

" 'Twas money, Leah—money will gain you anything. I had but to dangle my purse in front of her to discover she is as greedy as anyone and more greedy than most.

'Rig out m'girl like a lady,' I told her, and when she allowed as how she was busy, I said I expected to pay the pretty for her services."

Leah sighed, seeing where he was leading her again. "Papa, 'tis foolish to think clothes will make me a lady. No matter how much you wish it, I shall never grace the reception rooms at Almack's, nor will I ever be presented at court. And you must not think I mind it, for I do not. I am not of that world, Papa," she added gently.

"Because I am a Cit." He sighed heavily and nodded. "Aye, I can buy and sell most of the bucks in London, and I am still naught but a Cit to 'em, I suppose." His eyes traveled to the portrait of a lovely blond woman who seemed to be looking down on them with love in her eyes. "But I promised her—I promised Marianna you would have your due, puss—and so I shall."

"But I don't *want* to be a lady! Can you not understand that? Papa, I am what I was born—I am a Cit. Do you think I aspire to routs and balls and masquerades and . . . and whatever else they do?" Her voice gained an impassioned intensity as she paced before him. "It is an empty life, Papa. I watch the ladies come and go from Hookham's almost every week, and as far as I can tell, they are but decorations for rich men's houses." Pausing to collect her argument, she sought the means to explain how she felt about the Quality. "Just yesterday I saw the most pitiful climbing boy—his master was whipping him because he would not climb a chimney that was on fire. Do you think any of the fine ladies stopped? Of course they did not! Do you think they even felt sorry for the child? Well, they passed him as though he did not exist! And if I were to even attempt to enter such a world, they would ignore my existence also."

"Where is the boy now?" he asked suspiciously.

"Monsieur Lebeau is teaching him to work in the kitchen, and he appears to be a clever child. Perhaps you would see he is apprenticed in an easier trade." And in the face of his resigned sigh, she defended what she'd done. "Well, he could not stay with that awful man, after all, and I bought him."

"Leah . . . Leah. Your heart's too soft, girl."

"Papa, there ought to be laws against such things! How can a country that bans slavery allow indentures for small children?"

"There is a law, but it is seldom enforced," he retorted. "Too many fancy lords have narrow chimneys themselves, and without the boys, how would they clean 'em?" Catching her thoroughly disgusted expression, he relented enough to mollify her. "All right, all right—mayhap I can find a place for the boy at the dock, but do not expect me to do it until the India Company's ships come in."

"Thank you, Papa," she murmured demurely.

"Sly puss, ain't you? Ought to bend down and let me box your ears, you know. You are just like your mother, God rest her soul. But I'll tell you what I used to tell her: it ain't the gentle fellows who make fortunes in this world. Old Jeptha didn't get rich by being weak, and don't you forget it."

"Yes, Papa," she responded dutifully, despite having heard the speech more times than she dared count.

"Yes . . . well, did that man-milliner of a dance master come today?" he asked, remembering where they'd been before he'd heard of the chimney sweep. "And can you waltz yet, or am I paying him for nothing?"

"Master Jennings tells me that I am quite his best pupil."

"Do not be using that tone with me, miss! I know you think it an old man's fancy, but I'll see you a fine lady yet—I will. It stands to reason that if every fellow you meet makes a cake of himself, then there's a fancy lord somewheres as would want you." He met her eyes defiantly and nodded emphatically. "There ain't a man alive that don't admire you if he knows you, Leah."

"I'd sooner be a spinster, Papa, than be married for my money," she declared flatly. "And I warn you that you will not persuade me to marry any old fool just because he has a title."

"No, no—of course not. Did I say I wished for an old fool?" he retorted. "Silly chit! I am looking for a real out-and-outer for my girl, I can tell you!"

"You relieve my mind then," she answered sweetly.

"There is no out-and-outer who would have a Cit. No, we shall go on as we have always done, I think, and I will be a comfort to you in your dotage." Reaching to pat his head affectionately, she relented enough to allow, "But it is a harmless enough amusement for you, I suppose."

He sat quiet still for a long time after she left him, wondering where it all would end. He could leave her rich beyond her furthest imaginings, but somehow that was not enough. No, he had to see her settled very soon for his peace of mind. Finally he sighed heavily and raised his head to stare at his dead wife's portrait again, and the girl looked down, smiling at him as she had in his youth. If only Leah could have known her mother, then she would understand how much it meant to him to make her a lady in title as well as manners. Idly he wondered if Marianna would look the same when he saw her again—if somehow they would be as young lovers once more in eternity. It seemed to him that her portrait beckoned him even now.

"Well, Marianna," he said softly, "what say you—shall I inquire as to what sort of man this Lyndon is?" For a moment he thought he could read her answer in her painted eyes. "Aye, damme if I won't do it."

4

The glowing rows of yellow gaslights illuminated St. James Street, inviting Tony to enjoy a gentleman's evening of social entertainment. Having missed his friends Gil and Hugh earlier, he set his glossy top hat at a rakish angle, retrieved his brass-handled walking stick from the floorboard of his curricle, and waved his groom on with the admonition to return precisely at three in the morning, before he set off whistling softly in the direction of White's. Already the windows of the gaming establishments that lined St. James were warm with light, beckoning the elite who had money in their pockets.

After exchanging a few words of greeting with Raggett, the proprietor of White's, Tony handed his hat and stick to Piggles (Mr. Pigg, actually) and made his way through the carpeted salons toward the games in back. As he passed, fellow members of the club looked up from baize-covered tables to hail him.

"Hallo—thought to see you earlier, Tony," Gil Renfield greeted him without looking up. "Got the devil's own luck tonight," he murmured as he cast the dice again, to the appreciative whistle of Hugh Rivington. Raking in the pile of notes, he straightened and nodded. "Gentlemen, I leave you to Hugh—may he be kinder on your purses."

"Not me," Rivington responded. "My pockets are to let until quarter day, and even if they were not, my stomach rumbles for food. Hallo, Tony," he added, rising. "Missed you at Boodle's earlier. Do you sup or play tonight?"

"Both."

"Did you give my regards to the duchess?" Hugh asked curiously. "Can't think why you humor the old girl myself—she don't like me above half. Daresay it's because she's *your* great-aunt by blood and mine only by marriage. Got no expectations of her, you know."

"Aunt Hester will take her blunt to perdition with her before she parts with it," Tony responded, grinning. "But as long as she keeps her oars out of my water, I rub along tolerably with her."

"Called you to book, eh?" Gil cut in. "Thought she would when I read the *Gazette*—told Hugh there'd be the devil to pay when she saw it."

"She cannot abide anything that loses money," Rivington observed dryly. "I've not a doubt but she read a rare peal over you."

"She did." Unwilling to discuss his fortune or supposed lack of it with anyone, Tony changed the subject abruptly. "Tell me something," he asked casually, "either of you ever hear of a Leah Cole?"

Hugh furrowed his brow for a moment, then shook his head. "Don't think so. Why?"

"Gil?"

"Not that I recall—who is she?"

"The fairest Cyprian of them all, by the looks of it. I cannot remember ever having seen a lovelier creature," Tony declared solemnly. "I mean to have her."

"You want to enter it in the books? Three to five that Lyndon mounts—what's her name . . . Leah Cole?—that Lyndon mounts Leah Cole for his next mistress?" Hugh asked Gil.

"You must think me a veritable babe," Gil retorted. "A man'd be a fool to bet against it, and well you know it. If she's female, Tony'll have her set up snug in a week."

"Your confidence reassures me, but I'd as lief not have it bandied about," he warned Hugh. "I have a distinct aversion to being the latest *on-dit*, thank you. I am not, however, against supper," he added, his disclosure about Leah Cole at an end.

"Egad—there's Rotherfield!" Gil hissed.

A ripple of silence traveled before the tall, austerely clad man, and a low murmur followed him. That he was immensely unpopular with the gentlemen of his class never seemed to weigh with the earl. Tony watched him with grudging admiration, an admiration not shared by many members of the *haut ton*, and wondered how it was that he had the courage to show his face. He'd killed not one man, but rather three, and all over someone else's wife, an unpardonable sin, and then to compound his error, he'd returned to England, expecting to go on as though nothing had happened. At first, there'd been a cry to ban him from the clubs, but there were none foolish enough to tell him. It had been decided more or less amongst everyone that the best course of action was simply the cut indirect, although there were those who argued it was as dangerous to ignore him as it was to speak to him.

When he drew even with them, his black eyes met Tony's for a moment. "Your servant, Lyndon," he murmured in that cold voice of his.

"Hallo, Marcus," Tony answered easily while Gil and Hugh drew back perceptibly, their distaste for Rotherfield all too plainly written on their faces.

"It surprised me to see you about today. I'd more than half-expected you to take a repairing lease in the country after I read the *Gazette*. But then one cannot always believe what one reads, can one?"

"Not much of it, anyway, and almost none of what one hears," Tony responded.

"How true. You know there are those who have you three-quarters of the way to Newgate already."

"I never dignify gossip, Marcus. Did you come to play?"

"Actually, I had thought to observe your game. I do not suppose you have discovered the fair Leah's direction, have you?"

"No, and I would not share it with you if I had. As for my game, 'tis my intent to sup first, but you are welcome to join me later," Tony offered.

"Not tonight." With a slight inclination of his black head, Rotherfield moved on, leaving Gil to mutter, "Can't think why they let him in—fellow's as cold as they come. By the looks of it, he'd as lief run a man through as talk to 'im."

" 'Tis what he would have you think," Tony retorted, his eyes still on the earl's back.

"Deuced unpleasant sort, anyway," Hugh decided. "But then he don't waste his breath talking to me. Wonder why he came if he didn't want to play?"

"To discover if I found La Belle Cole," Tony guessed.

"Talks to anyone when it suits him—whether they wish for the discourse or not." Gil shook his head as he turned from contemplating the earl to Tony. "Deuced silly to offer to play him—nobody comes about at his expense, you know."

"I have played him before."

"But under different circumstances. Now you cannot afford to lose—gives him the edge, you know," Hugh observed dryly. "And the man is dangerous when he calls the tune."

"Thank you, Hugh—I will try to remember that," Tony muttered sarcastically. "Your belief in me is comforting."

"It ain't that, Tony—'tis just that you got a hot temper, and I'd hate to see—"

"I know very well what you mean to say, and I'd as lief not hear it. If you think me foolish enough to call him out, you are empty in the cockloft, my friend. Now, do we sample the lobster patties or not?"

Both of them murmured a hasty assent, with Gil attempting the role of peacemaker. "No sense quarreling about what ain't going to happen, is there? I say we eat and hear more about this Cole female."

Tony let himself into his town house quite late, or early, as the case could be argued, depending on whether the one counting the hour was master or servant. The hall was deserted and the candles in the sconces nearly guttered. Loosening his cravat, he groped his way to his library, where he lit the brace of candles on the table. One of these days, he was going to have to consider gas lighting, he supposed as he sorted through the papers left by his secretary. Usually John Maxwell was a prince when it came to doing almost everything, and Tony hoped for success in his quest. Squinting in the flickering light, he read and discarded half a dozen sheets of paper until he discovered what he looked for—the Scotsman's bold scrawl fairly leapt from the page beneath the heading "Leah Cole." But as he read further, Tony was destined for disappointment. The usually thorough Max wrote merely:

> Cannot determine anything about a Miss Leah Cole, a Mrs. Leah Cole, or anything similar beyond what is already known to you. She has a subscription to Hookham's library, but the proprietor refuses to divulge her direction or any information about the young woman. A clerk there did make it known to me that it is Miss Cole's custom to frequent the establishment weekly, usually on Thursdays, but that she missed today.
>
> I also took the liberty of inquiring of the various theaters and opera companies, but there is no one of her description amongst them. Aside from that, there are Coles too numerous to note amongst the lower classes, and she could be relation to any of them. It is my considered opinion that the greatest likelihood of encountering this person again is at the library itself.
>
> Y'r obedient, etc.
> John Maxwell

Crumpling the paper, Tony threw it in a ball across the room to vent his frustration. It was impossible that any female who looked like Leah Cole could be unknown. A girl like that had to have other pursuits besides reading. The image of her floated before him as clearly as if he were seeing her now, and he felt that dryness of mouth he associated with desire. Moving to a sideboard, he poured himself a glass of sherry from a decanter and contemplated his next move. He could not, would not, let Leah Cole elude him. Not even if Rotherfield were interested in her himself.

Finally he took a seat at the table and reached for the

inkstand. Leaning close to see in the yellowish light, he dipped his pen and instructed Max:

> I do not care if it becomes necessary to employ runners—I would have Miss Cole found. You have my leave to do all that is necessary to the search, and as you are a resourceful fellow, I quite depend on a satisfactory conclusion. Perhaps discreet inquiries of solicitors may yield information as to whether anyone has recently settled money on her or whether a house has been let for her.
>
> Lyndon

It would be like looking for a particular grain of sand on a beach, he knew, but he had to find her. And a female like that simply could not disappear without a trace.

Draining his glass, he leaned back in his chair and contemplated the problem. Already there was a faint rosy glow of dawn filtering through the crosspanes, a reminder that he ought to seek his bed. But he was strangely exhilarated at the mere thought of another meeting with the lovely Leah, and he had to admit he'd not felt such a strong and immediate attraction for any beautiful woman before—the feeling was as intense as the first calf-love of his salad days.

5

Despite his best efforts, it was a full week before Tony saw Leah Cole again, and then he had to haunt Hookham's on a Thursday morning to do it. Lingering over a subscription card, he kept an eye on the door, hoping she meant to come despite the light gray drizzle that enveloped the city. Impatient, he checked his watch several times in the course of an hour, until he was certain the rain had dissuaded her. Reluctantly he tucked his first selection under his arm and gave up. Feeling quite foolish about having wasted his morning, he emerged into the street to whistle for his driver just as the elegant black-lacquered carriage pulled up to discharge its passengers. He congratulated himself on this stroke of fortune and turned back, adjusting his beaver hat jauntily on his head as he waited for her to step down.

A glimpse of a slim stockinged ankle came first, followed by a lithe body clad in one of those simple muslin dresses whose very simplicity denoted expense. She twitched the narrow skirt down over slim hips and reached to straighten an altogether fetching chipstraw bonnet over the honey-blond curls that peeped from beneath its brim. She saw him then, and her eyes widened a fraction before meeting his coolly. She spoke first. "Good morning, Lord Lyndon."

"You are out early, Miss Cole," he acknowledged with his most winning smile.

"But of course. I have it on strictest authority that no lady dares venture into Bond or St. James Street after noon, my lord." There was the barest hint of a challenge in her low voice.

"And why do you think that is, Miss Cole?" he quizzed her.

"It is obviously because gentlemen of fashion seldom rise before noon—or so I am told. This way there can be no untoward discourse between the sexes. That, I suppose, is reserved for soirees, routs, and balls—and Almack's, of course."

His smile broadened. "You cannot have ever been to Almack's if you think that."

"I have never been to Almack's," she admitted candidly. "And I cannot quite think I should like the place."

He thought he detected a hint of defiance in the jut of her chin. "I am sure you would not—I think it rather stuffy myself."

"Yes, well . . . you remember Annie, do you not?" She turned to her abigail, murmuring, "Are you quite ready? Do you have the books?"

"You do not appear to have suffered any injury from young Hawkins' wreck," he hastened to add, unwilling to let her go.

"I did not."

"You look well." He felt as green as a boy just come down from Oxford for the first time.

"I am never ill, my lord, nor am I given to taking to my bed with imagined ailments. Now, if you will excuse us, I am determined to obtain a book that Mr. Parkins has reserved for me. Good day, my lord."

For the second time in as many meetings, she had coolly dismissed him, something that never happened to him. Moving with alacrity to get the door, he bowed slightly. "After you, Miss Cole. Actually, I just took out a subscription myself—perhaps you could recommend an edifying book?"

"Edifying?" she appeared to consider, then shook her head. "No. It is not likely that our tastes would be similar in the least."

Piqued—and even more intrigued than ever—he let her pass. Nearly every other female of his acquaintance would have artfully batted her lashes, spoken archly, fanned herself prodigiously, or otherwise flirted with him, but Leah Cole was obviously unimpressed, a singularly unexpected circumstance. Telling himself she could be merely seeking to whet his interest by her indifference, he decided to persevere.

He was surprised by the obsequious treatment she received from the proprietor, who came out from behind the desk to greet her personally. As he watched, three volumes were produced from a shelf and handed to her. Tony moved closer to peer over her shoulder.

"*Glenarvon*? My dear Miss Cole, 'tis naught but a thinly veiled pack of lies written for revenge. Caro Lamb—"

She stiffened and her expression grew a trifle pained. "If you do not mind, Lord Lyndon, I would very much rather read it myself. Since I do not personally know any of the principals, I shall merely be diverted."

"You read romances then?"

"Actually, I read anything." Turning back to the old man, she spoke in that low, husky voice Tony found so pleasing. "Thank you, Mr. Parkins. Annie wishes to borrow *Mansfield Park* again, if it is available."

"Oh, miss!"

"Nonsense, Annie—'tis my treat for you."

A clerk approached Tony with an offer of help, and for want of any other excuse, he ordered a volume of Shakespeare's sonnets, and tried to overhear Leah Cole as she spoke pleasantly with the proprietor. This time, he was going to learn her direction if he had to follow her home.

"Good day, Mr. Parkins," he heard her say. "And good day, my lord."

"Wait!"

He grabbed his books and started after her, catching up with her on the sidewalk. When she turned around, he favored her with another smile. "Actually, Miss Cole, I came in hopes of seeing you again," he admitted.

He was rewarded with a faintly skeptical lift of her eyebrow. "But whatever for? You do not even know me, sir."

"Ah, but I have hopes of remedying that. Indeed, I thought perhaps I might call on you now that you are recovered—unless of course you fear my doing so might displease your . . ." He paused to make his meaning clear without saying it. "And if 'tis impossible to meet there, I'd take you for a turn around the park, where none need know of it but ourselves."

"I do not think—"

"If not today, then perhaps tomorrow—or Saturday even. I pray you will not be hasty until you hear my offer."

She had not the least notion of his meaning, but she knew full well that gentlemen did not offer to take ladies up without paying calls on them first. And she could not quite forget the positively brazen way he'd looked at her earlier.

"I am sorry, my lord, but—"

"Look, I do not know what arrangement you have with your current protector, but—"

"Lord Lyndon, I believe you must be mistaken," she cut in coldly as she caught his meaning. "I have no wish to further this acquaintance. Good day, sir."

She'd spoken so abruptly that he wasn't certain he'd made himself quite plain. The chit had rejected him before he could even make the offer! Moreover, she'd wasted no words in dismissing him in no uncertain terms. Surprised, he snapped, "Perhaps 'tis you who are mistaken, Miss Cole. I am interested in making you a generous offer, and, unlike your current protector, I would not be averse to showing you about—taking you to the opera, theater, that sort of thing. A woman of your looks should not be hidden away. You are meant to be admired, my dear."

Mistaking her outraged silence for consideration of his offer, he moved closer and reached for her hand. She flushed to the roots of her hair when he touched her, and jerked away angrily. Beside her, her abigail gasped at his effrontery.

"Are you offering me *carte blanche*, my lord?" Leah Cole demanded awfully. "For if you are, you have entirely exceeded the bounds of decency!" Biting off each word and spitting it at him, she concluded with cold fury, "Let me make myself quite plain, sir—I neither wish for nor welcome your protection. So you see, you have quite wasted your time waiting for me when it could have been spent searching the gutters. Come on, Annie."

Angered by the finality in her voice, Tony grasped her arm. "On your high ropes, eh, Miss Cole? Do you think I cannot tell what you are? And do not be trying to pass yourself off as Quality, for it won't fadge! This is Tony Barsett—I have seen your kind before. Now, let us be reasonable—"

"Reasonable? Listen to me, you insufferable oaf! I was prepared to assume you merely offensive, but now I think you are escaped from Bedlam!"

"How much do you want?"

"*And* you are obtuse in the extreme! If you do not unhand me this instant, Lord Lyndon, I will set up such a screech that you'll regret it. I do not know what sort of loose screw you are, but you are definitely empty in the cockloft!"

"Coming it too strong, Miss Cole!" he snapped. "I am making you a reasonable offer—what will it take to get you?"

"Do you understand plain speaking, sir?" she demanded angrily. "I am not a Cyprian but a Cit!"

"Mr. Parkins! Mr. Parkins!" The woman Annie ran back into Hookham's for help while a small crowd of interested bystanders gathered. Two coachmen jumped down from Leah's carriage and advanced on Tony. Feeling the fool, he dropped his hand and stepped back, trying to regain his lost dignity. "Your pardon then. I have obviously mistaken the matter."

"Obviously." She looked down to where he'd held her arm, and her voice grew even colder. "I am a Cit," she repeated, "and a proud one at that. For the last time, good day."

"Miss Cole—"

"Good day," she repeated firmly. "James, hand me up, if you please." When one of the coachmen looked as though he'd like to take his fancy lordship down with his fives, she shook her head. "No, leave him be, Thomas—Lord Lyndon is dangerously deranged."

Once home, Tony relived every moment of the humiliating experience until he could stand it no longer. He'd made a cake of himself, and for the life of him, he could not quite decide how he'd come to do it. He'd meant merely to discover her direction, to converse with her, and to pursue her in leisurely fashion, but some devil in him could not wait, and he'd blurted out his intent like a green youth. He, Tony Barsett, the accomplished flirt, had succumbed to those gray eyes like a boy in the first throes of summer love.

And for the life of him, he could not fathom why he'd done it. If only she'd played the game—played the coquette a little—then there would be less to blame. But she hadn't. She hadn't encouraged him in the least. And in his eagerness to have her, he'd overlooked the obvious: he did not know her because she was a Cit. Drinking deeply of a glass of sherry, he stared morosely into the empty fireplace.

The door creaked open beneath a knock behind him. Reluctantly he swung his tall frame around. "What is it?"

"My lord . . . ?" It was the footman, Dilkes, easing into the room like a rabbit ready to run. "My lord, there is a person here to see you."

"Then send him away."

"He was most insistent—said his name was Jeptha Cole, sir, and that he had business of some importance with you."

Jeptha Cole. For a moment Tony couldn't place the name, and then recognition dawned. Old King Cole, they called him in honor of the fortune he'd made at the docks. His fleet of trading vessels plied the seas independently of the India Company, carrying cargoes of sugar, Spanish tobacco, Jamaica rum, timber, and rice. But what the deuce was he doing at Lyndon House? Although Tony had heard of him, they'd never actually met.

Then a horrible suspicion reared in his mind. Jeptha Cole. Cole, as in Leah Cole. With the perversity of one who seeks punishment, Tony nodded. "Send him in—and bring another bottle and a glass." Resolutely he drained the last of his sherry and prepared to face an irate father.

"Lord Lyndon?"

Tony acknowledged the greeting with a nod. "Mr. Cole?"

"Aye."

Cole was shorter than he'd imagined him to be—a plump, plainly dressed, balding man with sharp, penetrating eyes. He crossed the room to pump Tony's hand perfunctorily, and stated without preamble, "I believe you have made the acquaintance of my daughter, Leah."

The wine could not prepare him for the impact of those words. To hide his embarrassment over the earlier incident, Tony rose and gestured to the nearest chair, offering, "Er . . . would you care to take a seat and have some sherry?"

"Damme if I won't. Sit yourself." Cole dropped his bulk into the deep leather upholstery and drew out his handkerchief to mop his brow. "Fine-looking girl, my Leah—don't favor me at all," he began without preamble. "Looks like her mother, my late wife, God rest her soul." Looking across at Lyndon's totally arrested expression, he hastened on. "Oh, do not be thinking I mean to waste your time, my lord, 'cause I don't."

Cole reached to take the glass of sherry from the footman and waited for the fellow to withdraw. Tasting the wine, he savored it, nodding his approval. "Good stuff, my lord. Here, take a seat yourself, that I may look at you. Aye, that's better. Thing is, Leah's my only issue, my lord," he explained between sips. "Been reared like a lady—governesses, abigails, ladies' maids, tutors, dance masters, music masters, modistes—everything money can buy her. 'Course she ain't a lady, 'cause I'm a Cit—ain't ashamed of it—that's the way of it, you know. But she *ought* to be a lady."

Pausing to drain the glass, he sighed. "Promised her mother: 'Our girl's going to have a title,' I told her—reason I named her Leah, I liked the sound of it—Lady Leah, you know."

"I fail to see—"

"Run off your legs, ain't you? Well, I ain't! Jeptha Cole's got the blunt to bring you about, Lord Lyndon, and to do it handsomely." Leaning forward, the old man stared at Tony from beneath thick, brushy brows that contrasted incongruously with his shiny head. "Aye. When Leah came home last week and said she'd met you, I knew I'd heard of you. Made a few inquiries myself, if you want the truth of it, my lord. And now that I see you, I know I am right."

"Mr. Cole, I assure you—"

"No, no," the older man interrupted, "let me open my budget afore you answer me. My Leah's a good girl—not too biddable, I admit it, but good-hearted. Pretty too. She won't disgrace you with her manners or her appearance, I promise you. And don't you worry none that I am the encroaching kind—Jeptha Cole knows what he is. I'd be as out of place at your fancy balls as you would be in my docks."

For a moment Tony was stunned. "Am I to understand you are offering me your daughter, Mr. Cole?" he asked when he found his voice.

The old man nodded. "Good business arrangement for you—your title for my money. But if you wasn't interested, then let me tell you that there's an earl that's pretty badly dipped, maybe worse than you."

"Mr. Cole—"

"Ain't too high in the instep for the likes of Jeptha Cole, are you? You know, if you wasn't such a handsome devil, I'd go for him anyway. I mean, an earl's an earl, ain't he? And I know he'd take my offer—headed for debtors' jail, for one thing." His eyes were fixed on Tony's face as though he meant to see his thoughts. "But there's one thing wrong with him: he ain't the sort of husband to take a young girl's fancy, if you take my meaning, and you, me fine buck, fit that bill."

Stunned by the offer, it took Tony several seconds to realize Cole was indeed serious. Impatient at the delay, the old man snapped, "What think you—she ain't good enough for the Barsett name?"

"You cannot have mentioned this to her," Tony decided.

" 'Course I did not! Had to see you first, didn't I?"

"I do not think—"

"Then hear me out," Cole interrupted again. "I've got forty thousand that says she's as fine as any lady. And that's but the settlements, Lyndon. Leah stands to inherit more than thrice that and more again when I'm gone.''

''Forty thou . . .'' Tony opened his mouth and closed it abruptly as his brain assimilated the enormity of the offer.

''Thought that might bring you around.'' The old man nodded smugly.

''I doubt your daughter would welcome my suit,'' Tony admitted in bald understatement.

''D'ye think I made my fortune with a pea brain? 'Course she ain't going to like it! But she'll come around—bound to when she gets a better eyeful. You look like one of them damned Greek heads Elgin brought back—the ones he wants to tax us for—for one thing, and I hear you are well-versed in the petticoat line, which ought to help,'' he digressed briefly. ''Bound to know how to please my girl, Lyndon—bound to!''

He lowered his voice and leaned closer. ''But I won't have you trifling with her affections, you understand? She ain't ever to hear of any other lights-o'-love—a woman don't take kindly to that sort of thing. Be discreet, Lyndon—be discreet—'tis all I ask.''

''Mr. Cole, I am trying to tell you that she has taken me in dislike,'' Tony interrupted patiently.

''Aye, she did mention as how you was overbold with her when you met,'' Jeptha Cole allowed. ''But females get queer notions, don't you know it? A little address, a few compliments—she'll come to see it our way—you can take Jeptha Cole's word for it.''

Tony thought of Leah Cole as last he'd seen her and knew she would refuse such a match out of hand. Besides, his pockets were far from let, rumors notwithstanding, and he was not certain any fortune was worth the end of his salad days. Offering to set Leah Cole up as his mistress was one thing, marrying her quite another. There was no way to wrap it up in clean linen—the girl, however beautiful, was still a Cit. And if his great-aunt complained of trade, he could well imagine her reaction to the lovely Leah.

When Tony didn't answer, Jeptha Cole wondered if he'd mistaken his man. The Quality was queer in some respects—sometimes it seemed they'd rather go to Newgate than rub elbows with the merchant class. "Tell you what, my lord—come dine with us tonight," he coaxed. "You don't have to give me an answer until then. And once you see my Leah at her best, I think you'll be pleased to take her."

"You do not give a man much time," Tony muttered.

"I may not have much time, my lord." Cole touched his chest apologetically. "D'ye think I'd go about it like this if I did? Damned Frenchie doctor says the heart's bad—got to rest more, he says," he snorted. "Well, I cannot. But I mean to see my girl settled, and I'd like to see a grandson ere I go—gives a man pride to know his blood goes on."

Tony could almost see the look on her face when her father presented him as a prospective husband, and decided that alone would be worth the dinner. And he had to admit that the mere thought of her was enough to send his pulses racing.

"I am promised to dine with friends at White's," he began slowly, and as the older man's face fell, he relented. "All right, I'll come, but I don't . . ."

Pleased with the apparent success of his mission, Jeptha Cole smiled broadly. "Just wait until I tell my Leah—a viscountess!" Then, catching sight of Tony's frown, he remembered himself and sobered. "Well, that's not to say you'll take her, of course," he added hastily. "But I'm a fool if you can look at her and not think her worthy of a title, my lord."

6

"*Lyndon*?" Leah screeched indignantly at the mention of his name. "The man's a dashed loose screw! No, I could not even be civil to him—no."

"Aye, you will. I asked him to dine with us tonight, and he has accepted," her father told her smugly.

"*Tonight*? Papa, how *could* you?" Jutting her chin mulishly, she met her father's eyes defiantly. "I shall keep to my room then," she declared. "I refuse to sit at the same table with him."

"Now, now, there's naught to dislike in the fellow, I assure you. I daresay 'tis all a mistake on your part, my dear, for—"

"A mistake on *my* part? Papa, you have no notion how 'twas!" Her voice rose dangerously and her gray eyes flashed angrily. "You were not there!"

"Well, you were overset by the curricle, no doubt," he said soothingly.

"It was no such thing!" she sputtered. "And . . . and even if I was, that does not account for his odious behavior today. The man had the . . . the *effrontery* to insinuate that I was some sort of lightskirt! He offered me *carte blanche*—said he'd be generous to me—to *me*, to your daughter, Papa! And it wasn't even as if he knew me! Are you so lost to propriety that you would expect me to entertain the lecher here?"

"Now I know you are mistaken," he pointed out mildly. "Can't have offered you a slip of the shoulder even—he's got no money, Leah. Very good sort of a fellow, actually, the way I see him."

"Very good sort . . . the way . . . Papa, you are quite

certain we are speaking of the same gen . . . the same *man*?'' she choked.

''Ain't but one of 'em.'' He was positive. ''Devilish handsome fellow—too pretty by half, actually, looks like that Greek . . . what's his name?''

''You are thinking of Alexander the Great most probably,'' she answered dampeningly. ''And even if he does, that cannot compensate for his total lack of manners!''

''Now, now, puss . . .'' He attempted to mollify her. ''If he acted queer in the attic, which I don't admit he would, then it must've been over his losses—fellow lost everything when his ship sank a couple of weeks back, like I told you. You ought to pardon anything under the circumstances—I mean, stands to reason he ain't thinking clearly just now.''

For once in her life, Leah was bereft of speech. Unable to believe her father would dismiss Viscount Lyndon's insult to her so lightly, she paced the floor to cool her temper.

'' 'Tis all over London, Leah—fellow ain't got a feather left to fly with,'' he continued in the same vein. ''Heard where he's taken to the gaming hells to bring himself about—''

''And you would have me be civil to a . . . a hardened gamester, Papa? Are you so taken with this . . . this *unprincipled* rakehell's title that you will forgive him anything?'' she demanded.

''Leah . . . Leah . . .'' He extended his hands again to placate her. ''I would see he does right by my girl, and well you know it.''

''I will not dine with him.''

''Have to—that is, he is expecting to see you, my dear,'' he informed her patiently. ''Went to see his lordship just this afternoon—told 'im I'd bring 'im about, pay his debts and settle on him handsomely.''

As his meaning sank in, she stopped pacing and spun around. ''You *what*?'' she demanded awfully.

He hadn't meant to give her his news quite so abruptly, and he could have bitten his tongue for saying it, but there was no help for it now, he supposed. Nodding, he plunged into his scheme. ''He'll make you a lady, Leah.

You ought to have been born one, you know—ten times prettier than them that are—and it's my fondest wish to see you fixed in society ere I am gone. Thought to be choosy," he went on as the wrath in her eyes increased, "but there ain't too many lords as wants to mix with Jeptha Cole, and my time's passing, Leah. Now, Lyndon's fine-looking—got a good, aristocratic bloodline too—and he can't be too nice in his tastes if he is to come about by marriage."

"You offered Lord Lyndon money to marry me?" The color drained from her face momentarily as she faced him, and her voice dropped to a husky whisper. "Papa, how *could* you?" And then it rose again to a near-shout, and the flush returned to her cheeks. "Of all the humiliating circumstances . . . Well, I won't do it! D'you hear me?"

"Leah . . . Leah . . ."

"No! Not only will I not consider him eligible, I will not even come down to see him," she declared flatly.

"Aye, you will—my heart is set on the match."

"Papa, are you *daft*? I tell you the man has insulted me beyond bearing, and you tell me you have offered him money to marry me!"

"Make you a viscountess, my dear," he maintained stubbornly.

"And I do not care if he could make me a royal duchess! I'd sooner wed Prinny himself than Lord Lyndon—do you hear me?"

"Aye, I hear you—and so does everyone else in this house." His own patience at an end, he advanced on her. "Now, let me tell you something, missy—I have not paid for all these fancy lessons to see you wasted on a nobody!"

"Perhaps I should prefer a nobody," she sniffed.

It was an idle threat and Jeptha Cole knew it—he'd not guarded his daughter carefully, refusing to send her away to school even, for nothing. "You don't know one! You listen to your papa, missy—I promised your dying mother you'd have what was due you, and so you shall! I have let you indulge yourself in those silly novels and all manner of foolishness, and now 'tis time to pay up. I have turned away offers every day from men who have not even seen you—rich men, too—while I waited for a titled lord. Well, the time is now! I have found the one I want."

"But I don't want him! Please, Papa—"

"You ain't no simpering miss, Leah! You are nigh to twenty and 'tis time you wed. You will be pleased to be all that is civil to Lord Lyndon!"

"Papa, I have taken him in active dislike. Surely—"

"Would you rather have Rosswell? He's nigh to fifty, if he's a day, but he'd take you in a trice. Which is it, missy—countess to an old earl, or viscountess to a young viscount?"

"Neither!"

"Leah . . ." He spoke in a calmer voice, but the veins stood out ominously on his shining head. "I did not make my fortune by being soft. Do not make me treat you as I would any other. Indulge me in this—use Lyndon to your advantage, Leah. Wed him and live your life as a lady," he coaxed.

"Lord Lyndon is a rake and a gamester, Papa—and an odious person in the bargain. I do not care how pure his blood is—the man himself is beneath contempt."

"Then change him!" he snapped, abandoning his brief effort at reasoning. "Bring him to heel with my money, if you will, and make what you want of him! I tell you my mind is set on him!"

She knew it was useless to argue with her father when he used that tone to her, and further words would only make him more adamant. No, the only way to circumvent his ridiculous plan would be to discourage Lyndon himself, and if his lordship were indeed in such straitened circumstances, that task could prove difficult.

"What time is he to arrive?" she asked finally.

"Now, that's the girl I like to see, Leah." His voice softened perceptibly, and the harsh lines on his face relaxed at her apparent capitulation. "He comes at eight, and I have already instructed that Frenchie cook to provide an elegant repast, you can be sure—'Make something unpronounceable for his lordship,' I told 'im, 'and don't be stintin' on the expense.' Damned fellow would have it that he could not do so on late notice, but I gave him the right of it,'' he grumbled. ''It ain't a wonder that they lost the war if they cannot run a tighter establishment than that—'tis the French character, that's what it is!'' His voice dripped with disgust until he remembered the main point of Lyndon's visit. ''Yes . . . well, that ain't got nothing to do with you, my dear. You run along and put on some of that finery I've ransomed. And do not forget to have your dresser pinch those cheeks for you—'tis too pale by half you are, and I'd not have Lyndon think you unhealthy.''

''Yes, Papa,'' she murmured with feigned docility.

Her whole body seething at the thought of meeting Lord Lyndon again, she sought her chamber and plotted her strategy. So Lyndon thought to look her over like a horse at Tattersall's before he bought? Well, she'd give him something to look at, all right. She did not have much time, to be sure, but she intended to make an impression he would not forget.

Calling for her dresser the moment she crossed the threshold, she ordered, ''Find the paste and rouge pots, Jeanne—I think Annie had some when she threw her hat over the windmill for Mr. Thirkell's second footman—and rip the lace from the bodice of my blue dress, if you please.''

''The lace? But, mademoiselle, 'twill be indecent!''

''Let us hope so,'' Leah muttered under her breath. ''If Lord Lyndon would see a lady, I mean to show him a harpy—'tis what he thinks I am anyway.'' Aware of the little dresser's shocked expression, she added forcefully, ''And I would have all the tall plumes you can discover.''

7

It was precisely at eight o'clock that Anthony Barsett lifted Jeptha Cole's brass knocker. Located in Hans Town, the house reflected the prosperity of the merchant class, with Corinthian pilasters and cornices across the wide porch, huge carved double doors beneath an arch of leaded glass, and exterior proportions that were both pleasing and ostentatious.

As the uniformed butler opened the doors to him, Tony glimpsed the wide expanse of hall, its highly polished rose marble floor reflecting the lights of the multitiered chandelier above. Stepping inside, he could not resist the temptation to look around him, and he was surprised at the tasteful elegance of the merchant's home.

As he looked up, Leah Cole came out into the hall above him and started down the steps, and the sight of her made him wince. Her slim fingers seemed to skim lightly over the polished cherrywood of the curved banister as she descended, her carriage erect, her head held high. She was dressed in a gown of deep blue moiré taffeta, which rustled seductively with each step she took but it was the bodice, or rather the lack of it, which caught his attention immediately. It was as though it had been designed to display her charms—deeply and widely cut, exposing the crevice between her breasts just short of baring the mounds themselves. The gown was as good as sleeveless, with but tiny puffs at the shoulders, giving Tony a good glimpse of creamy neck, throat, bosom, and arms. As his eyes traveled upward, he could scarce credit what he saw, for she'd rouged her cheeks and reddened her lips with the liberal hand of a brothel procuress. And above her painted face, her dark blond hair was a mass of corkscrew curls à la Medusé, springing forth wildly, and above the disarray, rising like a phoenix, was a bizarre assortment of curled ostrich plumes.

"Miss Cole," he managed, despite a twitch at one corner of his mouth.

She stopped mid-stairs at the sound of his voice, and her body stiffened noticeably. A frown of displeasure, much like that of one forced to do something distasteful, crossed her face momentarily. "Lord Lyndon," she acknowledged with a barely civil nod. Her gray eyes traveled over him, taking in the exacting cut of his deep blue woolen coat, his snowy cravat done in a fall of his own design above a crimson silk waistcoat, his smooth-fitting narrow pinstripe trousers, and his plain leather pumps, all a sharp contrast to the affectations of the wealthy merchants' sons she knew. Her eyebrow rose a fraction, betraying her surprise.

"Well, do you come down that I may apologize, or do I come up?" he asked finally. "I shall feel like the veriest cake up there, but I am willing to lie prostrate at your feet for a well-deserved kick, Miss Cole."

"I would not advise it, my lord. I should kick you down the stairs, I fear," she responded acidly. "Indeed, I should relish the task." Her hand still on the railing, she negotiated the last few steps, being careful to balance her outlandish headdress.

"I am quite sorry, you know," he murmured, now fighting to suppress an outright grin. "I can see now that I quite mistook the matter. I—"

"I assure you there is no need for this, my lord," she cut in abruptly.

"Then you will forgive me?"

"No. But that is quite beside the point. Nothing you could say would convince me that your opinion of me has changed for any reason other than the discovery that I am the daughter of a wealthy man—a wealthy Cit, to be exact, Lord Lyndon." She used the word "Cit" rather than "merchant" openly, almost challenging him to dispute it. "That is what people of your class call us, is it not?"

"Miss Cole—"

Her hand went up to steady her hair. "Do you like

it?'' she asked archly. '' 'Tis the latest in Cit fashion, you know.''

'' 'Tis charming—particularly the cut of the gown.'' Bending over her hand gallantly, he sought to kiss her fingers.

Clearly he was not recoiling as she had hoped. Snatching her hand back quickly, she tried again to give him a disgust of her. ''Lord Lyndon, let us not play games with each other when plain speaking will serve us best. I quite know why you are here, and I intend to accept your suit—provided, of course, that you mean to take me to Almack's and all of the other elegant places a fashionable lady is seen.'' Pausing to inspect with studied insouciance a garish bracelet she'd borrowed from the belowstairs maid, she added coquettishly, ''You do mean to introduce me to the swells, do you not? That is, I shall expect it.'' Leaning backward to flutter her soot-blackened eyelashes at him, she lost part of the effect when two of the teetering plumes chose to fall out.

He bent to pick them up and his eyes traveled from her toes to her face slowly, bringing a blush in their wake. ''Miss Cole, you seem to be laboring under a misapprehension that I have made you an offer.''

She stared blankly for a moment, unable to believe the relief she felt. ''You mean you have *not*?''

''No. I have made no offer of marriage, Miss Cole—not to you or anyone. 'Twas my belief that your father invited me to dine.''

''Oh, but . . .'' For a moment she was nonplussed, feeling like the veriest fool. ''But I thought . . . I mean, did he not offer you money to take me?''

''There was some mention of it, I believe, but I did not commit to the offer. My title, Miss Cole, is not for sale.'' He watched her, enjoying her discomfiture immensely, taking in the parade of dismayed emotions that crossed her painted face.

''Ah, there you are, my lord. Cozy little *tête-à-tête* with m'daughter, eh? Taking little thing, ain't she?'' Jeptha Cole boomed from the hall above them.

''I cannot say the discourse between Lord Lyndon and

myself has been of a particularly friendly nature, Papa,'' Leah replied.

''Still up on your high ropes, eh?'' the old man observed imperturbably. ''Well, you'd best come down from 'em, 'cause m'mind's settled in the matter. It ain't like I brought home a man-milliner or one of them fops you see parading Bond Street in the afternoon, is it? There,'' he managed as he executed the last step and stopped to mop his brow. ''Got to catch m'breath—your pardon, my lord. Egad, *girl*!'' he choked when he actually saw her. ''What is the meaning of this? Cover yourself!'' Turning quickly to Lyndon, he sought to smooth over the effect of her garish appearance. ''My lord—''

''Papa, Lord Lyndon assures me that he has not the least desire to wed with me,'' Leah informed her father sweetly. ''That being the case, I do not think you should press him.''

''Leah!'' His eyes still on Tony, the old man raised his hands in supplication. ''The chit needs a firmer hand than mine, my lord, but she ain't as empty in the cockloft as she looks just now, I promise you.''

But Tony's eyes were still on Leah. ''No, you mistook the matter, Miss Cole,'' he pointed out evenly. ''I said I had not made an offer of marriage—yet.''

''You said your title was not for sale!'' she accused.

''Here, here now, miss!'' Jeptha Cole roared. ''Where's them pretty manners I paid for?''

''Wait—are you saying now that you *are* going to offer for me?'' she howled indignantly. ''You cannot!''

In that moment Tony Barsett forgot what he owed his name, forgot that he stood in the foyer of a merchant's house, forgot the presence of Jeptha Cole even. Staring down at her flushed upturned face, meeting those incredible eyes of hers, he knew he desired her above all others. It did not matter that her father offered forty thousand pounds in the bargain, it did not matter that she was a Cit's daughter, and it did not matter that she'd refuse him. A slow smile of anticipation spread over his handsome face as he made up his mind to take her. ''Yes. Yes, Miss Cole, I am,'' he decided abruptly.

''Well, I'll be damned! If this don't call for some

brandy! Wilson! Wilson! Damme, where's a footman when you need one?'' The old man clapped his hands excitedly and called for the butler, who'd withdrawn discreetly at the first sight of Miss Leah. ''Crome!''

''Aye, sir?'' Thomas Wilson, the lower footman, was the first to reach them, followed by the aged and wheezing butler.

''Brandy for his lordship and me! And ratafia for m'daughter! In the green saloon, and be quick with it! Lady Leah—if that don't sound right! Lady Leah!'' The words rolled off his tongue as though he'd practiced them a hundred times.

Embarrassed by her father's exuberant enthusiasm, Leah stubbornly shook her head. ''No. Although I am cognizant of the signal honor you do me, Lord Lyndon, I must decline your offer.''

''Don't listen to her, my lord! She'll be pleased to have you—pleased to be a viscountess, I promise you,'' Jeptha Cole interposed hastily. ''As for you, miss, if you don't want to take ratafia, then see when the cook means to serve. Me and his lordship's got business!''

''Papa, you are selling me!'' Leah screeched.

''No, I ain't. Buyin' him,'' he retorted. ''Come, my lord, the brandy's excellent—got it from a smuggler off Cornwall. Fellow said it came from Boney's own stock.'' Taking a proprietary hold on Lord Lyndon's coat sleeve, he propelled him toward the green saloon determinedly. ''Females! Never know what gets into 'em sometimes—say no when they mean yes, if you take my meaning.''

Leah gaped, unable to believe what they'd done. Even given her father's recent moodiness, his behavior was so unlike what she'd come to expect of him. A ruthless man in business, he was now toadying to a rakehell—a gazetted fortune hunter even—for no other reason than the fellow had a title. She watched the door close after them and felt a sense of shame and disgust.

Inside the saloon, Tony took the glass from the footman and gazed appreciatively at the tasteful furnishings. Looking upward, he was surprised by the portrait of a lovely woman above the mantel.

''Your wife?'' he inquired politely.

Jeptha Cole nodded. "Don't do her justice, though—not as good as the one Lawrence did. I've got it in my library where I can just sit and look at her."

"She was very beautiful."

"Aye, there's been none to compare with her—not even Leah. I told her when we was married that I'd gain a fortune for her, to make up for what she lost in marrying me. Almost did it, too, but she died giving me the girl. Made me promise I'd not hold it against Leah—losing her, I mean. But every day I look on my girl, I see Marianna in her."

"How old is Leah?" Tony asked quietly.

"Be twenty next month. Oh, I know girls go for their Seasons before they are eighteen, but I took my time with Leah. I remember how it was for my Ma—" He stopped abruptly. "No, you'll not fault what you get in Leah Cole, my lord. I've seen she has the accomplishments of a lady—and a good head too."

"But she has not gone about much," Tony reminded him.

"Kept her at home—didn't want some Cit fixing his interest with her, nor any half-pay officer neither. Couldn't have all the bucks ogling my girl, knowing what I know about the *ton*. Well, I mean, think on it: you was trying to give her a slip of the shoulder yourself, wasn't you?"

"I am not proud of my mistake, Mr. Cole." Tony had raised his glass to take a drink when he heard Jeptha Cole's sharp intake of breath, the sound that came with acute pain. Looking down to where the older man had taken his seat, he saw the profuse sweat break out on his balding head and noted the white knuckles that clutched the arms of his chair. Even as he watched, the man's color turned ashy gray and his breath came in gasps. Alarmed, Tony rushed to his side while yelling, "Your master's ill . . . Mr. Cole is ill!"

"No . . ." Cole managed in a weak half-whisper.

Leah heard Tony's call all the way back in the kitchens, where she was sampling the sauces. Gathering her skirt above her ankles, she ran to the front of the house.

Throwing open the door, she nearly collided with the butler and footmen, who'd come up from the cellar.

"Papa! Are you . . . ?" One look told her he was not. "Oh, *Papa*." She knelt at the side of his chair across from Tony and began massaging Jeptha Cole's hands vigorously. "Someone send for Dr. Fournier in Half Moon—please hurry!"

"He cannot breathe," Tony muttered. Rising, he leaned over to loosen the older man's cravat and unbuttoned the waistcoat over his ample stomach. "Get a wet cloth," he ordered curtly.

"You cannot order me—" She stopped, biting her lip to hold back her bitter retort. Her father was obviously in great pain, and there was no time for quarreling. "All right." Meeting the housekeeper, who stood in the doorway wringing her hands, Leah urged her, "You heard his lordship—bring us a wet cloth."

"Yes, miss."

When Leah turned back to Lord Lyndon, he was mopping her father's brow with his handkerchief, and her father's pain was easing. Relieved, she noted his returning color.

He blinked his eyes and looked up at Lord Lyndon. "Damme," he rasped, "thought I was stickin' my spoon in the wall that time." He craned his neck toward his daughter, and his hand reached for her. "Can you not see how it is that I must have you settled, puss?" he managed. Seeing the tears well in her eyes, he shook his head. "None of that now—'tisn't the first time, if you want the truth of it, but one of these days, 'twill be the last." His hand closed over hers and held it. "Marry Lyndon here—he at least knows something about shipping . . . can keep his eye on my business, you know." His fingers tightened as his eyes pleaded with her. "Make your mama and me proud, Leah—be a fine lady."

"Papa—"

"No sense lyin' to you anymore is there? Might be here a year from now, or I might be gone tomorrow. Either way, I've got to see you settled. Take Lyndon—please."

Her teeth cut into her lower lip to still its quivering;

but she managed to nod assent. Slowly her father relaxed his grip on her and leaned back.

Mrs. Crome, the elderly housekeeper, returned to flutter about them with the wet cloth, while her husband, the butler, tried to reassure everyone that the doctor had been summoned. "Don't need 'im now," Jeptha Cole snorted. "Go on about your business, both of you—got to have supper with my son-in-law-to-be!"

"No, sir," Tony contradicted. "I think you should take to your bed and wait for the doctor. You will wish to dance at the wedding, after all," he coaxed.

Jeptha Cole shook his head. "I'd not shame you afore the *ton*, my lord—told you I ain't the encroaching kind."

"Can you stand, sir?" Tony asked, leaning over him to offer his hand.

"Of course I can stand!" the old man exploded as he lurched to his feet. "Damme, Leah, if he don't try to manage me. Got to have dinner—invited him, didn't I?"

"Papa, I think Lord Lyndon is right. You must not be about until the doctor sees you."

"You, fellow," Tony ordered a stunned footman, "assist me in getting your master to his bed."

"It ain't seemly," Jeptha Cole protested weakly as the two men helped him from the room and Leah hovered anxiously at his side, admonishing him to be quiet.

"Well, I never—and him a fancy lord at that," the old housekeeper muttered, shaking her head. "Thought they was useless—the Quality, I mean—but he don't seem to mind missing his dinner. Lud, but won't he lead her a merry dance?"

"No, Mrs. Crome, he will not," her husband told her flatly. "Our Miss Leah will lead him the dance."

Shooed out of Cole's bedchamber by the valet and footman, Tony faced Leah in the hallway. "I think your father is all right for now, but he bears watching," he told her soberly. "If aught is needed in the night, you can send to me." Abruptly his manner changed as he glanced wickedly at her nearly bared bosom. "Really, Miss Cole, there was no need to go to such lengths to bring me up to scratch. I have a fair enough imagination."

Flushing behind the rouge on her cheeks, she groped for an appropriate set-down, but the sound of the doctor's arrival cut her short. Still grinning, Tony leaned forward to brush her startled lips with his. " 'Tisn't much of a betrothal kiss, I admit, but sometime I will do better by you."

Wiping her mouth with the back of her hand, she stared after him as he lightly trod the steps. At the bottom, he took his hat from Crome and tipped it jauntily. "Good night, Miss Cole," he called up again. She stood rooted to the carpet runner until she realized Dr. Fournier was coming up the stairs. Glancing down at her dress, she turned hastily and fled to make herself presentable.

In the safety of her chamber, she scrubbed her face thoroughly and changed into one of her most demure muslins. She'd made a fool of herself, she knew, and in appearing as Haymarket ware, she'd not discouraged him in the least. Dragging her comb angrily through her tangled curls, she nearly cried, knowing he'd outfaced her.

8

It was still early when Tony left the Cole house. Swinging up into his town carriage, he leaned back against the blue velvet squabs and contemplated what he'd done. Given the old man's enthusiasm for the match, Tony had not a doubt in the world that the announcement of the betrothal would be inserted as soon as possible in the *Gazette*, the *Morning Post*, and any other place Cole could think to have it printed. And that gave him pause. If his great-aunt had caviled at his venture into the shipping business, Tony knew that she would be incensed at his marriage to a shipping merchant's daughter.

He rapped on the roof of the carriage with his stick, calling out to the driver and coachmen, "Davenham House, if you please!" Settling back, he smiled to himself. By the time he was through with her, the old girl would be more than grateful to think that she had not had to rescue him herself. Hopefully, by the time she discovered she'd been had, she would have come to like Leah.

The streets were still clogged with carriages as the fashionable set off in their pursuit of the evening's pleasures. Tony's stomach rumbled, reminding him that he still had not eaten. Well, he would beard the old girl first, and then he would press on to White's for supper. A coach drew even and the dark-haired female occupant waved a greeting, reminding him that he'd not seen Elaine Chandler in over a week—not since he'd first encountered Leah Cole. A pang of regret assailed him momentarily and faded. That was one piece of business he'd have to attend to, but he had little anticipation of unpleasantness. Elaine was no simpering miss—she'd entered their association as candidly as he had—and it was not likely that her mercenary heart had even been touched. No, a handsome gift handsomely bestowed ought to put an end to any sadness on her part.

By the time he reached Davenham House, the watch was calling ten-thirty and Tony's stomach was becoming insistent. Noting with no small measure of satisfaction that the lights were still on in the front saloons, Tony stepped down from the coach, admonishing his driver to wait for him. Adjusting the sleeves of his coat, he whistled a soft tune and prepared to beard the lioness in her den.

Stodgill, belatedly answering Tony's determined knocking, stepped back to allow him admittance. "Lord Lyndon," he acknowledged with the imperturbability born of his occupation.

"Hallo, Stodgy—m'aunt still about?"

"Taking her brandy before retiring. I shall—"

"No, I'd as lief announce myself, if you do not mind," Tony murmured, stepping past the aging butler. "Rose room?"

"Aye, my lord, but—"

"Thank you."

The old fellow shrugged perceptibly and moved back. Lord Lyndon had run tame in the house since he could walk and had never been known to stand on ceremony with the duchess anyway. "As you wish, my lord, but her temper's not the best tonight."

Tony found his aunt and Mrs. Buckhaven sitting before a small fire, his aunt sipping her brandy and Bucky quietly plying her embroidery needle to what appeared to be a pillowslip. He moved into the room before clearing his throat audibly to gain their attention. Startled by the intrusion, his aunt's mousy companion jumped visibly.

"Oh, my lord!" she tittered with the nervousness born of sudden fright.

"Eh . . . what . . . ?" His aunt twisted her neck around to survey him irritably, and then she relaxed her frown enough to greet him with, "Oh, 'tis you, Tony. Naughty boy—you have overset Bucky." Her black eyes traveled over him, taking in his evening clothes. "Humph! In my day, a gentleman wore silks and satins at night—don't know why they call 'em dandies now when they are plain as Methodists! Well, well, do not be standing there gaping, Anthony! You ain't here for dinner, but you must have reason, else you'd not have come."

He crossed the room to plant an affectionate kiss on her rouged and wrinkled cheek. His eyes twinkled as he leaned closer to tease her, "I am come to share my good fortune with you, you old Tartar, but now I've half a mind to hold my tongue."

"Is this going to cost me?" she demanded suspiciously.

"Not a penny, I promise you."

"They found your ship afloat, and 'twas but rumor it sank," she ventured to guess, intrigued in spite of herself.

"Alas, no, but I think you will be pleased."

"Humph! How can I be expected to be pleased when my only nevvy's wasted his fortune on a leaky ship?" she queried tartly. "And don't tell me you ain't in dun territory, Tony, because 'tis all over town that you are." Out of the corner of her eye she noted Mrs. Buckhaven's acute interest and put a damper to it. "Bucky, see if Mrs. Cox has any of those sweet cakes left over in the kitchen. I'll be bound that Tony'd have one or two if he was offered 'em."

She waited impatiently for the woman to reluctantly lay aside her needlework and go in search of the dessert. "And pray close the door behind you." Turning back to Tony as the latch clicked shut, she fixed him with those sharp eyes of hers. "Now, I'll not be put off, Anthony—out with it."

"Poor Bucky," he murmured, drawing out the suspense. "If you do not take care, you'll find yourself alone one of these days."

"Humph! Much you know of it then," she retorted. "If you was around here more, you'd know I am more of a companion to her than she is to me. Poor thing cannot seem to do anything but sew, you know. But I did not send her away to speak of her—'tis you who concerns me."

He appeared absorbed in adjusting his coat sleeve for

a moment, and then he looked up, flashing her that engaging smile of his. "Have you ever heard of Jeptha Cole, Aunt Hester?"

"Cole? Oh . . . I collect you mean the fellow who made all that money building ships," she decided.

"Not building them, Aunt—sailing them. He speculates on rich cargoes, trading at ports all over the world. Rich as Croesus, by all accounts."

"Shows you that you ought to leave trade to men of his class," she sniffed. "They know what they are doing."

"Wish me happy, Aunt Hester."

She blinked, unable to quite assimilate the sudden shift in the direction of his conversation. "You are getting married Tony?" she asked blankly. "But just last week—"

"Jeptha Cole is to be my father-in-law."

"*What*!" she gasped in shock. "You cannot be *serious*! The man is a Cit!"

"A rich Cit," he reminded her bluntly. "I thought you'd be pleased," he added untruthfully.

"*Pleased*?" Her voice rose in a shriek of displeasure. "You cannot have thought such a thing, Anthony Barsett! Do you not know what you owe your name, Boy? No, I won't have it—I'll not countenance such an association with *my* family!"

"He offered forty thousand in settlement." He had the satisfaction of seeing her eyes widen in shock at the enormity of the offer. "Just so—a man in my circumstances would be a fool to reject such a sum."

"Forty *thousand*?" Her mouth made a round O, emphasizing the "thou," and she sank back in her seat. "Surely not," she managed weakly. " 'Tis a fortune." Her bony hands gripped the padded arms of the chair until the veins stood out even more prominently than usual. Then, as the initial shock waned, she exhaled heavily and shook her head. "Even so, you should have come to me if your pockets were let that badly, Tony."

"You said you would not help me," he reminded her. "Jeptha Cole will."

"Yes, I did say that, didn't I?" she admitted. "But I

also told you I'd not let you go to Newgate. If you'd only explained the extent of your losses, Tony, I'd have seen you come about—and you cannot say you did not know it."

"I did not want to know. 'Tis not your responsibility to pay for my mistakes, Aunt Hester."

"Do not be getting noble with me, Tony Barsett!" she snapped. "I'd as lief settle your debts myself as see you marry a Cit! I suppose the girl smells of the shop—or have you even see her?"

"Leah Cole will be a credit to you, I promise. There is nothing displeasing in her looks, and as for her manners . . ." He stopped, recalling the way she'd looked earlier. "Well, all I can say is the chit's as high in the instep as you are. In fact, she views me with about as much enthusiasm as you view her. And she's got a devil of a temper."

"She didn't want you?" his aunt asked incredulously. "Surely not—not with your looks and address. I'll not believe it. Why, you are a veritable Corinthian, Tony! And you are a Barsett, after all."

"Think on it—I'll not be the last one if I marry," he cajoled.

"But this Cole person—everyone knows that he is but a Cit. Tony, even if this girl is a paragon, which I am not ready to concede, there is Mr. Cole."

"On his last legs. Wants to see his girl settled before he pops off."

"That kind live forever," she countered. "I ought to know—been threatening it for years, but I don't mean it."

"He had some sort of attack tonight, Aunt Hester. I thought for a moment he'd bought his ticket already." He leaned closer and put his hands on her chair arms. "She is his only child, Aunt Hester."

"Even so—"

"She stands to inherit a fortune as big as yours—bigger maybe." Backing off, he walked over to lean on the mantelpiece. "Not that I want the old fellow to pass on, you understand. Miss Cole is uncommonly fond of her parent, by the looks of it, and I'd not distress her for the world.''

The duchess opened her mouth and closed it without uttering a sound. After eyeing him suspiciously for a moment, she found her voice. ''Tony,'' she asked finally, ''have you thrown your hat over the windmill for this girl?''

It was his turn to be silent as he considered the answer. ''I don't . . . Yes, Aunt Hester, I think I have.'' He met her eyes almost sheepishly, nodding. '' 'Tis rich, isn't it—Lyndon caught by a Cit, of all things.''

''Well, why did you not say so?'' she uttered bracingly. ''Puts an entirely different complexion on the matter! When you speak to me like a gazetted fortune-hunter, I know the cheese is rotten! Have too much pride to marry for money! Dash it—you are a Barsett!'' She hobbled to her feet and made her way to face him. ''But if it's the gel herself you want, and not her father's fortune, then that's a different tune.'' Her black eyes softened as they scanned his face. ''Will I like her, do you think?'' she asked him.

He was taken aback by her sudden about-face and knew not what to make of it. He'd expected to insinuate that he'd had to take Leah Cole out of desperation and to enlist her aid in presenting his betrothed to society. Never in his furthest imagination could he have thought she'd see through the ploy. But she was a downy one, when one considered the matter. In spite of himself, he grinned. ''I don't know,'' he answered truthfully. ''She'll put every Incomparable on the Marriage Mart to shame, I can tell you, but she's not insipid in the least. And she's certainly not in the conventional style. I have never seen eyes like hers.''

''You sound besotted.''

''Oh, I am not blind to her faults, Aunt Hester—I suspect she's a bluestocking and a reformer—but I am willing to wager you will think her an Original.''

''As long as she ain't peculiar-acting. Well, you have seen enough females to know your mind, I suppose,'' she decided. ''Then there is no help for it, is there? If you are caught, we will have to see the girl established.

I would not for the world behave shabbily to your wife, Tony, and I'd not see her cut by the *ton* either. Mind you, I do not like it that she is a Cit, but if she carries on the Barsett line, I'll give her her due."

"Interrupted by a timid knock at the door, the old woman barked impatiently, "Yes—what is it?"

The door opened slowly to admit Mrs. Buckhaven bearing a small tray of sweet cakes. "Cook did not have many left," she apologized as she set the tray down.

"Sweet cakes! Humph! Ring the bell-pull and see if there's aught substantial left of dinner, Bucky! M'nevvy's nigh famished—ain't you?" she asked Tony. "Well, whilst you eat, we shall plan how best to present Miss Cole this Season. Bucky"—she turned her attention to her companion again—"we are opening Davenham House for a party in honor of m'niece-to-be. Tony's marrying an Original! And, Bucky, do get my glass and a pen—we've got a guest list to plan. I mean to set the *ton* on their ears! Invite everybody! Give 'em enough to gossip about each other so's they'll leave the gel alone!"

"Everybody, Aunt Hester?" Tony asked, suppressing a grin.

"Everybody! Don't mean to leave any of 'em out! Rakes, gamesters—the whole lot of 'em!"

"But, Your Grace—the Season calendar is set for April, I am sure," Mrs. Buckhaven ventured timidly.

"Nonsense! London's thin of company yet, ain't it? Besides, 'tis Davenham House I am opening to them, Bucky—they'll come."

9

Having spent a sleepless night tortured by her fears for her father and nightmares of Lord Lyndon, Leah rose early and invaded her father's chamber. To her relief, he looked much better, his color having improved greatly, and he was his usual irascible self. As she entered the room, she heard him muttering to his valet, "Damned Frenchie doctor."

"I collect you were wishful of your morning coffee," she greeted him as she took a tray from the retreating footman. "Well, Dr. Fournier says 'tis not a restful drink, and therefore—"

"I say hang Fournier—aye, and his prohibitions also," he grumbled. "Afore long, there'll not be a thing left to enjoy. A man might as well die and take his chances with perdition."

Having listened to the doctor's opinion last night that her father did indeed have a weak heart, she forbore to argue for fear of oversetting him. "Humor him and see to his rest," he'd advised. So she held her tongue and set the tray on a bedside table, saying brightly, "You have not even looked to see what Monsieur prepared this morning, have you?"

"Don't have to—ten to one, it ain't fit for a man." He raised his head to watch her lift the warming cover, then lay back. "Porridge! Ought to have known—pap fit only for a babe, I tell you! Well, I won't have it, miss, and so I have told Wilson already! 'If 'tis some damned horse mash,' I told him, 'I don't want it.' " He eyed her with disfavor and shook his head. "And now here you bring it back to me."

Unperturbed, she reached for the napkin and tucked it under his chin. "It will not make you as bilious as sausages will,'' she observed mildly as she dipped the silver spoon into the bowl. Leaning over him, she held the spoon in front of him and waited.

''Overreaching yourself, ain't you, missy!'' he snapped. ''I ain't a babe to be fed.''

''Of course you are not,'' she said soothingly, ''but you must eat if you are to feel better. Hunger makes you ill-tempered, you know, and you must not overset yourself.'' She held the spoon steadily. ''If 'twere I who was sick, you'd do the same for me.''

''I ain't sick—'twas but indigestion. Damme if I'm going to let you feed me, Leah. You can take that mess back from whence it came.'' He struggled to sit up higher on the pillows, barking at his valet, ''I'll have my bath and my clothes now, I tell you. Ain't missed a day at the docks in twenty-five years, and I'll be hanged if I miss today—d'you hear me? And you, miss—d'you hear me also?''

''Very well, Papa.'' Tears welled in her eyes as she rose from her perch on the edge of his bed. ''You must forgive a daughter whose only wish is your health, for I know not how I shall go on when you are gone.'' Slowly she replaced the cover over the bowl and started for the door with the tray. She had her hand on the doorknob before he called her back.

''Oh, very well!'' he snapped. ''Bring the nasty stuff back, puss, but for God's sake let me feed myself!'' He could not see the expression of triumph before she paused, her back still toward him, to school her face into bland meekness. ''I said I'd eat it!'' he repeated, goaded. And when she returned, he picked up the spoon, ready to eat. ''Aye, you think you are a sly one, don't you? Well, I ought to box your ears, but I daresay Lyndon'll have to do it for me.''

''Papa, about Lord Lyndon. I—''

''I ain't listening to it! My mind's settled, Leah, and that's all there is to the matter. I don't know what Fournier told you, but he's been pretty open with his budget to me, 'cause I asked 'im the first time I had a spell like last night. Got to give up all my pleasures, and I ain't so sure I want to live without 'em.''

"Papa—"

"Thing is," he continued, ignoring her interruption, "I got two things I care about in this world—you and my business, Leah—and it looks to me like I can take care of 'em both with Lyndon. Man's got a good head for the business—oh, I know he lost his ship and cargo, but you can't blame typhoons on 'im, you know. He was in a fair way to making a profit afore it happened." He looked up at her troubled frown and shook his head. "I know you think him an empty-headed fool like the rest of the pack that call themselves Quality, but I don't think so. Don't know what it is about him, but I like him." His piece said, he dipped his spoon into the cooled porridge and took a bite, shuddering with distaste as he swallowed.

"But one wants a different sort of man for a business partner than for a husband," she offered helplessly. "I don't—"

"You don't like him," he finished for her. "Well, that ain't as important as you was to think. For one thing, you don't know him yet, and for another, it don't matter. Manage him. I ain't seen a female yet as couldn't get what she wanted from a man, if she went at it right. And I don't mean sniffling and sniveling and giving 'im the cold side of your shoulder, either."

"Just what do you mean?"

Instead of answering, he took another spoonful of the porridge and gulped it down. "Ugh! Well, I wish your mother was alive now more than ever, puss, 'cause there's some things it ain't proper for me to tell you, and I got no one to do it for me. Thing is, you are a fine-looking female, Leah, and if you was to play your hand right, you'd have Lyndon in your pocket—don't look at me like that, dammit!"

"You want me to toadeat him—well, I won't," she muttered.

"Not toadeat—damme, girl, but for a bluestocking, you ain't got good sense! What I am asking you to do when you are married is to . . ." He hesitated, floundering about for the words, and finally finished lamely, " . . . well, be nice to him. You know, well . . . that is . . . Dash it, Leah! You've got to make him love you!"

"And just how am I to do that?" she asked with deceptive sweetness.

"How should I . . . Oh, the devil take it, Leah! You ain't a slowtop! Make him want what he's got at home, and he won't go out lookin' for something else."

"If you think I am going to throw myself at Lord Lyndon's head, Papa, you are very wide of the mark. I find his behavior offensive."

"Back to that insult business, eh? Well, he knows better now—besides, you are to be his wife. He'll give you your due—I am certain of it." Before she could turn on him, he managed to get another congealed dollop of cereal into his mouth.

She bit back a sharp retort, reminding herself not to overset him. Instead, she merely sighed expressively and nodded. "Well, I hope you are right, Papa. 'Tis just . . . well, does it *have* to be Lord Lyndon? I mean, I think I should prefer even Rotherfield to him—and I do not even know the earl."

Jeptha Cole choked and spit the cereal into a napkin. "Now *that* shows you ain't been out! No, take Lyndon and be done. Go on—out with you, and let's have no more of this nonsense." As she leaned down to kiss him, he caught her hand, squeezing it. "Trust me, Leah—I am your papa. You run along and leave me be. It ain't seemly for me to get up with you here." He waited while she leaned down to brush his forehead with a kiss, and then he caught her hand. "Trust me in this, Leah."

Even as she emerged into the upper hall, she was surprised to hear Crome greeting someone below. Curious, she leaned over the railing to see Viscount Lyndon in the foyer, looking up at her.

"Good morning," he called out.

"I thought fine lords did not rise so early," she muttered.

"We tend to sleep late after dissipation, Miss Cole, but as I retired early last night, I am for a turn in the park this morning. I thought to stop by and inquire of your father—and to see if you might be persuaded to drive out with me."

"Alas, I would not. As for my father, he is more than

a trifle hagged, but his temper is strong, and that is a good sign, I think."

"I do not suppose you would come down, that we might converse in a more normal tone of voice?" he coaxed.

She started to tell him she had nothing to say to him, but thought better of it. "All right, but you find me scarce ready for company, my lord."

She didn't suddenly start patting her hair into place or smoothing her gown nervously, and Tony liked that instantly. It denoted an unconscious acceptance of her beauty and made her even more attractive when compared with the young misses of his acquaintance. Most of them would titter nervously and fret about their looks until a man couldn't converse decently with them. He watched and admired as she came down the wide steps, the hem of her sprigged-muslin day gown touching the polished wood softly. Her glorious hair had been brushed until it shone, and it hung down past her shoulders artlessly. In that moment he wondered how he could ever have mistaken her for a Cyprian.

"Very well," she announced crisply as she stepped off the last stair, "I am here. What is it that you wished to discuss with me?"

"Is there someplace where we may be more private?"

She looked up at him suspiciously, trying to discern his motives, but his brilliant blue eyes were friendly and his smile disarming. Despite her prejudice against him, she found herself responding to that ready smile of his. "Yes," she answered, "my father's library—the maids are cleaning the front saloon."

She waited for him to follow her into the richly paneled room, tall bookcases lining its walls. As she left the door slightly ajar, he moved to examine the nearest shelves appreciatively. "Your father has all the classics," he murmured in approval.

"Those are mine—as are all of them on this side of the room." Noting his skeptical expression, she added, "When one does not go about much, one reads. Alas, but you have contracted yourself to a bluestocking, my lord." Unbending slightly, she gestured to the opposite wall. "My father's are over there and make for dull reading. You would not credit it, but he has one entire shelf devoted to the construction of ships. Papa," she added proudly, "has never been a sailor, but I'll warrant he knows every board in one of his vessels."

"And I admire him for it," he responded sincerely. "Miss Cole, you must not think that I look down on trade. I have owned a ship myself."

"Yes, of course—the one that went down."

"A deuced bad piece of luck, but I shall come about. It was not my only investment, despite what everyone thinks."

"Of course you will come about—with my money," she countered acidly. Moving to lift the rich drapery that darkened one of the tall windows, she looked outside. The sun was shining warmly and there was not a sign of a cloud in the sky. Spring flowers blossomed in profusion in plantings that ringed the house, bringing with them the promise of summer. Her thoughts immediately went to her father, and the lowering thought crept into her mind that he might not live to see her entry into the world he'd so desperately sought for her. She dropped the curtain as her spirits sank.

"I think my father is very ill," she said quietly, as much to herself as to Lord Lyndon.

He came up behind her, and without thinking placed his hands on her shoulders. "I hope not. But if you would wish a consult, I can arrange—"

"No. Dr. Fournier understands Papa, and that is important. I doubt another physician would have the patience to deal with him, for Papa can be quite obstreperous when he wishes." She drew away and turned to face Lyndon. "Your pardon—I am merely blue-deviled today."

"Perhaps with good reason, my dear."

Her eyes widened at the sympathy in his voice. Kindness was the last thing she'd expected of a man like Lyndon, but then he wished to share her father's fortune. Resolutely she steeled herself to remain aloof, to ignore his efforts to win her goodwill.

"Lord Lyndon, it is imperative that we understand each

other—I am *not* your 'dear,' as you chose to put it," she told him firmly, striving to keep him at a distance.

"A manner of speech, merely, Miss Cole—but it does become tiresome calling you 'Miss Cole' when we are betrothed." He favored her with a rueful smile that threatened to disarm her. "Think how we shall be remarked when we go about in society together whilst persisting in such formality."

"You are funning with me, my lord."

"I assure you that I am not. I think that if we are to establish you amongst the *ton*, Miss Cole, we ought to pass this off as a love match." This time he emphasized "Miss Cole" so heavily that he made it sound ridiculous. "Unless, of course, you wish it to be said that I have been bought with your father's money."

"But you *are* bought with my father's money," she reminded him.

"But do you wish to hear everyone say it?"

"I do not care what they say!" she retorted.

"Miss Cole, I do not care if you fling epithets at me when we are private, but in public you will call me by my given name—'tis Anthony, but my intimates call me Tony."

"I do not intend to be one of your intimates!"

"Not at all?" he asked with a faintly injured air. "A man has the right to expect certain things from his wife, you know."

"You may expect Papa's money. If I were to be plain on that head, sir: if I could think of any way to decline your offer without oversetting Papa, I should do so on the instant. I do not particularly wish to be a titled lady. In fact," she added dramatically, "I do not even wish to know you."

"You are forgetting the matter of my succession, Miss Cole—you behold the last Lyndon Barsett."

"That, sir, is no concern of mine."

There was no point in arguing the matter now, Tony decided, for he was still reasonably certain that he could change her mind once they were wed. Instead, he tried another tack. "At least flirt with me when we are in company."

"I should not know how."

"I never met a female who wasn't born to it."

"Obviously you have known the wrong sort of females."

His temper snapped under the weight of her persistent rebuffs. "I do not know who you think you are, Miss Cole, and I do not know where you got the maggot in your brain that you make the only sacrifice in this marriage! You are mistaken, you know, for I have enjoyed my freedom immensely."

"Then cry off and keep it! You cannot come in here and tell me how 'tis to be—how I am to go on amongst your tonnish friends. I'll not have it! My father wishes me to appear the lady, not the fool!"

"Here now, miss!"

She spun around guiltily, and to her horror discovered her father dressed to go out. "Papa, you must not—"

"I ain't going to lie abed—got things to do, damme if I don't. Now, what is the meaning of this?"

Tony was the first to recover. "I came to see how you fared, sir, and to tell Leah that my aunt Davenham means to present her at Davenham House Thursday next."

"Told you he was relation to the Duchess of Davenham!" Jeptha Cole crowed triumphantly at his daughter.

"The dowager duchess," Tony corrected him. "Actually, I am related to all of them, but 'tis the dowager who gives the party. Owing to a digestive complaint, my cousin's wife is taking the waters at Bath this spring."

"There is no need to educate my father, Lord Lyndon," Leah cut in coldly.

"Didn't take it amiss, my dear—have to know that sort of thing if you are to succeed in this lady business, after all."

"Your pardon, Miss Cole—'twas not my intent to instruct so much as to tell which duchess gives the party," Tony fired back. Turning to her father, he added easily, " 'Tis the warmest day yet this spring, and I am on my way to take a turn about in the park. Perhaps I could persuade you to drive out with me? I have a new pair to put through their paces."

"No . . . no, my lord. Ain't expecting you to put me before the world—it wouldn't be seemly."

"Nonsense," Tony dismissed this objection briskly. "If you think I mean to hide you in the family closet, you are mistaken. Besides, I should like your opinion on the rum market, sir."

"Rum is always sound—men of all classes will drink rather than eat, my lord. But if you was to ask me about speculating in that market, I could tell you a thing or two, I suppose. Now, if 'twas me, I'd hedge a bit—not put all my blunt in one pocket, you know. Damme if I don't think I will go, sir—that is, if you was truly to want me."

"Of a certainty."

" 'Course, it ain't seemly . . ." The older man hesitated again. "I mean, what if you was to meet some of your fancy friends, my lord?"

"I'd introduce you as my papa-in-law-to-be," Tony answered firmly.

"Well . . ."

"If he does not wish to go, my lord—"

"The air will do him good—better than an office on a day like this," Tony argued.

"Now, you leave me and his lordship alone," her father intervened. "We got things to talk about."

Following the older man to the door, Tony turned back to grin at Leah. "Good day, Miss Cole. I shall be back to take you up tomorrow." And while she glowered at him, he had the impudence to wink.

10

Leah tugged nervously at her pearl eardrops as her maid pinned an errant strand of blond hair into place. She had no doubt about the elegance of her toilette or her appearance, yet she approached her impending introduction to the *haut ton* with considerable trepidation. That she was guest of honor at a party given by Lord Lyndon's elderly relative gave her no illusions about her acceptability, particularly not since the dowager had not even called in person to discuss her plans.

"Please, mademoiselle, but you must sit still if I am to finish this," the petite French maid complained. "You will wish to be beautiful for Lord Lyndon and his friends."

"If you would have the truth of it, Jeanne, I care not what they think of me. They will let me know soon enough that I am not of his world."

Leah rose from the dressing table to survey herself in the cheval glass. Lyndon had made it quite plain to her father that she should wear something simple and white for her debut, and she did not think the color became her nearly so well as almost any other. But then Lyndon was quite free with unwanted advice, and she was not inclined to take much of it. For well over a week, he'd fairly haunted them, spending much of his time with her father, so much in fact that she'd tasked him with it. But her pointed hints had fallen wide of their mark, and he'd merely smiled and replied that he rather liked the old fellow.

"I shall look the veriest dowd," she muttered, taking in her reflection in the mirror. "They shall dub me 'the milkmaid' or some such sobriquet, and I shall not have a chance."

"*Mais non*, *mademoiselle*," Jeanne protested. "All the gentlemen will think you *trés belle*—I swear it."

Leah eyed herself doubtfully and smoothed the softly clinging white material with damp palms. The Grecian drape of the gown clung to the curves of her breasts and hips almost indecently, she thought, and yet Lyndon himself had chosen it, remarking that he wanted to be certain she did not appear again in blue taffeta and plumes. "He probably is more used to the company of Cyprians than ladies, and does not know how I should look, if the truth were known," she groused under her breath.

The maid shook her head. "You will have all the beaux in London at your feet, mademoiselle."

"Ah, Jeanne, you are just like Papa," Leah sighed. "You forget that without my money I am a totally ineligible female. And even with it, 'twill be said behind my back that I am an encroaching upstart, probably even by those who deign to speak to my face."

"Lord Lyndon awaits, Miss Leah," one of the upstairs maids announced through the closed door.

"I thought 'twas unfashionable to be punctual," she grumbled as Jeanne stood on tiptoe to repin a Grecian curl that nestled at the nape of her neck. "Have done—'tis time for this travesty to begin."

She swept out into the hallway and paused briefly at the head of the curved, stately staircase. Her hands and feet felt like ice as her wrapped kid sandals trod the first few steps slowly. She stopped to take a deep breath at the landing, unaware that the sunset framed her through the sparkling leaded panes behind her.

Tony looked up and his breath caught almost painfully in his chest. Despite Crome's pointed remark that "Mr. Cole is in the library, my lord," he'd chosen to wait for her to come down. There was something so regal, so graceful about her on the stairs that he thought he'd never tire of seeing her thus. And tonight she looked like a grand painting, a portrait that ought to be forever captured for posterity. He made a mental note to have Lawrence paint her if he could be enticed back to England. He'd have her just as she was now, with that draped gown, her hair piled in cascading curls, her neck and shoulders bare save for the single strand of pearls at her throat. The effect was stunning—he'd be the envy of every man he knew once she was seen.

He moved with easy grace to stand at the foot of the staircase, where he caught her hand as she executed the last step and carried it to his lips. "Venus descending," he murmured over her fingers. "Your hands are cold, my dear," he added, chafing them between his warm ones.

" 'Tis the evening air, no doubt." She quickly pulled away as though she were afraid to touch him.

To the footmen and maids who peeped from the service-stairs doorway, they were a breathtaking pair. "Gor—he's beautiful!" one of the girls sighed dreamily, only to be brought to book by a footman, who shook his head. "Naw, Miss Leah outshines 'im."

"There is no need to play the lover here, Lord Lyndon," Leah hissed in a low undervoice.

"Tony," he reminded her.

"Pray save the informality until we are in company."

"Look like a god and goddess," Jeptha Cole said in approval from the library doorway. "Ain't a soul there as won't think you was a lady born once you are seen, Leah—looks like a queen, don't she, my lord?"

"She does that," Tony agreed sincerely.

It was then that Leah noticed her father wore his plain brown coat and his tan kerseymere pantaloons. "You are not coming?" she demanded in panic.

"Now, don't be in a taking, puss—you and Lyndon make my regrets to Her Grace the duchess. I've not a doubt but what his lordship here'll see to everything for you, anyways."

"But—"

"I'd not disgrace you, Leah." He shook his head definitely and turned to Tony. "You understand, don't you, my lord? I'd not spoil it for her, and if I was to go, there'd be somebody to say I smell too much of the shop."

"I assure you—"

"No, no," he cut Tony short. "I know you don't hold it against me anymore, but there's them that would. You run along and take her with you—it does me proud just to look at the two of you afore you go. Just wish Marianna could've lived to see you, though."

"Papa, you are quite certain you are feeling well?"

"Right as a tick," he reassured her. "Tired, that's all. Going to read a bit over my brandy—and don't say I cannot have any, 'cause I ain't had any today. Now, go on with you—the duchess is waiting to meet you!"

"Oh, Papa." Leah brushed past Tony to embrace her father and brush a kiss against his cheek.

He patted her awkwardly, as though he feared to ruin her gown. "There, now, missy—enough of this," he told her gruffly. "You got Lyndon for that sort of thing now. Off with you both."

He watched proudly as Tony took her fringed Norwich silk shawl and draped it around her bare shoulders, and then he walked slowly back into the library. Uncorking a decanter, he poured himself a stout glass of brandy and held it up beneath the blond woman on the wall.

"Well, Marianna, 'tis better than we ever hoped for—fellow pleases me more every time I see him. Now, if I can just stay to see m'first grandson, I'll be content."

Leah and Tony rode the better part of the way to Davenham House in silence, each viewing the approaching party with misgivings. Twice Tony attempted to make polite conversation to alleviate the tension, only to be rebuffed by her terse answers. Finally his patience snapped.

"I sincerely hope you are more animated at your betrothal party, else everyone will think I have contracted myself to a peagoose," he muttered after her last monosyllabic reply.

"A *rich* peagoose," she corrected.

"And that rankles you, doesn't it? *Your* sex is to be congratulated when you ensnare rich men, but mine is to be condemned for fortune-hunting when we marry well."

"They'll not congratulate you for wedding a merchant's daughter."

"With a title and money, one can be forgiven almost anything, Miss Cole," he retorted. "When you are a viscountess with heirs in your nursery, there will be few to remember you were ever anything else."

She gave him a pained look in the dimness of the carriage interior. "I thought I had made myself plain on that subject. And not even the promise that I shall be accepted by a group of selfish nobs could tempt me otherwise."

"You know, Miss Cole, for someone who's never been amongst the *ton* at all, you have deuced queer notions about how wellborn ladies behave." He saw then that she was nervously twisting the folds of her gown in her lap, and his irritation faded to sympathy. Reaching across to still her hands, he smiled wryly. "Come—am I truly that difficult to take?"

"Yes, but I cannot expect you to understand it, I suppose," she sighed. "You at least are gaining something for your sacrifice."

"Have it your way." He nodded, releasing her hands. "I am some ogre come to carry off your gold."

When she did not answer, they lapsed into silence again until the coach drew up to the portals of Davenham House. He could sense her body tensing and he heard her exhale sharply as the coach halted. He jumped down and reached up to assist her to the ground, where he turned her around expertly and twitched her skirt into place.

"You seem to have much experience with women's gowns," she commented dryly while stepping back. "No doubt it comes from a long association with opera dancers."

"An extremely improper comment from a lady, Miss Cole. It is indelicate for you to acknowledge the existence of such creatures—I trust you will remember that when we are inside."

Another carriage rolled to a halt behind them, prompting Tony to offer his arm quickly. "For your papa's sake, Miss Cole, remember that this is a love match," he hissed. "Now, buck up, and call me Tony."

11

Curiosity replaced Leah's fears the moment Stodgill admitted them to Davenham House itself. The place was grand—grander than her own home, in fact—and the atmosphere was decidedly aristocratic, from the tall portraits of Havinghurst and Barsett ancestors to the austere, museumlike character of the cavernous entry hall. Even the chandelier, suspended on a heavy brass-plated chain, hung a full two stories above them.

Directed to the ballroom at the rear of the house, Tony tucked her fingers in the crook of his arm and prepared for their grand entrance. Despite their leaving Jeptha Cole's house early, they'd been stalled in streets clogged with carriages, making them late for their own betrothal party, and a number of guests already stood waiting to see Tony's Cit. Conversations stopped in mid-sentence while the curious watched him present her to that grande dame of the *ton*, the dowager duchess herself, and then they queued up to meet the merchant's daughter.

The frail dowager, rouged like an aging madam, pulled him down to plant a kiss on her wrinkled cheek before she acknowledged Leah. Leah, on the other hand, took in her hostess's plumed turban and had to resist the urge to giggle. Her headdress bobbing with every dip of her head, the old lady craned her neck to greet her great-nephew.

"Dear boy! I vow I feared that you would miss your own betrothal party, and Bucky and I should look ridiculous without you! And this is Miss Cole?" The black eyes traveled sharply over Leah as though she could count every penny expended on her gown, and then she smiled. "Charmed to make your acquaintance, my dear—truly I am. I'd not thought to see Tony leg-shackled before his dotage, you know—made me fear the end of the Barsetts." Extending two fingers to be shaken, she dipped her turban again in approval. But the duchess's next words made Leah stiffen as the old woman spoke lower to Tony. "She will do, I think. No, no, do not take offense, my dear," she told Leah. "One never knows until one sees one."

"One what?" Leah's voice was deceptively sweet as she faced the old woman. "A Cit?" She could feel the viscount's arm tense beneath her fingers, but his determined smile never betrayed him.

"Well, she ain't one of those milk-and-water misses, is she?" the duchess commented. "But she cannot care a chip what anyone says." Turning once again to Leah, she bobbed her turban knowingly. "That's not to say you won't have much to bear with my scapegrace nevvy. He was right, you know—you are an Original. Bucky!"

A rather colorless female of indeterminate age hastened to the duchess's side, her pale blue eyes beaming at Tony. "Is this—"

"Miss Cole," the duchess cut in, "I present my companion, Mrs. Buckhaven—flighty, but she ain't got a dissembling bone in her."

"Mrs. Buckhaven." Leah inclined her head politely.

"Oh, my lord, she *is* lovely," the woman said breathily. "Pleased to make your acquaintance, Miss Cole."

Somehow Leah managed to smile beneath the open appraisals of the men and the cold stares of the women as the duchess's guests filed past her. Tony, on the other hand, chatted pleasantly with people whose names were synonymous with the *haut ton* itself.

The musicians struck up the first dance at almost the same time as the line ended, and Tony leaned to whisper for her ears alone, "You do waltz, do you not?"

"Will you cry off if I do not?"

"No."

"Then I suppose I waltz."

He led her through the expectant crowd and whirled her into his arms, and she immediately discovered the difference between an effeminate dance master and Anthony Barsett. At first, she hesitated, stiffening at the warm feel of his hands on her waist, but as he guided her gracefully across the polished floor in perfect time to the beautiful music, she began to relax. His arm tightened, pulling her closer until their bodies nearly touched. The fragrance of his Hungary water floated down to her, and despite its faintness, it was extremely pleasant. She was struck by two things as his arm tightened again and her gown brushed against his clothing—his strength and his obvious masculinity. At first, she found it difficult to concentrate on her steps within his embrace—it was no wonder that Byron had termed it the seductive waltz. Finally the loveliness of the music soothed her and she almost forgot her dislike of the man who held her.

"Lean into me—'tis a love match, remember." He spoke softly, his breath on her ear sending a shiver down her spine.

"I don't—" Before she could protest, he held her even closer, until she could rest her head against his broad, muscular shoulder. "My lord, this is most improper," she protested low. "I insist you give me room to breathe."

"Tony," he reminded her. "And you are breathing—I can feel it when you do."

She thought she ought to pull away, but then she did not truly wish to make a scene. Looking up at him, she realized her father had been right—Viscount Lyndon did look much like a Greek god. Studying him covertly though thick lashes, she had to admit she was not entirely invulnerable to his handsomeness. He was quite tall, probably six inches taller than she, and he wore that softly waving blond hair of his brushed forward in the classical style. His chin was well-defined, unlike some of the more inbred of the nobility she'd seen, his nose was as patrician as an ancient Roman's and his eyes were the deep, brilliant blue of a lake on a bright summer's day. The total effect was devastating to a female's peace of mind.

"Well, do I pass your inspection, my dear?" he murmured with a slightly wry twist to his altogether too sensuous mouth.

She jumped guiltily and nearly missed a step. "I do not know what you mean, my lord," she muttered. "I was but trying to appear interested, according to your instructions.''

"Well, are you?'' He gazed lazily down, meeting your eyes.

"Of course not.''

"Then do keep up the pretense, for I quite enjoy it.''

"There is no end to your conceit, is there?''

He turned her expertly to the last notes of the waltz, and almost immediately she was claimed by a distant cousin of his. "I say, Lyndon,'' the pleasant-faced man greeted Tony. "You cannot stay in her pocket all night—'twould be monstrous unfair to the rest of us.''

"Davenham,'' Tony acknowledged. "Leah, you recall Arthur, from the receiving line, do you not? He inherited from Aunt Hester's husband.'' His eyes twinkling as he handed her over, Tony bowed in her direction. "Sets are forming, my dear, and I collect he wishes to lead you out. Servant, Coz.''

Irritated by her betrothed's almost cavalier dismissal of her, Leah flashed the expectant duke her most enchanting smile and took his arm. Tony, on the other hand, stepped back to watch them, his face sober for a moment, and then a satisfied smile warmed his eyes. For all her words and airs, Leah Cole was more like other females than she would care to admit. And he had not a doubt in the world that he could win her. Slowly he walked from the dance floor.

"I say, Tony—Miss Cole *is* an Incomparable!'' Gil Renfield caught his sleeve to halt him. "It ain't fair, but you have stolen the march on all of us, you know.'' Leaning closer, he added under his breath, "But I own I was surprised to read you was marrying her—until I discovered her papa is Jeptha Cole.''

"Dashed shock,'' Hugh Rivington murmured behind them, "but I daresay it don't matter she's a Cit when one counts the settlements. Give it to the duchess, though—thought of everything, didn't she? Can't understand why she invited Rotherfield, though, unless she wanted the tabbies to talk more about him than your Miss Cole.''

"Rotherfield—here?'' Tony gave a surprised start and observed dryly, " 'Tis not his sort of amusement.''

"Came in while you was dancing with Miss Cole. Thought you knew of it—I mean, he stood right here and watched you, didn't he, Gil?"

"Uh-huh. Said she looked good enough to grace *his* table, if you could credit it."

"Well, he's—" Tony stopped in mid-sentence, his attention suddenly riveted on the dark-haired woman who stood in the doorway. "You will have to pardon me."

"Now, I *know* the duchess did not invite her," Gil said with certainty.

But Anthony Barsett had already left him standing as he moved quickly to intercept Elaine Chandler. He caught her before she'd actually entered the ballroom, but he was still too late—already her presence had been remarked, and there was a ripple of malicious interest moving through the crowd.

Looking over the duke's shoulder, Leah saw her also and noted the smug glances. "That woman—the one over there—who is she?" she asked curiously, certain that something was amiss. Her partner looked where she directed, and in his shock, missed his step. "The woman in the green gown? Why . . . uh, I believe that is Mrs. Chandler." He coughed apologetically and turned her away. "Can't think that Aunt Hester meant to invite her. In fact . . ." His voice trailed off as he caught himself and shook his head. " 'Tis no concern of yours, Miss Cole—Tony will tend to the matter, I am sure."

Her interest now thoroughly aroused, Leah craned her neck uncomfortably for another glimpse of the beautiful Mrs. Chandler, and could not resist asking, "I collect she is one of Lyndon's Other Interests then?" This time the duke went into a full paroxysm of coughing, and she knew she'd hit the mark.

"Miss Cole," Davenham managed in strangled accents, "it is not a fitting subject to discuss with a lady."

"As if I did not know of such things," she scoffed, trying to appear unconcerned. "Besides, it is not as though this were a . . ." Biting back the worlds "love match," she finished lamely, "Well, I daresay she is not, then, after all." She had no intention of letting anyone other than Lord Lyndon himself know how very affronted she was.

Mercifully, the music finally ended, and she turned to leave the floor. Noting the malicious satisfaction of the women around her, she determined to find Barsett, despite the clamor of gentlemen who vied for the next dance with her. Involuntarily, her eyes went to the door—just as her betrothed took Mrs. Chandler's arm and left the crowded ballroom. Resolving to hide her chagrin, Leah moved to stand alone in front of a row of tall potted ferns.

"Surely Hester did not invite that creature!" she heard someone on the other side exclaim in astonishment.

"I shouldn't think so—but then she cannot approve of Lyndon's betrothed either, can she? My dear, the chit positively smells of the shop!"

Tittery laughter came through the ferns as the first woman answered, "But what can she do about it, after all? I have heard his pockets were entirely let, and she cannot have wanted him hanging on *her* purse."

"Well, I had it of Charlotte Edgeworth that Hester tolerates the situation because his circumstances were quite desperate, although they are giving out that it is a love match."

"Nonetheless, 'tis lowering to think we shall be expected to receive the girl."

"Well, I for one do not intend to do it. Oh, I shall not give her the cut direct—Tony can be such a hothead, and he will protect her, if for no reason than that she is to be his wife. I shall simply avoid her."

"My dears, did you see that ridiculous gown?" Yet another voice joined the gossips, and it carried with wounding clarity. "She obviously aspires above her station."

"Men are such fools—my own dear Bertrand stood like a gaping fool when he saw her. But of course it does not signify, for even he admits that she's naught but an encroaching little Cit."

"That dress must have cost a hundred guineas."

Leah's cheeks flamed dangerously, more from anger than hurt, anger that Tony had left her unprotected from their malice. Seething, she turned to confront them herself.

"You must not let the barbs of jealous females overset you, my dear. Before he lost his fortune, most of those same tabbies had hopes that Lyndon could be brought up to scratch for their silly daughters."

She spun around at the sound of a very masculine voice and was startled to see the strikingly handsome man behind her. Her eyes widened, taking in his tall, well-proportioned frame, his raven-black hair, black eyes, and sardonic smile. He was attired almost entirely in black, save for his snowy white shirt and cravat, and even those were extremely plain above his black silk waistcoat. Large diamond shirt studs that winked in the light were his only apparent affectation. "Lord Rotherfield." She brightened, glad for the diversion. "So kind of you to come."

He bowed slightly, surprised by the warmth in her voice. "I am seldom kind, Miss Cole." His black eyes met hers and held steadily. And then one eyebrow rose skeptically. "Dear me, can it be that you are unafraid of this notorious earl?"

There was a bitter inflection on the last words that roused her curiosity. "You have the advantage of me, sir, for I scarce know you," she admitted candidly. "But I am pleased to further the acquaintance."

"Do not be so certain of that, Miss Cole. The stories told of me are seldom pleasant."

Startled by his frankness, she shook her head. "Well, I daresay gossip never gives the right of anything, my lord. You do not appear . . ."

"Evil," he supplied when she hesitated.

"Well, I was not going to say *that*, precisely. Indeed, you appear less frightening to me than half of the people in this room."

"Then I may have the pleasure of this dance?"

Her eyes strayed to the empty doorway, a gesture he did not miss, for he said, "Yes, I believe Lyndon is occupied just now, but if you fear that he will be displeased—"

"Oh no! No, of course not!" The reminder of her betrothed's outrageous behavior was enough to make her reckless. "It is not very much to the point what Lord Lyndon chooses to think, anyway, my lord."

"Then?"

"I should enjoy it."

Noting the gasps from those members of the *haut ton* they passed, Leah felt a certain sense of satisfaction as Rotherfield led her onto the floor and put his hand on her waist. She might shock them, but at least she would not be an object of false sympathy. To her pleasure, the earl proved to be an excellent dancer, nearly as light on his feet and as graceful as Anthony Barsett. Moreover, his conduct was correct in the extreme, and unlike her unwanted betrothed, he did not keep pulling her closer.

"You dance quite well, Miss Cole," he observed quietly.

"Thank you. Does it surprise you that a Cit can dance?"

"Certainly not, my dear. Had I wished to say such to you, I would have."

"My apologies, my lord. Not knowing Rotherfield, I did not know that."

"At least you speak your mind, do you not? I was afraid you would prove to be one of those simpering misses who are all looks and no brains, but I find myself mistaken." A faint smile played at his lips, softening the harsh handsomeness of his face. "One word of advice, Miss Cole—you must forget you are a Cit before anyone else will. And above all, to rise to the gossip's bait is fatal. Ignore them as I have done, and they will seek their sport elsewhere. I know."

At the end of the music, he led her back through the crush of people to the refreshment table, where he stood conversing with her for several minutes. But even as she spoke with Rotherfield, she cast about the room for her missing betrothed.

"As for my second word of advice," the earl murmured low, "you must not appear to be in Lyndon's pocket. He will come to expect it."

At that moment Lyndon chose to reappear in the doorway with the lovely Elaine Chandler hanging on his arm. His face was flushed, and to Leah it was obvious that they had been enjoying an intimate *tête-à-tête* somewhere. Her sense of ill-usage complete, Leah turned impulsively to the earl.

"I should like to go home."

At first Rotherfield was not certain he'd heard her aright, and he shook his head. "You cannot wish to give up the field to the gossips, my dear."

"No, I wish to leave Lyndon here," she snapped tersely. "I should prefer they laugh at him rather than me." Looking up at her companion's intrigued expression, she asked suddenly, "Do you have a carriage here, my lord?"

"I did not come in a rented hackney, Miss Cole."

"Then would you be so kind as to take me home?"

"You wish to leave with me?" His black eyebrow shot up in surprise. "Are you quite certain you have considered the consequences?" he asked gently. "Association with me is dangerous—and Lyndon will be angered."

"I do not care if he is furious. And you cannot possibly be worse than the man my father would have me marry."

"And you are not afraid I will molest you?" There was a gleam of amusement in the black eyes that studied her. "You must surely be the first of your sex to trust me in many years."

"No—I think you a gentleman."

His smile widened as he offered her his arm. "Then, Miss Cole, you are probably the only woman in the room to hold that opinion."

Still absorbed with ridding himself of Elaine Chandler, Tony did not note Leah and the earl. Literally pulling his sleeve from Elaine's grasp, he shook free of her. "Enough of this—you are creating an unpleasant scene," he hissed. "You should not have come."

"Please, Tony—only say you'll come to see me later."

He ran his fingers distractedly through his hair and yet tried to appear uninvolved to the interested parties around them. "You'll have to leave, Elaine—'tis unseemly to humiliate Leah like this."

"A Cit!" She spat out the word like something too unpleasant to swallow.

"My betrothed," he reminded her coldly. "I'll get your shawl."

"But you will come?"

"I . . ." He knew her renewed interest in him was a mercenary one, and he could have cursed himself for not bidding her good-bye earlier. But he had to get rid of her now any way he could, before Leah got wind of her. Reluctantly he nodded. "All right."

"Tony!" Gil Renfield tapped him on the shoulder and hissed in his ear, "Whilst you have been making a cake of yourself with La Chandler, Miss Cole has left with Rotherfield."

Beset by the knowledge that his aunt would cut up a dust over Elaine, Tony snapped, "Gil, I am in no mood for jests."

"Ain't jesting—saw it with m'own eyes, I swear it."

"Lud!" he groaned. "And you did not stop her?"

"She ain't my betrothed—and I ain't putting myself before Rotherfield, anyway. I ain't a fool," Gil retorted.

Alarmed, Tony forgot Elaine and everything else. Leah was no match for someone like Marcus Halvert—she was not up to his weight at all. "When did they leave?" he demanded tersely.

"Can't have been above five minutes. Wait—where are you going?" Gil called out.

"After her. Tell Aunt Hester that Leah has the headache and Rotherfield's taking her home," Tony flung over his shoulder.

Dumfounded by it all, Gil stared after him, scratching his head and mumbling doubtfully, "It ain't going to fadge—the old girl ain't stupid enough to believe anybody'd send a female home in Rotherfield's company. Shocking bad *ton*, for one thing, and for another . . ." He stopped. It didn't make any difference what he thought—Tony Barsett was already out the door in pursuit.

12

Lord Rotherfield had barely taken Leah home, escorted her to her door, and departed before Anthony Barsett arrived. Pushing past the astonished butler, who was already confused by her precipitate arrival home in the company of another man, Tony confronted her lividly.

"There you are, my girl! What the devil did you mean by leaving my aunt's like that? I doubt even she can scotch the *on-dit* now!" His face flushed with anger, he tapped his foot on the marble tiles. "Well, I am waiting to hear what you have to say for yourself, Miss Cole," he snapped.

"Your're waiting for an explanation!" Her own cheeks grew red as she faced him, and her gray eyes flashed fire at the challenge. "You're waiting for an explanation?" The sarcasm dripped from her rising voice. "That's rich, it is!"

"Well?"

Her bosom heaving at the effrontery of it all, she exhaled deeply to calm herself before answering. "You will not call me to book, my lord, when 'tis your scandalous behavior that has exceeded all bounds!"

"*My* behavior! 'Twas not I who left with Rotherfield, Miss Cole, giving rise to all manner of unpleasant gossip!"

"How dare you, sir! How *dare* you? You left me to be the butt of cruel gossips whilst you dallied elsewhere—and during *my* betrothal party! And you think 'tis I who owe you an explanation? Well, I do not—and what is more to the point, Lord Lyndon, you may consider you have whistled my father's fortune down the wind! Our betrothal, sham that it was, is at an end!"

"You are yelling, Miss Cole!"

"You are shouting, sir!"

"You still have not explained how you came to leave with the Earl of Rotherfield!"

"Did you not hear me? I owe you nothing! Nothing on earth could induce me to ally myself with such a . . . a *libertine*!" she fumed. "You and your fancy *ton* can go to the very devil, for all I care!" She turned to run up the stairs, but he caught her and pulled her into her father's library. Unceremoniously he pushed her into a chair and stood over her. "I am still waiting, Miss Cole."

"*Get out of my house*!"

"Listen to me, you little fool!" Lowering his voice, he managed to speak evenly. "I do not know what you think you saw, but I was attempting to persuade an unwanted guest to leave my aunt's house. No one invited Mrs. Chandler."

"Really? And just why was she not invited? 'Twould seem that everyone else was, sir. But could it be that she is perhaps your bit of fluff?"

"That liaison is past, Miss Cole."

"You must think me incredibly stupid, Lord Lyndon." She sneered. "Well, I am not so green that I do not know an insult when I have been given one. If, as you said, she was uninvited, you could have had the servants escort her out."

" 'Tis you who are incredibly stupid, Miss Cole!" he shot back. "*You* left with Rotherfield! Being seen with a man of his reputation puts you beyond my or my aunt's help, you goose!"

"His reputation! Sir, were I not so angry, I would laugh in your face, I assure you. His reputation cannot possibly be worse than your own, I'll warrant! You are a rakehell, a gamester, and a . . . a gazetted fortune-hunter, Anthony Barsett! How dare you impugn anyone else's character when yours is just as black? Indeed, I found Lord Rotherfield to be all that is gentlemanly," she finished defiantly.

"Aha! I think you are jealous!" he crowed in triumph.

"Jealous! she shrieked. "Listen to me, you idiot, and

listen carefully—I do not care if you have a hundred mistresses, do you understand me? But you will not have Papa's money to support them!" She looked up to where he leaned, one hand on each arm of her chair. "Now, you will pardon me, but I intend to retire."

"I think not—not just yet, Miss Cole." He bent closer, and to her horror, she feared he was about to kiss her. His face blurred, and she closed her own in preparation for the worst. But his lips never met hers.

"My dears! What in heaven's name is this unseemly commotion?"

Tony jerked his head back at the sound of Jeptha Cole's voice, and straightened guiltily. In the doorway, the old man was still tying his dressing gown over his nightshirt. Ignoring their red faces, he addressed his daughter.

"Did you not pass an agreeable evening at the duchess's, my dear?" he asked with a perfectly straight face.

She remembered with a pang of remorse how he'd beamed so proudly at her when they'd left, and she could not bring herself to tell him how it had been. "Yes, Papa—'twas a splendid party," she lied.

"And Leah outshone 'em all, didn't she, my lord?"

"That she did, sir," Tony admitted.

"Then what brought this quarrel on?" the old man demanded, looking from his lordship to his daughter.

"Lord Lyndon did not approve my standing up with so many men," she invented, her eyes daring Tony to dispute it. " 'Twas but jealousy, I suppose," she added sweetly as she met his thunderous look.

"Everybody talking about my Leah, eh?"

"I think it can be truthfully said that there was not a person present whose tongue did not wag with her name, sir," Tony answered, his double meaning obvious only to her.

"Well, it was to be expected, you know." Cole nodded smugly. " 'Tis quite a girl you'll be getting, if I was to brag about it."

"She is that. I can scarce wait for the wedding."

The old man cocked his head to look knowingly at his prospective son-in-law. "So that's the way of it, is it?" he asked, grinning. "I might've knowed she'd win you also. Well, well, we'll have to tend to the matter then, won't we? I'd set m'mind on a big wedding, mind you, but I'll not cavil at a Special License, I suppose.''

''Papa!'' Leah choked in horror.

''What's this, miss? You never put much stock in fripperies, anyways, did you? Always said you did not,'' her father maintained stoutly.

''No, but—''

''Then I leave it to Lyndon—when would you have her?'' Turning to Anthony Barsett, he waited for the answer despite Leah's indignant gasp.

''It should not take me above a week to get my affairs in order, sir—I'd thought to take her to the Continent, Paris perhaps.'' With a spark of mischief in his blue eyes, he looked at Leah. ''Or would you prefer Italy, my dear?''

''I'd as lief not go anywhere with you, my lord.'' She gritted out the words tersely.

''But of course you will have a wedding trip! 'Tis her nerves, my lord—you must not mind her,'' Jeptha Cole reassured Tony. ''Pick your place and I will provide the passage myself—a wedding gift to the both of you.''

''But, Papa . . . your health . . . I'd not leave . . .''

''Nonsense!''

''But I have no trousseau!'' she exclaimed desperately.

''I believe I can remedy that, my dear,'' Tony said smoothly. ''I am not without influence with Madame Cecile, and I believe I can contrive to obtain what you require. Indeed, I shall take you up at ten o'clock this morning, that we may have you fitted early.''

''But I do not need clothes!''

''Set your mind one way or t'other, missy!'' her papa snapped. ''Which is it? I ain't educated, but to my way o'thinking, clothes and trousseau is one and the same!''

''Papa, I need time! I cannot—''

''Time for what?'' he demanded. ''So's you can become even more missish in the matter? No, I ain't got the time!'' Even as he spoke, he clutched the back of a chair and waited for the pain in his chest to stop. ''Forgive me, my lord . . . got to sit . . .''

Responding with alacrity, Tony eased him into a seat.

Her anger forgotten, Leah went white with fear and guilt. "Papa—"

"No, no, 'tis past." Slowly the older man relaxed to mop the perspiration from his forehead with the sleeve of his dressing gown. "Now, as you was saying, puss?"

"'Tis nothing to the point, Papa." Sighing, she knew when she was beaten. "I will be available at ten, Lord Lyndon." Gathering her dignity about her, she held her chin high. "But I find myself overwearied just now. If you will pardon me, I shall leave the both of you to discuss my future. Good night, Papa. Good night, my lord."

Tony stared after her, sensing her desolation, and he wished he'd had the time to pay proper court to her. But her brief, however innocent, encounter with Rotherfield had given him pause. If she had attracted the earl's interest, he risked gaining a dangerous enemy. No, it was better to marry Leah Cole first and win her later, he was certain, for Marcus Halvert might be less inclined to pursue a married lady, since he'd been burned at that before.

"Oh, about our discussion, my lord . . ." Jeptha Cole's words cut into Tony's thoughts. "I still don't see the difference, but if you was still wanting the loan rather than the settlement . . ."

Reluctantly Tony turned back to him. "I'd have you settle a respectable sum on her, of course, sir—say, twenty thousand? But I'd as lief earn mine."

"Got your pride, ain't you? Don't want to be bought, I suppose." Seeing Tony's shoulders stiffen, he nodded. "Don't see the difference myself—'twill all be yours when I am gone anyway, but I mean to settle however you wish it."

"I will see you are repaid, sir."

"'Course you will—got a good head for the business. Just wish you'd let me give you the money."

"As you said, I have my pride."

"Hot to have her, ain't you?" Cole changed the subject abruptly.

"Yes."

"Aye, I know the way of that." His eyes lifted to his dead wife's portrait. "'Twas the same with me. When I saw Marianna standing in the posting house with that portmanteau, I knew I had to have her. And whether you credit it or not, I'd sampled my share of the other kind also. Yes, well . . ." His voice trailed off, and his eyes misted for a moment before he collected himself. "Forgive the maundering of an old man, Lyndon. I know you'll do right by my girl."

"I mean to."

"Got to give her her head sometimes, though—like my Marianna. Now, she was one to have her own way until I gave it to her. Then I'll be damned if she wasn't downright reasonable."

"Yes . . . well, sir, would you like help up the stairs ere I go? If I am to be back at ten, I'd best seek my own bed."

"No, no. Be off with you then." Cole reached a hand to Lyndon's, clasping it warmly. "Don't worry—you'll tame each other, my lord. Forgive me if I do not see you out."

He leaned back in his chair after Lord Lyndon left and contemplated Marianna. "Well, my dear, the die is cast, ain't it? What d'ye think of our fine Corinthian?" His eyes intent on the well-memorized face, he nodded slowly. "Aye, I knew you'd like him. But 'twill be as Petruchio and Katharina, I fear, before 'tis done." Then a self-satisfied smile broadened his face. "I'll warrant you thought I'd forgotten taking you to that play, didn't you? Well, I ain't—I ain't forgot a day."

13

Elaine Chandler opened the door of her house herself, and her welcoming smile froze on her face as her visitor stepped into the foyer. It was obvious from the sheer confection she wore that she'd expected someone else.

"You!" she choked with loathing.

"My dear Elaine . . ." The expression on his face was pained, but a faint smile played about his lips. "What have I ever done to warrant such a greeting from you? Was I not generous to a fault?"

He walked around her still-stiff body and into the small formal saloon off the front hall. Taking out his quizzing glass, he inspected some of her more recent acquisitions—a Sèvres vase, an ormolu clock, and a handsome marble figurine. Glaring, she followed him.

"Carrington," he hazarded knowingly as his fingers touched a particularly exquisite jeweled box on the mantel. "For 'tis doubtful that Lyndon would waste his money on such trinkets. But then who knows," he added softly. " 'Tis certain he will come into a great sum of money soon, is it not?"

"What is it that you want here, Marcus?"

"Nothing *here*, my dear." He turned around and raked her with those cold black eyes. "Alas, your charms faded for me years ago."

"Then get out!"

"Ah, yes—the company. I collect you are expecting Lyndon, are you not?" His mouth twisted and the irony in his voice was unmistakable. "Can you not spare a few moments for an old friend?"

"For God's sake, Marcus—leave!"

"Surely you do not think he would mistake me for one

of your lovers, do you? If he does not take exception to these . . . er . . . tokens from others, my dear, he must be quite tolerant—more tolerant than I had imagined him to be, actually."

"Get out."

"But then perhaps he does not pay all your bills," he continued, ignoring her request.

"If you do not leave on the instant, he *will* think you my lover!" she spat at him. "And since you no longer pay them, 'tis none of your affair."

"In due time, Elaine—in due time. I come as your friend, you know," he murmured with deceptive softness. "If you seek to hold Lyndon, I stand ready to assist you in the endeavor."

"You?" Her eyebrow lifted scornfully and her lip curved in a sneer. "You'd not give aid to a dying man unless it suited you."

"Elaine . . . Elaine . . . such rancor." He shook his head, feigning injury. "And after so many years."

"I can think of no reason why you would wish to help me," she told him flatly.

He moved to study the clock on the mantelpiece before answering. "I do not wish him to marry Leah Cole," he announced with his back to her. "And that, my dear, makes us natural allies, does it not?"

"Tony needs her money—'tis all over London that he is done up."

"I am willing to pay to remove him from my path."

"You wish to mount Tony's little Cit?" she demanded incredulously, coming up behind him. "From all I have heard of it, Cole has too much money and influence to allow such a thing."

He paused in his examination of the ormolu clock. " 'Tis an expensive piece, my dear—quite fine," he decided. "Actually, my interest in the matter need not concern you."

"Are you like the rest of them?" she asked curiously. "Somehow I cannot see you dangling after a Cit for any reason."

He set the timepiece down abruptly and turned around. "I do not believe I owe you an explanation, Elaine," he told her coldly. "My reasons are and shall remain mine own. But she is a beauty, you must admit—and so fresh and unspoiled, unlike some of the more experienced of my acquaintance."

The barb struck home, sending a new tremor of misgiving through her, for she'd been stunned when she'd seen Lyndon's Cit. For the first time in her career, she'd actually worried about her position, coming home to examine her own face in her mirror, wondering if she should perhaps accept Carrington's suit, after all.

"You must want her very much," she said bitterly.

"I want Lyndon out of my path, Elaine."

" 'Tis no concern of mine!" she snapped.

"And I thought you wanted him back—or did you not know 'tis common gossip that he lives in her pocket now?"

"Because he has to! For God's sake, Marcus, leave me be! If he stands attention for her, 'tis for her father's money!"

"I wonder . . ." He let his voice trail off speculatively, knowing full well he'd touched on her vulnerability.

" 'Tis all over London that his pockets are to let. If you have not heard it, you are deaf."

"I own I had thought it so also, but now that I have seen Miss Cole, I am not so certain. Perhaps he is merely smitten."

"Tony? You jest, of course! My dear Marcus, nothing but money could bring him to wed below his station—and well I know it."

He picked up the marble statuette for a closer look and then replaced it. "We digress, my dear," he reminded her. "I have no interest in why he is betrothed to her—I merely wish to end the arrangement between them."

"But she *is* betrothed to Lyndon—she is to be Lyndon's lady. I fail to see—"

"We will remove him, of course."

"But how . . . ?" She stared, her expression reflecting her dawning horror. "Oh, Marcus, you would not!"

"That would be the last resort," he admitted. "But actually I mean to rely on you to keep him out of my way, Elaine."

"But he has to marry her. I cannot . . . You saw . . ."

"Tut, my dear. I had thought your avaricious spirit able to scheme better than this." His black eyebrow rose skeptically as he watched her with those black eyes of his. "Or have I mistaken your greed?"

"Tony is worthless to me if he is in dun territory, my lord. He has to marry the Cit."

"I may decide to buy him off, and he may take my offer—if he thinks she is lost to him anyway." Moving closer, he reached to lift a strand of dark hair away from her temple as she shivered in recoil. "A good bargain, I believe—he does not have to wed for money, and he can yet afford you—or another like you."

"And what do I get?" she demanded suspiciously.

"Lyndon perhaps?"

"No. 'Tisn't as though he would ever marry me. No, Marcus, I do not come so cheaply. 'Twill cost you a thousand pounds for my assistance."

"Come now, Elaine, I saw that little scene you played out at Davenham House earlier tonight. It prickles your pride that he has left your bed."

"He amuses me." She held out a slender arm and admired the winking light reflected off a diamond bracelet that Lord Carrington had given her. "Actually, I prefer things of a more permanent nature than the gentlemen themselves."

"Mercenary jade," he said approvingly.

"I do not mean to end my days in some cramped room somewhere when I grow aged, Marcus. One thousand pounds the day the betrothal is broken."

" 'Tis cheaper to kill him," he complained.

"One thousand pounds," she repeated evenly. "And I have changed my mind—I'd have it now, I think."

"Elaine . . . 'tis Rotherfield you bargain with," he murmured. "As you recall, I pay only for what I get. One thousand pounds *if* one of them cries off." His black eyes raked over her, lingering where the sheer fabric clung to her breasts. "Ah, Elaine, 'tis such pleasure doing business with you, for you always have your price."

"And what if I cannot do it? What if I cannot stop Tony's marriage—what then?"

"In that case . . . Well, let us not contemplate that just yet."

"You'll kill him. Marcus, you are positively evil."

His eyes as hard as obsidian, he stepped back. "I make no apologies for what I am, Elaine. But now that we understand one another, I shall leave you to Lyndon, my dear, and wish you good fortune."

"But how . . . ?"

"That is your affair—you are not anything if not resourceful, my dear. 'Tis *always* such a pleasure engaging in business with you," he repeated softly.

After he left, she sat up far into the night, waiting for Anthony Barsett. The candles were guttered and the wicks were sputtering before she could be brought to admit to herself that he was not coming. Alternating between rage and despair, she finally could stand it no longer. Pacing the floor, she pondered just how to bring him back to her now that he was going to be rich again. She even contemplated warning him about Rotherfield, but then thought better of that. She had better hope of the thousand pounds.

Her foray to Davenham House had been a calculated risk and a serious mistake. Her first look at Lyndon's thunderous, almost murderous countenance had told her that—long before he put his rebuff into words. He'd dragged her into the duchess's kitchen—the kitchen yet . . . she seethed as she remembered—and he'd told her that he could not allow her to embarrass Miss Cole. As if Miss Cole were actually somebody! Miss Cole—a damned Cit.

Her brief glimpse of Leah Cole had done little to soothe her jangled nerves either, for the chit was beautiful in an unusual way. Had she not heard Sally Jersey whisper to Mrs. Drummond-Burrell that the girl was going to take? And had not young Harry Campbell pronounced Miss Cole an Incomparable? On reflection, she had no illusions that the girl would even be openly cut. Oh, the men would flock to her, and the women would be cool to her, but if Tony married her and the duchess promoted her entrée into society, Leah Cole would establish herself.

Elaine toyed with her bracelet, admiring it again. The

gift of an aging roué who was becoming decidedly partial in his attentions, it was a reminder that she need not exert herself to throw a spoke in Tony's wheel. There was something to be said for the security of another marriage, even to the wheezing Lord Carrington. But then everybody would assume she'd lost the handsome viscount to Leah Cole, and that would be unbearable.

Resolutely she sat at her writing desk and composed a conciliatory message to Tony. There would be no recriminations and no begging—just a brief missive stating her regret over the incident and promising to remain his "friend." As an afterthought, she sprinkled a few drops of his favorite scent on the envelope for a reminder of better times between them. Retiring, she regained her confidence. She was, after all, skilled as a lover, and the Cole chit was naught but a sheltered virgin.

Across town, Marcus Halvert stayed awake until well past dawn considering just how far he wished to go to get Leah Cole. And his ultimate conclusion surprised even him.

14

Leah rose early, not so much because Lord Lyndon was to take her up, but rather because she could not sleep. After a night of turmoil that left her drained, defeated, and ill-tempered, she had to admit that Anthony Barsett had utterly outfaced her. She wavered back and forth, telling herself that she could fight the marriage still, and then admitting that she was a mere female, after all, and what did females have to say to such matters? Not nearly enough, as far as she was concerned. Oh, she knew the daughters of the nobility had been bargained into marriage for centuries, but, dash it, she was a Cit.

No, whether she liked it or not, she was going to fulfill her father's fondest wish and be a titled lady. As Jeanne dragged a comb through her tangled hair, she considered his advice. *"You don't like him . . . well, that ain't as important as you was to think . . . manage him . . . you've got to make him love you!"* The words echoed in her head over and over again. And just when she almost had herself argued into accepting the truth of her father's advice, Jeanne hit a particularly bad snarl, bringing tears to her eyes. No! What about Lyndon himself? Why was it not up to him to make her love him? Why should she give everything in the bargain? He had her money, after all. Besides, she'd seen the Chandler woman, and who could possibly wish to compete against a beautiful mistress?

" 'Tis enough, Jeanne," she snapped impatiently. "Just pin it up and have done."

"But, mademoiselle—"

"No."

The steady drizzle of a spring rain did nothing to raise her spirits either, and the sound of a carriage halting in the street added to her sense of ill-usage. Damn the fellow—was he never late? Leaning forward to study her face in the mirror, she knew she looked positively hagged.

" 'Tis enough, Jeanne," she muttered, rising.

"But 'twill come down. Just a few more pins—"

"I have to get down before he persuades Papa 'tis Gretna Green today. Every time they are alone, Lyndon manages to turn my father up sweet, Jeanne. Fetch me the paisley shawl—no, best hand the spencer with the military trim instead . . . and the cossack hat, I think."

"The cossack? But—"

"The cossack." Leah slipped the spencer jacket over her dark blue crepe walking dress and worked the frogs with her fingers. "And have Annie tell Crome to have Lord Lyndon wait in the green saloon. I do not wish Papa disturbed." Taking the military hat and setting it over her curls until only a few peeped out, she reached for the black kid gloves that would complement her toilette. "Well, what do you think?"

"I think he will think you mean to do battle."

"Good—I may be beaten, but I mean to let him know I am not defenseless."

Belowstairs, Tony Barsett paced the floor in the green saloon, having been informed that "Miss wishes you to wait here, my lord." He too had spent a sleepless night sorting out his own mixed feelings about the marriage. Part of his rational mind told him he was a fool to ally himself with a female who came not only from the merchant class but who also did not want him. For despite his many conquests amongst the female sex, it could be truthfully said that he'd never before pursued anyone who did not truly wish to be caught, and certainly none who did not play the coquettish games of enticement. Nor did he ever dally with respectable females, raising hopes he did not intend to fulfill. And he definitely was not given to rapine—indeed, the thought thoroughly repelled him. The world was full enough with willing women, anyway, women who knew what they were about, who gave themselves quite liberally both for pleasure and for money.

But Leah Cole was quite a different matter. All

thoughts of her father and his money aside, she was the most attractive female of his memory. And despite the fact that he'd wanted her for his mistress from the moment he'd seen her, he was becoming reconciled to marrying her. She possessed not only beauty but also wit and intelligence, a combination he'd despaired of finding in the same girl. She exasperated him, but she didn't bore him.

The cynical side of him insisted that what he felt for her was desire and the exhilaration of pursuit, but the rational side advanced the wholly novel idea that he could love her. And as for that nonsense about a business arrangement . . . well, he'd never met the female he couldn't win. In fact, 'twas usually that they pursued him whenever he exerted himself to be charming.

Absorbed in his thoughts of her, he did not look up until he heard her enter the room. Then, to hide the pleasure he felt at the sight of her, he flicked open his watch.

"Well, Miss Cole, you are almost prompt."

" 'Tis but ten now, my lord, and—" Her words were cut short as his eyes flicked over her with what she considered a shade too much familiarity. "And I wish you would not look at me like that!" she snapped.

" 'Tis too early for carping, my dear, so I beg your pardon for however you think I am looking at you." A smile lifted the corners of his mouth and crinkled the edges of his eyes. "But I own I am surprised. Er . . . am I to take it that you fear I mean to storm the citadel?"

She looked down at the black braid frogs on her spencer and gave him a grudging smile. "My citadel, sir, is fortified for the siege and cannot be taken."

"Still guarding your gold, eh?"

"No, sir," she shot back. "My person."

"Actually, you look lovely today, my dear—you will positively inspire every man you meet to buy his commission."

"Thank you. Are you quite ready, sir? For if you are, I should like to be done with this. I have hopes of being home before nuncheon."

"Actually," he announced cheerfully as he got the door, "I have made plans for the day, my dear. I had thought to go to Cecile's for a fitting, to Burle's for slippers, to Clark and Debenham's or Botibol's for bonnets, and—''

''Surely not. 'Twill take all day, and I—''

''And then nuncheon out, followed by ices at Gunther's,'' he continued, unperturbed by her dismay. ''And of course there is the park at five o'clock. 'See and be seen,' my aunt Davenham says, so that last night's contretemps will but be set down as a small lovers' spat.''

''And may I remind your lordship that we are promised to some sort of musicale tonight?'' she asked with deceptive sweetness, while ducking under his arm. ''How, pray tell me, am I to ready myself for that?''

''I shall set you down here at six-fifteen promptly and return at eight-thirty to take you up. 'Tis but Mrs. Chatsworth's small affair, after all. You will wear something simple and maidenish.''

''Now, really, my lord. I think that I—''

''Your appearance tonight is to still the tongues you set wagging last night, Miss Cole.'' He grasped her elbow to guide her down the steps while his coachman sprang to open the carriage door. ''I should have preferred an open vehicle, of course, but as 'tis raining, I thought you would wish to be dry.''

Cecile's was already alive with activity, but nonetheless the proprietress herself hurried to greet them, bobbing deferentially to Viscount Lyndon, ushering them into a private room with chairs and a table laden with fashion plates. '' '*I am not without influence with Madame Cecile*,' '' Leah mimicked low. ''Just how many mistresses has she dressed for you, my lord?''

''Several.'' Turning to Cecile, he announced, ''We shall require traveling dresses, walking dresses, pelisses, spencers, day gowns, evening wear, and a court dress. Everything save the court gown needs to be readied by next Wednesday, and I am prepared to expend the necessary to hire additional seamstresses for the task.''

After minor haggling over the haste required, they set about determining what Leah should have, poring over sketches and plates, making adjustments to designs, and choosing fabrics from book after book of swatches. At first irritated by the difference in deference between that afforded even a wealthy Miss Cole and a future viscountess, Leah nonetheless forgot her ire and became caught up in the selection process. Tony's taste in ladies' apparel was as flawless as in his own—he had an unerring eye for both line and color, and he knew exactly what he wanted. Deciding "Peach becomes you, my dear—bronze does not," and "This brings out your unusual eyes," he pulled out a stack of silk, taffeta, muslin, bombazine, and twill samples.

In general, the three of them agreed as to what flattered her best, but one design pushed forward by Cecile brought a frown to his face. As they were all standing now, holding up first this fabric and then that, Tony stepped behind Leah, slid his arms under hers, and put his hands over her breasts to indicate the height of neckline he wished. "She does not wish to display her charms like Haymarket ware, madam—if we are to take this style, 'twill have to be raised to here." Dropping his hands as her face flamed crimson, he stepped around to the front and traced across her shoulders with his fingertip. "And cut it thus—'tis more flattering. She has good bones here—show more shoulder and less bosom."

As Cecile turned around to mark on the sketch, Leah pushed his hand away, hissing, "Had I a hatpin just now, Lord Lyndon, you would be skewered with it."

"Your pardon, my dear."

"And you cannot stay here when they begin pinning the patterns."

The selection process, the pinning and repinning of cloth patterns, the marking and trimming, and the standing required infinite patience. For nearly two hours Tony paced in the outer parlor while cutters and seamstresses worked to assure that everything would be fitted exactly to Leah. And when at last she emerged, she declared forcefully, "I hope I never see another pair of scissors, nor pins, nor ribbons, nor braid again."

"We are nearly done—there are but slippers to match these samples and some hats left to order. Then I am for food, a lemon ice at Gunther's, and a leisurely drive in the park, by which time I am certain your feet will welcome that as much as mine.''

The rain had stopped by the time they emerged from the modiste's, and the equipage that rolled to the curb to take them up was his curricle rather than his carriage. ''I sent it home,'' he explained as he handed her up. ''You are better seen in this, after all.''

Their errands finished, it was slightly past three when they managed to put away the last of their ices in Gunther's front parlor. Despite all they'd accomplished, it had been for the most part a pleasant day passed between them. Laying aside his spoon, Tony leaned across the table. ''I have just thought—you have never seen Lyndon House, have you? If you are to live there, perhaps you would like to inspect the place, that any changes necessary to your comfort may be made whilst we are abroad. And you will wish to meet the servants, of course.''

''Of course,'' she murmured. ''I should like to inspect my chamber most particularly.''

To Leah, Lyndon House proved to be a pleasant surprise. Though not so large or commodious as her father's residence, it was nonetheless quite elegant and showed positively no signs of the viscount's recent financial distress. Indeed, it abounded with expensive pieces of furniture and artwork, all tastefully displayed against lovely carpets and damask-covered walls. Treading the front stairs to the second floor, she followed Tony as he threw open doors to all the rooms and stood aside for her to look at them.

His bedchamber was particularly attractive, with a tall postered bed, exquisite dark green canopy and hangings, well-polished chests and tables, thick Aubusson rug, and soft green silk-covered walls. Walking past her, he opened the door to an adjoining chamber. ''These were my mother's rooms—there is the bedchamber and dressing room. You will, of course, wish to have it done to reflect your own taste, I am sure.''

She glanced around, taking in the ornately carved bed, whose headboard rose almost to the ceiling, with gauzy drapings extending out to ornate hooks that were suspended from the ceiling and falling softly like a cloud of gossamer to surround the bed itself. The furnishings were in the gilt-washed French style of Louis XIV, both elegant and feminine. And for her boudoir, the last viscountess had chosen patterned damasks in hues of blue and green. He came up behind her to ask, "Do you like it?" as though it mattered to him if she did.

"It . . . it's very lovely."

"We can change the colors if you would like."

"No." She spun away, afraid he meant to touch her in the intimacy of a bedchamber. " 'Tis lovely as it is, but I prefer the one that overlooks the garden in the back, my lord."

"Ah, I see," he murmured, appreciating her reasons with a sardonic gleam in his blue eyes. "The one at the *far* end of the hall."

"Yes. 'Twill suit me quite well, I think. 'Tis light and pleasant, and the view is excellent. I can sit and read in the window. Now, is there anything else you wish me to see?"

"No, but have you considered that the servants will think it odd that you choose to . . . er . . . sleep so far away from your husband?"

"If it becomes a subject for gossip, you may insinuate that I dislike your snoring," she answered with a perfectly straight face.

"You will certainly have been the first to note it."

"Ah, yes, but then the house's other residents sleep upstairs, do they not? Unless you are in the habit of dallying with the maids, I suppose."

"No. Miss Cole, are you always so frank?"

"Candor is a virtue—I cannot remember who said that, but I have quite taken it to heart, my lord." Reaching into her reticule, she retrieved her kid gloves and drew them on. "We really must go, sir, if we are to arrive in the park for me to be properly seen."

Reluctantly he stepped back to allow her access to the door, and his eyes traveled almost wistfully around the room. Somehow, he could quite imagine her living in it. Catching up to her, he offered, "There is a key, after all."

"Yes, but no doubt there are two of them."

15

The second time Tony saw Christopher Hawkins, the boy was getting fleeced. Having decided that Leah needed an evening alone with her ailing parent, he'd gone to White's, prepared to endure both curiosity and a good ragging over his betrothal. And even as he handed his hat and stick to an attendant, his acquaintances hailed him, berating him for everything from desertion to a mesalliance. The overbearing Baron Bagshot was attempting quite openly to pry into the nature of the settlements when Tony's eyes caught sight of the boy.

"Just spoke t' the duchess t'other day," Bagshot confided. " 'Lyndon's a fine figure of a man—real Corinthian, that is—out-and-outer, if you was to say it. 'He'll come about,' I told her, and damme if he didn't!" Turning to Tony, he asked outright, "How warm d'ye think Old Cole'll cut up when 'tis done—hundred thousand?" But Tony was watching Hawkins push his money forward on the green-baize-covered table. "Well, from all I have heard," the baron answered himself, "it could be even twice that even—I doff m'hat t' ye for your good fortune, old fellow. Why, there's some as don't like it one bit that the chit's a Cit, but I say for that sum, I'd take a Turk!"

"Your pardon," Tony murmured, his attention riveted on the play, as he decided to intervene.

"What the devil ails him?" Bagshot demanded as he left. "Didn't bother to answer me even!"

"And for that you may be grateful," Gil retorted. "Tony don't like to bandy about his affairs, you know, and if he'd been listening, he might have called you out."

"Over a Cit?" the baron scoffed.

"Over the lady he's wedding." Now even Gil's curiosity was whetted. "By the looks of it, 'tis Skeffington with another green 'un primed to fleece. But it ain't like Tony . . ." Shaking his head, he watched his friend bow to Lord Skeffington and greet the boy. "Well, daresay he must know 'im."

"Lyndon!" Hawkins beamed up at Tony with the enthusiasm of a pup. "My lord, 'tis Lyndon himself," he announced to his partner, unaware of that lord's scowl. "Do you join us, sir?" he asked Tony eagerly. "I apologize for our last meeting, my lord—hadn't been to town long enough to know who you was. Why, when I told m'uncle I'd met Viscount Lyndon, he said you was a real Corinthian—a true whip—and allowed as you must've thought me a veritable gapeseed. *Have* you boxed with Jackson, sir?"

"I am certain that Lyndon is wishful of supping," Skeffington cut in hastily. "Whist is scarce his game."

"Actually, I like it, and am a fair hand at it. And I cannot say I have boxed so much as I have studied the science of it," Tony answered both of them. "Deal me in, my lord," he addressed Skeffington.

"And I should like to play also."

The baron whitened visibly at the sound of that chill voice. "Egad, my lord!" he expostulated. "But you ain't a hand to play."

"Perhaps it affords me amusement tonight." Rotherfield's voice was silky, his eyes hard. "Unless, of course, there is some reason you do not wish Lyndon and me to play?"

"No . . . no. 'Course not—heh-heh," Skeffington tittered nervously. "Just surprised, that's all."

"Hallo, Marcus," Tony greeted him without turning around. "Hawkins, you remember Rotherfield."

Gil pulled up a chair and straddled it to watch, his interest now thoroughly piqued. Jason Skeffington was not known amongst the *ton* as Jason of the Golden Fleece for nothing, having earned a reputation for introducing green youths to the pitfalls of gambling. More than once the baron had been accused of cheating, but as his victims were almost always nobodies, the charges had never stuck. Well, if it were just Tony against Skeffington, Gil would wager his friend would not lose a farthing, but the fact that Rotherfield had chosen to join them was cause for concern. It was not usually the earl's lay to insinuate himself into games, and the fleeting thought crossed Gil's mind that he meant to take on Tony.

Obviously Skeffington had been outmaneuvered by both Lyndon and Rotherfield, for he sat glowering from beneath heavy brows at both of them, while his victim blithely welcomed them. Tony immediately called for a new deck from an attendant, broke the band on it, and shuffled.

"Whist, is it?" he asked Hawkins, ignoring the baron. "Oh . . . and keep the sherry coming," he ordered the attendant who'd brought the cards. "Cannot play without it."

It was equally obvious that Tony had not only come to play, he'd come to win. Pushing the first bottle toward the boy, he told him to drink up, and that also surprised Gil Renfield, for Tony usually kept a clear head when he played.

"My lord, I'd as lief be called Kit, if you do not mind it—all of my friends call me thus."

Shuffling quickly, Tony dealt deftly, wagered moderately, and won the first game. It was as though he were testing the waters, so to speak, to determine the sort of money best wagered. After three more hands, of which he won only one, he suggested higher stakes, raising brows amongst those who'd gathered to watch once word had spread that 'twas Lyndon against Rotherfield. The assumption was immediate and unspoken that the viscount meant to come about at the tables.

"Thought he'd found a rich Cit," was the lone furtive whisper that further expressed everyone's opinion. "Didn't think he needed to play deep."

But play deep he did. In less than an hour, Skeffington withdrew and attempted to persuade Kit Hawkins to leave with him, suggesting supper, but the boy held to his determination to play until he could come about. Skeffington's place was taken by a dandy who immediately went down a hundred pounds.

Rotherfield played judiciously, neither winning heavily nor losing, choosing to pass on some games, playing on others, and all the while watching Lyndon with that enigmatic look he affected so well. Bleary-eyed gamesters gathered to watch as the hour grew late, and drifted away to waiting carriages when it turned early, and still Kit Hawkins played desperately in the hope he could recoup his losses, which were mounting at an alarming rate. Empty bottles now littered the table and were strewn about on the floor beneath them.

Long before dawn, the boy ran out of his purse and pressed Tony to take his vouchers. Against the protest of Gil and several others, Tony agreed. Rotherfield finally withdrew from play altogether, announcing his departure. Leaning over the table behind Tony, he murmured, "You've had the devil's own luck tonight, Lyndon. 'Twas my intent to speak with you on a matter of some import between us—perhaps I should call later today?"

"No, I am committed elsewhere, Marcus, but I shall be at home tomorrow."

"Tonight?"

"Tonight is the Wicklow affair."

"Until tomorrow then." Nodding a curt farewell, he left.

"Didn't know you was friendly with him," someone observed to Tony as he again shuffled the cards.

"Neither did I," Tony admitted. His eyes met Christopher Hawkins' across the table. "Do you wish to quit?"

"Can't," the boy mumbled, his head drooping from fatigue and too much wine.

"Tony, he's had enough," Gil insisted. "He cannot come about."

"Have you had enough?"

"Got to come about." Kit's speech was softly slurred now, but his determination was firm.

This time, Tony risked five hundred pounds, and the boy wrote furiously to cover it. Winning again, Tony picked up the slips of paper that littered the table and stuffed them into his already bulging pockets. Behind them, the attendants swept the floor, picking up coins carelessly dropped in play, and still Kit Hawkins clung to hope.

Slivers of gray light filtered through the front windows,

and the watch outside cried eight o'clock. Finally Tony Barsett pushed back from the table and announced he was done. Gil, who'd observed the entire debacle, watched in disgust as he collected his winnings. It was the first time he'd ever seen Lyndon deliberately set out to fleece anyone, least of all a green youth.

"I am for home then," Gil announced heavily. "Do you need taken up?"

"No, I told my driver to come back this morning." Tony's own eyes heavy, he turned to the boy, who now slumped over the littered table. "I am taking him home."

"Can't go—got to come about," Hawkins mumbled.

"Another time. Come on, up with you." Tony hoisted him to his feet, balancing him against his shoulder, and began walking him to the front of White's.

When the boy stumbled, he righted himself, muttering thickly, "Pardon."

Tony walked him, weaving from Hawkins' weight against him, to the front of the establishment, where he collected both their hats and his own stick. Once outside, Kit Hawkins revived slightly in the cool morning rain. One of the coachmen jumped down to help Tony get his companion into the closed carriage.

Pushed, the boy lurched across the seat to lean his head against the cool pane. As the coach moved into the street and picked up speed, he was silent—so much so that Tony feared he was sick. Finally Christopher Hawkins turned a stricken face to him.

"How must dith . . . did I loosh?" he managed thickly.

Tony pulled out the wad of banknotes and vouchers from his pocket and hazarded, "About three thousand pounds."

"Three th-thous-thousand?" The boy fell back, scarcely able to comprehend the enormity of what he'd done. Sobered suddenly, he stared out into the London Street. "I . . . you . . . pay you," he mumbled almost incoherently as tears welled in his eyes.

"Actually, I think it may be a little more than that, but I shall not know until I have a chance to count it fully. I am uncertain as to what I had to begin with, but I do not recall more than five hundred pounds." After he finished emptying the rest of his pockets, he straightened the wad of banknotes and separated out the vouchers. Peeling off and pocketing several notes, he reached to press the rest into the boy's hand.

" 'Tis a bitter lesson, is it not? Pockets to let and no money to refill 'em—a debt bigger than a quarter's allowance."

"I . . ." Kit blinked, trying to make sense of what Lyndon had done. "I don't . . ."

"No. I have kept approximately one hundred pounds of your money for the lesson. Suffice it to say that Skeffington is a known fleecer—he gets his money from fellows like you, fellows too green to know what they are about even."

"Got it all wrong. I was—"

"You were winning. They always do at first, some for longer than others, depending on how badly he is dunned by the tradesmen. But after a night or two, he takes 'em to the hells he frequents, and then they always lose." Tony tapped on the roof to remind his driver to stop. "But we have arrived at your uncle's."

"Must think me a fool," Hawkins muttered.

"Yes, but hopefully a wiser one."

"Got t' pay . . . gennulman pays if he plays."

Tony shook his head. "I never fleece the infants, Kit—play me again sometime when you reach your majority." Leaning down to retrieve the boy's hat, he picked it up and set it over the reddish locks. "Now, begone with you—and don't play where you cannot pay."

Kit Hawkins stumbled from the carriage and had to be helped to his door by a coachman, while Anthony Barsett watched and wondered why he'd bothered with the boy. Leaning back against the squabs, he slid his own hat forward to shade his itching eyes. His obsession with Leah Cole must be making him dicked in the nob.

16

The room was crowded, the air stifling at the Wicklows' ball, for Lady Wicklow was determined that Miss Amanda's come-out should be a success. And, given the thinness of the social calendar on this particular evening, the event had turned into a true crush. The dance floor had narrowed by the press of people until it was overheard that " 'Tis far too crowded for a country dance, and so close that the waltz becomes positively indecent."

Tony had no more than relinquished Leah's hand to a dashing young Irish peer than the Earl of Rotherfield edged his way through the departing dancers to her side. His black head gleaming beneath the gaslights, his dress characteristically both expensive and austere, his manner abrupt in the extreme, he managed to insert himself between her and her would-be partner.

"Ah, Barrasford—I believe I am promised this dance with Miss Cole."

Not ready to give up the field tamely, the handsome Barrasford raised a barely civil eyebrow. "A Banbury tale, if I ever heard one, Marcus. You are but just arrived, and Tony put her in my care."

"Ask Miss Cole." Rotherfield shrugged indifferently and waited for Leah's answer.

Perplexed, she looked from one man to the other, and her interest was piqued by the earl's self-assurance. "Yes, 'tis true," she heard herself say to the disappointed Barrasford, "but I did not see Lord Rotherfield and thought he meant to forget me." She smiled apologetically at the younger man, murmuring, "But I shall be happy to save another one for you."

"Now, that was well done," the earl approved as he

led her onto the crowded floor. "You are learning early how to keep them dangling, aren't you?"

"How could you have known I would do that?" she asked, looking up at his face. "I did not know it myself."

"I knew it."

"Well, I think it quite shameless of me, actually."

"You could have said I was mistaken." He spoke softly, drawing her into his arms.

"I suppose I wished to thank you for taking me home the other night—'twas most kind of you. I find it difficult to reconcile what is said of you with the man."

"Lyndon will tell you I am quite dangerous." He smiled down at her, and for once his black eyes were warm. "You ought to listen to him."

" 'Tis a case of the pot calling the kettle black then, I am sure," she responded easily, "for there's naught that can be said of you that cannot be said of him."

"Almost true," he agreed readily. "But thus far, no one has accused him of killing a man."

Her eyes widened and she nearly missed her step at the casualness of his admission. "You are a duelist then?"

"In my youth."

"And you are so positively elderly now, my lord, that you are ready for the grave," she teased lightly. Then noting the sudden sobering of his expression, she grew serious. "Well, I daresay you were exonerated."

"Your pardon—I should not have touched on a matter I have no wish to discuss. As for my age—I am seven-and-twenty, no matter how old I appear to you. A misspent youth sits heavily on one's face, you know." His black eyes warmed again as he looked down on her. "You cannot know, Miss Cole, how utterly refreshing it is to meet a female who does not either recoil from my reputation or simper at my title."

"Actually, I like you," she admitted candidly.

"You must surely be quite brave to voice such an unpopular viewpoint, my dear. Tell me—how is it that you find yourself betrothed to the irrepressible Tony Barsett?"

"I thought you knew—indeed, I think everyone does."

She colored slightly, remembering the gossip she'd overheard, and spoke into his shoulder. " 'Tis but a simple business arrangement between him and my father—his title for Papa's money, if you would have the truth of it."

"What—can it be that you are so unlike other females that you have not fallen victim to Lyndon's charm?" he quizzed her. "Can it be that you are impervious to the dashing Tony Barsett?"

" 'Tis difficult to be charmed by a rakehell and a gamester, my lord," she retorted stiffly.

"Your pardon. 'Twas not my intent to overset you."

"I am not overset."

Suddenly he stopped almost mid-step and quickly turned her away, putting himself between her and something. Curious, she craned her neck to see what he'd seen, only to have him step into her line of vision.

"What is it?"

"I'd not have you unnecessarily wounded, Miss Cole."

"I do not wound easily, my lord, and neither do I suffer from an excess of sensibility," she snapped irritably. "I do not even have a delicate constitution."

Even as she spoke, he allowed her to turn in time to see her betrothed escorting Mrs. Chandler from the crowded room. Those around them stared at her, spitefully waiting for her reaction, only to be disappointed when she smiled coquettishly at Marcus Halvert and did not even miss a step.

"Well done, Miss Cole," Rotherfield commented above her ear. " 'Twill be said that you do not care."

Her earlier charity with Tony Barsett forgotten, she answered, "I do not. I do not care a fig what he does—'tis all of a piece with what I know of him, anyway."

"Perhaps in the months before the wedding, your father will come to realize he has chosen unwisely."

"Months? You mistake the matter, my lord," she answered bitterly. "We are to wed by Special License."

"Without the banns?" For once, the earl's face betrayed his dismay, and then he recovered almost immediately.

" 'Tis mutually agreed between them—Lyndon cannot wait for Papa's money, and my father fears he will not live to see me a lady, I suppose. Please—I would not discuss it."

He nodded sympathetically, his mind working to digest her startling news. "I own I'd heard he was badly dipped, but lately I thought he'd begun to come about. When I saw him last night, he was winning heavily of young Hawkins at White's—beggared the boy, in fact," he mused aloud.

"Hawkins?" This time she did miss a step. "But he is but a boy!" Collecting herself, she sought to refute the idea. "Surely Lyndon would not . . . That is, I cannot think he . . ."

"Do not overset yourself unnecessarily, my dear—I should have held my tongue. Er . . . I'd forgotten you knew the boy."

"Yes . . . no—that is, I do not precisely know him. You were there also—'twas when his curricle jumped the curb. Poor Mr. Hawkins."

"Well, 'tis no uncommon thing to introduce young men into gambling establishments, after all," Rotherfield offered as an excuse for Lyndon.

"To think he would stoop so low as to take a boy's money—I do not care how deeply he is in debt—and when he is to get Papa's also." Her disappointment in Lyndon was rapidly growing.

Satisfied that he'd accomplished enough, the earl turned the subject away to the polite inanities, discussing the spring flowers, the weather, Hyde Park, and the Princess Charlotte's interesting condition, expressing the commonly held hope that the baby would be male. As for Leah, this brought forth her assertion that she rather agreed with Jane Austen, who despised the Regent for his treatment of his wife, the Princess Caroline.

"Then you cannot have ever seen her," Rotherfield murmured, "for an uglier, more uncouth female cannot exist."

Her reply was lost as the music ended. Abruptly the earl grasped her elbow and propelled her toward the double French doors leading to the Wicklow garden, where a hundred gaily festooned lanterns winked and floated in the cool air. " 'Tis too hot for speech in here, my dear."

Just as they reached the doorway, Leah turned back to see Lord Lyndon returning without Mrs. Chandler. His face darkened thunderously when he saw her with Rotherfield, and he began pushing his way toward them. The earl's hand clasped her arm in reassurance, but she shook her head. " 'Tis my quarrel, my lord."

Without a word to Rotherfield, Tony grasped Leah's hand and pulled her into the garden after him. She would have resisted, but she was loath to provide further amusement for the gossips, and therefore she held her tongue until they were out of hearing. Rotherfield stood there watching, a slight smile playing at his lips, knowing that Tony Barsett was about to make a cake of himself.

"This is unseemly, my lord," Leah protested as soon as they cleared the terrace steps into the garden itself. Wrenching her arm free, she turned angrily to face him.

"Unseemly? Miss Cole, I do not intend to tolerate your want of conduct!" Tony snapped.

"*My* want of conduct! Just who do you think you are, Anthony Barsett? If you think you can read me a peal for dancing with Rotherfield whilst you dally with that . . . that *brazen* jade, you are very much mistaken! 'Twas not I who arranged a little meeting with *my* bit of fluff! It seems to me, my lord, that 'tis you who wants conduct!"

"I cannot fathom what nonsense you are speaking, Miss Cole, but I warn you, I will not tolerate your association with the likes of Rotherfield!"

"And I do not mean to tolerate your public pursuit of that woman!"

"Pursuit?" he fairly howled. "You have a dashed queer notion of pursuit, if that is what you think I was doing. If you must pry, I was telling the fair Elaine to cease pestering me!"

"Oh, 'tis rich, that is! Are you so filled with conceit that you believe I will swallow that tale whole? If 'tis as you say, then why did you have to take her outside?"

"Would you have me humiliate her publicly?"

"You humiliate me!" Clasping her arms against her in the chill night air, she flung away from him and hurried back toward the glittering ballroom.

"Just a minute, Miss Cole." Catching up to her, he

grasped her shoulders and yanked her back. "If you would discuss humiliation, let us discuss the gibes and barbs you have cast my way since the day we met!" Catching the martial light that flashed indignantly in her eyes, he continued, "I have done my best to rectify my first mistake with you, you know. This betrothal is not without constraints on me also—I have given up some of my more nefarious pleasures for you."

"Oh? You must think me blind! You court my father for his money, and everyone knows it," she spat at him. "And I fail to see that you have given up anything—you are *still* a rake and a gamester!"

"What the devil are you speaking of?" he demanded.

"*Her!* Oh, I know 'tis fashionable amongst the *ton* to sport mistresses, but I will not countenance it, I take leave to tell you! And you fleeced that poor Hawkins boy!"

"I collect you had that from Rotherfield?"

"It doesn't make any difference where I had it, does it? 'Tis evidence of one of your nefarious pursuits you have not abandoned—and Mrs. Chandler is evidence of the other!"

"Ah, so I only have two vices, at least! Well then, Miss Cole, would you like me to enumerate your shortcomings also?"

"Yes!" Then, her face highly flushed, she caught her breath and spoke more calmly, retorting in a clipped voice, "They cannot possibly compare with yours, after all."

"I scarce know where to begin, my dear," he told her sarcastically. "In the first place, you seem determined to twit the very society you wish to enter, reminding everyone at every stop and turn that you are a Cit by your total lack of modest behavior."

"You know full well 'tis not I who wish to be what I am not, and as for modesty, would you have me turn into a simpering fool just to please you?"

"I'd have you cut Rotherfield before everyone cuts you."

"If you would ever take the time to stay and watch,

you would see that I am already cut. Do not think I am so deaf that I cannot hear what is said of me."

"You have not yet been given the cut direct. If you would but attempt to be all that is pleasing, you just might take."

"Pleasing to whom? Stiff-necked snobs who are too worthless to work a day in their lives?"

"In the second place, you put yourself forward as a bluestocking, Miss Cole, and 'tis not fashionable for a female to attempt the discussion of anything beyond an occasional novel."

"Oh, I see." This time it was her voice that dripped sarcasm. " 'Tis only men who are allowed any intelligence, is it? You wish me to be as empty-headed as those insipid misses who line the walls waiting to be noticed by some gentleman, too fearful of being left on the shelf to venture even the smallest original thought." Her bosom heaving with indignation, she blew an errant strand of hair out of her eyes. " 'Tis a pity you were not born earlier, else you could have told Mary Wollstonecraft she had no right to a mind."

"Well, I should scarce hold her up as all a female should be," he shot back. "She was quite free with her favors as well as her mind, from all I have read. And that brings me to another fault of yours—I heard of your climbing boy from your father, Miss Cole—you are a deuced reformer!"

"If we had to depend on *your* class to right any of the wrongs of this world, we should be in sad case indeed!" The strand of hair fell forward again, and she brushed it back irritably. "Indeed, 'tis the fault of fancy lords like yourself that there are climbing boys being beaten, starved, and burned every day."

"I have never beaten, starved, or burned anyone, Miss Cole!"

"Well, if you really wished to do something worthwhile with your life, you'd speak in the House of Lords on the problem—'tis the lords who refuse to stop it."

"Aha! And now I am to be faulted for the ills of the world also! What about the members of your class—those rich merchants who are so ready to turn a profit that they do not care whom they cheat?''

''I do not have to listen to this!'' Once again she turned to leave, flouncing angrily up the narrow rock steps set amongst the foliage.

This time he caught her and pushed her against a stone garden wall. Releasing her arm, he leaned to pin her there with a hand on either side of her. The light from the colored lanterns reflected in his eyes, giving him an eerie aspect and frightening her. Her own eyes widened when he leaned even closer.

His anger suddenly gone, he spoke quite softly. ''Do you know what 'tis, Leah? We are better matched than you think—we both have devilish tempers.''

Shrinking against the wall, she was not at all certain she liked the change, either. ''Release me this instant, my lord—else I shall scream.''

He was so close that she could smell the clean scent of lavender soap and she could feel the warmth of his body as he leaned into hers even before he touched her. His coat sleeve brushed against her bare arm, sending a shiver down her spine.

''You tempt a man, Leah—all that fire and spirit,'' he whispered.

''You would not dare . . .''

Her voice trailed off uncertainly as he blotted all else out with his head. The glittering light in his eyes was the last thing she saw before she closed her own to hide from him. His breath was warm and alive against her cheek, and then he brushed her lips lightly, sending another shiver that had absolutely nothing to do with the cold through her. His lips lingered there, warming her own, as his arms moved from the wall, one to cradle her head, the other to clasp her waist and pull her closer. Her mouth opened slightly in protest, only to be stilled by her first real kiss.

She was utterly unprepared for the sensation he gave her as the kiss deepened. For a moment she thought her knees would buckle, and she clung to him for support. She was both shocked and thrilled by the feel of his skin against hers, and when he finally released her lips, his cheek turned to nuzzle hers.

Behind them, small twigs snapped and leaves crunched, bringing both back to their senses. Leah stared wide-eyed in the starry darkness as Tony released her. Clasping her hand, he turned to face the intruder.

"Thought it was too cold for anybody to be out, told Letty so when she had 'em hang the damned lamps, but I guess I was mistaken." Their host took in Leah's expression and winked at Tony. "Daresay a little chill don't stop a hot-blooded buck, though. Damme if you ain't a hand with the females, Lyndon."

Tony felt Leah's fingers stiffen in his and he could have cursed Wicklow. "Miss Cole was overcome with the heat inside." He spoke evenly.

"Guess you are wishing me at Jericho, ain't you? Just came out to see what happened to you after Rotherfield left, that's all." Peering closer, he studied Tony. "Damme if I don't think this is a love match, after all."

"We were just going in," Tony lied.

"Ought to, I suppose. Ain't the thing to dally in the garden on a night like this—gel's probably dashed cold out here."

Embarrassed, Leah pulled her hand away and started back inside, leaving Tony to follow on her heels. Just inside the doors, she stopped, still shivering, and collected her disordered thoughts. Almost immediately, Lord Barrasford was bearing down on her, ready for his dance. She managed to smile, thankful that it was to be a country dance, for she did not think she was up to being held for another waltz.

Outside in the street, a very self-satisfied earl leaned back against the lushly upholstered carriage seat, his long legs stretched across the interior, his hat pushed back on his black locks. That strange half-smile of his played about his mouth as he surveyed the woman across from him. Lacing his fingers together across his flat abdomen, he noted, "You know, Elaine, if you exhaust all your protectors, you just might try for the stage."

Tears flowed unchecked down her lovely face, streaking her artfully applied rouge, while she stared silently into the street. "You know, Marcus," she said finally, "while you were enjoying yourself with your little Cit . . ." Out of the corner of her eye she saw him stiffen and his face tighten in the shadows, and she hastily amended, ". . . with your Miss Cole, then—while you were dancing with her, I was being summarily dismissed by Tony. I am afraid you will have to get the girl for yourself," she sighed.

Rotherfield shrugged. " 'Twas to be expected, I suppose —'tis said he is determined to hang in her pocket until the wedding. But," he added generously, "you still have Carrington. A trifle old, I'll admit, but rich enough to afford your tastes, and who knows, the old fool might even offer marriage."

"Leave me alone."

"Come, Elaine, 'tisn't as though you expected Lyndon to offer for you," he consoled.

"He means to have her, Marcus—I know he does."

"Then he is doomed to disappointment, my dear, for I have put my spoke squarely in his wheel."

17

Anthony Barsett awoke to the unwelcome news that the Earl of Rotherfield was paying him a morning call. Rousing himself from sleep, he glanced at the card on the tray and considered having his valet convey to the butler that he was not receiving. But there was something about the rather austere "Marcus C. W. Halvert, Earl of Rotherfield" that leapt from the cream-colored cardboard and demanded attention. And, as if reading his lordship's thoughts, the valet nodded, his own disapproval patent in his expression.

"Fitch says Lord Rotherfield has expressed his intent to wait however long 'tis necessary for an audience with you."

"Damn the man! What time can it be, anyway?" Tony leaned to open the cover of his pocket watch. " 'Tis but ten," he grumbled. "One would think he keeps country hours, when he is never in the country."

"Perhaps Fitch should—"

"No." Tony sat on the side of his bed and ran his fingers through his rumpled hair as though he could restore order to it. "Have James bring up some coffee—and tell Fitch to direct Rotherfield up."

"Up here, sir?"

"Well, I am scarce prepared to come down," Tony snapped irritably, "and I'd not have him in my house all morning, either. Hand me the dressing gown." Rising, he shrugged into the brocaded robe and fastened the black braid frogs. He knew instinctively that whatever the earl wanted, it concerned Leah, and after the night he'd spent, Tony welcomed the confrontation.

"Lyndon."

One thing he had to give Marcus Halvert—the man could make one word sound like a challenge.

"Hallo, Marcus," Tony acknowledged coolly. "Coffee?"

"No—I shan't stay long. I have come on business merely," he added, cutting immediately to the heart of the matter. For the briefest moment he appeared to be absorbed in the heavy gold-and-onyx signet ring he wore, and then his black eyes met Tony's. " 'Tis quite simple really—you find yourself in dun territory, and I am prepared to assist you out of it."

"You will of course forgive me if I take a cup?" Tony inquired politely, spooning a dollop of heavy cream into his coffee and stirring it. "Now, I do not consider myself sufficiently acquainted with you, Marcus, to discuss my affairs. The state of my fortune need not concern you." His eyes still on the earl, he lifted the cup and sipped. "Are you quite certain you do not wish some? 'Tis the best to be had of Johnathen's—excellent really."

"Do not be a fool!" Rotherfield snapped.

Tony's eyes went hard over the rim. "You have been misinformed, my lord—I do not require your aid."

"I am prepared to match Cole's settlement, Lyndon."

"My dear Marcus, you could not possibly. For one thing—"

"How much do you owe?" the earl broke in harshly. "Ten thousand? Twenty? Thirty?"

"As I was about to say, the lovely Leah is the most tempting part of Jeptha Cole's offer."

"She doesn't want to marry you."

"But her father approves the match."

"Name your price, Lyndon—I am not averse to your making a profit in the course of our agreement."

"I have no price, Marcus—none. Like you, I want the girl herself, so we are at cross-purposes, are we not?" Tony's voice was soft but there was no mistaking the will beneath. "So if you do not care for coffee, there's naught else to be said between us."

"I'd not thought you a foolish man—or a stupid one."

A chill ran down Tony's spine at the veiled threat in the other man's words, but his face did not betray him. "If you mean to call me out, Marcus, by all means do so. I am not afraid to meet you, you know—and unlike

Calicott, I am better than a fair shot. I am also less than half his age."

The muscles in the earl's jaw worked as his mind overruled his anger. "Thirty thousand today, Lyndon," he offered evenly.

Tony's face grew pained. "I thought I made myself plain on that head—I mean to have Leah Cole."

"Cole might prefer to make her a countess," Rotherfield countered.

"No. I can see she is received, my dear Marcus, which is something you cannot quite manage. And despite what you might think, the old man is rather fond of his daughter. So . . . we have reached *point non plus* between us, I think." Turning away, Tony set his empty cup on the tray and prepared to pour himself some more of the coffee. "Good day, Marcus."

Grasping the head of his walking stick as though he would strangle it, the earl executed the stiffest and slightest of bows to acknowledge his dismissal. " 'Twould seem the hand is yours, Lyndon," he murmured in that cold voice of his, "but the game is not yet done."

"A line worthy of the great Edmund Kean." Tony lifted his steaming cup in a mock toast to Rotherfield's back and then sighed heavily at the sound of the earl's measured tread on the stairs. Once again, he could have strangled his betrothed—through her he'd gained an enemy no man wanted.

Unable to dismiss the earl's visit lightly, Tony bathed and endured the ministrations of his valet before presenting himself in Hans Town to speak with Jeptha Cole. Consoling himself with the thought that Rotherfield's sudden ardor for Leah would probably cool in their absence, he prepared to discuss the wedding trip.

In the process of directing the cleaning of the marble floor herself, Leah was in the foyer when he rang. And, for once, she appeared self-conscious in his presence. As the door opened to admit him, her hand flew to the dust cap that covered her hair, snatching it off to hold it behind her.

"If you are looking for Papa, he has gone to Garraway's for an auction sale of salvaged goods,'' she offered, not meeting his eyes. ''Mrs. Crome, will you inquire of Millie if there are any polishing cloths left? I fear that 'twill take more than we have to do the task correctly. And, Timothy—do go with her to carry.'' Looking up quickly and then down again, she added to Tony, ''You find us at sixes and sevens with the cleaning, I fear. Whether there are guests or no, Papa would have the place shipshape for the wedding.''

''Miss Cole . . . Leah . . .''

''If you are come to apologize for kissing me last night, I—''

''Not for the kiss, Leah, but for the quarrel.'' Moving in front of her, he reached to take the cap and, flinging it aside, possessed both her hands. To his surprise, she did not pull away. ''Come, can we not cry friends, my dear? I shall promise to treat you with the respect you deserve in hopes that you will cease ripping up at me.''

This time, when she dared meet his eyes, they were searching her face soberly, and she felt an involuntary lurch in her chest. A man ought not to look at one quite like that. ''I daresay the fault was not all yours, my lord,'' she answered slowly. ''You are not the first to accuse me of a devilish temper, after all.'' Pulling her hands free, she turned her back on him and rubbed at a finger smudge on the highly polished staircase newel. ''I would, however, prefer that you not see Mrs. Chandler publicly. 'Tis narrow-minded of me, I know, but I . . . well, I would not be the object of false pity, my lord,'' she finished, stiffening her back.

''I do not mean to see her at all.''

''Never?''

''She is gone from my life, Leah.'' He came up behind her, but made no move to touch her. '' 'Tis not admirable of me, I know, but then you do not know how 'twas between us.'' When she remained silent, he sighed and sought to explain. ''I cannot expect you to understand everything, of course, but there are women who sell their favors outright, and there are those who flatter and pretend affection for gifts. Elaine Chandler is one of the latter, Leah. I was not her first protector nor am I her last.''

"How can you know she did not care?" Swinging around to face him suddenly, she looked up, demanding, "How can you just cast away someone?"

"I have reason to believe she had already sought another, wealthier man than I—that only word of my imminent rescue by your father brought her back."

"Oh."

"That and the *on-dit* that my Cit was quite beautiful. I think perhaps the gossip stung her pride. Elaine is rather noted for choosing her protectors, rather than for being chosen."

"And she came to the duchess's party to see you."

"Not me—you. That was my mistake, Leah—I sought to make her leave and drew even more attention to her. Had I the chance again, I should ignore her."

"But how can you?" Her gray eyes searched his face as she sought to understand him. "I mean . . . that is, after what she has been to you . . . well, you must have felt something for her once."

It was a highly improper conversation between them, but Tony realized that she deserved an answer. "No," he admitted baldly. " 'Twas merely a business arrangement. When I saw she sported Carrington's gifts, I knew our liaison was over."

"Carrington? But he is old and fat and ugly!" She nearly choked with revulsion at the thought of the aging roué she'd met at the Childredges' party. "Surely not!"

"Old men pay more to get what they want, Leah."

" 'Tis disgusting!"

"I suppose it is," he admitted, smiling at her innocence. "I find the notion distasteful myself, but 'tis the way of things. Now . . ." His blue eyes gleamed as he moved closer to lean his tall frame on the banister. "Having admitted my folly, I'd ask of yours, my dear—what is Rotherfield to you?"

"The earl?" She appeared taken aback by the sudden shift in direction the conversation had taken. "I like him—I'd count him a friend, I think."

"Leah, I think you should know that—"

"There are no more cleaning rags to be had, Miss

Leah,'' laundry is done, we shall have to contrive with what we have. And with the wedding coming so soon upon us, I don't know as how—'' She stopped and caught herself guiltily. ''Well, daresay it can be managed, of course, if you two was to get out of our way. Ain't a bit of sense to havin' four people standing about when two's got to work.''

''I cannot stay,'' Tony murmured apologetically. '' 'Twas my intent to take you driving, as the weather is quite warm.''

''Alas, but I cannot, my lord. I am scarce prepared to be seen, and I . . . well, there is so much to do. Despite the fact that there will not be many to eat it, Papa is determined that we have a particularly fine supper, and—''

''Enough! 'Tis comforting to know I shall be leg-shackled with some ceremony then. If you will but see me to my curricle, I'd have of you just where 'tis you would go on the wedding trip.''

''Oh, I had not thought . . .'' Looking around her, she caught the intense interest of the old housekeeper and the footman. ''Yes . . . of course,'' she managed, hiding her consternation at the thought of leaving her home forever with him.

He held the door open for her and followed her out into the early-afternoon sun. ''You did think to go somewhere, did you not? I seem to distinctly recall speaking of France or Italy, my dear.''

''I have never been away from London in my life, sir,'' she admitted frankly, ''and I have not the least notion of where to go. Indeed, I'd hoped that perhaps we could just stay here with Papa.''

He shook his head. '' 'Twould be too much remarked —and I should like to show you Paris if you do not object. However, if 'tis Italy you prefer, then I thought perhaps Florence or Milano—Rome is dirty and crowded.''

''As Paris is closer, I think I should prefer that—I'd not be gone from Papa overlong.''

''As you wish then. I shall send my man ahead to bespeak accommodations for us.'' They'd reached his curricle and he turned back to face her. "I think you will find the experience enjoyable, Leah."

The soft spring breeze caught his blond hair and ruffled it and the sun reflected warmly in his blue eyes as he looked down on her. The thought flitted through her mind that he did indeed look like the conquering Alexander. Sucking in her breath, she managed to nod. "But you will not forget our agreement, will you?" she blurted out finally.

A slow smile lifted both corners of his mouth and one eyebrow. "That your citadel is safe from me? Miss Cole, I herewith promise to make no direct assaults on your fort."

"And indirect?"

"Now, that depends on you. I am not above attempting to gain the keys to the gate, but then 'tis up to you to keep them."

"If that means you hope to charm me, Lord Lyndon, you will discover the task difficult indeed." But the sharpness of her words was eased by the mischief in her eyes. "Good afternoon, my lord."

He stood watching her as she skipped back up the steps and into the house. If that could be construed as a challenge, Tony meant to take it. Whistling softly, he took the ribbons from his groom and swung his tall frame up into the seat. Seeing the drapery lift slightly in the front saloon, he tipped his beaver-brimmed hat in that direction before clicking the reins.

As he drove out of sight, she let the curtain fall. If Tony Barsett thought to turn her up sweet with those incredibly handsome looks of his . . . She paused midthought, fearing that he just might be able to do it. He was a rake and a gamester—an unprincipled fellow who mounted mistresses and discarded them, she reminded herself severely. And as long as she could remember that, she could guard not only her citadel but also her heart.

18

With the bride's father's illness as an excuse, the wedding was a very private, albeit elegant affair. The dowager duchess, having ascertained that the Coles were not, after all, so terribly vulgar, deigned to lend her presence and that of Mrs. Buckhaven, as did lords Renfield and Rivington.

Owing to the grayness of a rainy day, the gaslights glowed invitingly in the green saloon as the party assembled. Leah, truly lovely in a simple dress of rose-colored raw silk, took her place beside Lyndon. As she walked, the silk rustled against the stiffened taffeta petticoat whose lace edging peeped fashionably from beneath the gown's hem. The single strand of perfectly matched pearls nestled in the hollow of her throat, while another strand had been woven into curls spilling from a knot at the crown of her head.

The vicar, summoned from Old St. Margaret's, cleared his throat and began with the ancient words, "Dearly beloved, we are gathered here . . ."

Leah stole a sidelong glance at the viscount, catching his somber profile and thinking, despite her misgivings, that he was certainly the handsomest man she'd ever seen. If only . . .

She was brought abruptly back to the present as her father placed her hand in Lyndon's and she heard the clergyman addressing him, charging him with the responsibilities of marriage, asking his response. Her eyes widened a fraction as his warm, almost frighteningly strong fingers tightened on hers and he answered clearly that he would. And she felt his body tense beside hers when the vicar turned to her, charging and asking the same. She hesitated momentarily, her gaze traveling to where her father sat in his best coat and breeches next to the small, deceptively frail duchess.

"I will."

It was as though she could feel Lyndon's silent sigh of relief. Turning again to him, the vicar took him through the age-old vows that bound husband and wife together until eternity, and Leah listened almost dispassionately as Tony repeated, "I, Anthony Edward Charles Robert Barsett, take thee, Leah Frances Cole . . ."

This, then, was it—she was no longer a daughter in her father's house, but rather a wife, mistress of her own establishment, responsible for the duties that went with her new and elevated status. Well, not for *all* of them, she reminded herself to bolster her lagging courage. Stealing another quick glance at Barsett's face, she wondered what was going through his mind. He too was committed forever now—if he should find another, if he should come to love someone else, he was no longer free . . .

"Repeat after me, please." With a start, she realized they waited for her now. Drawing in a deep breath, she nodded and followed his words, "I, Leah Frances Cole, take thee, Anthony Charles . . . that is . . ." Flustered for a moment, she hesitated and began again in a stronger voice, "I, Leah Frances Cole, take thee, Anthony *Edward* Charles Robert Barsett, to be my husband, to . . ."

In a matter of very few minutes it was done and they knelt on the soft woolen carpet for the blessing and benediction. Balancing herself awkwardly with her hand in his grip, she struggled to smooth her slim skirt and rise. It was over. For good or ill, she belonged to a man she scarce knew and had not wanted.

"Not quite," he murmured, as though he read her thoughts. Leaning so close that her senses reeled from the clean, pleasant scent of his Hungary water and from the warmth of his skin against hers, he brushed his lips across her mouth quickly and stepped back—but not before he'd seen her eyes flutter and heard her sharp intake of breath.

"Now?" she asked, trying to hide the sudden apprehension she felt.

"Now." His hand slid down from her shoulder to her hand again, sending a shiver in its wake. "You are cold as ice, my dear," he whispered. "Would you have me send for your shawl?"

"No—'twill pass."

"Well, now . . . Lady Lyndon. Let me be the first to congratulate you, my dear." Jeptha Cole's eyes brimmed brightly as he surveyed her proudly. "Aye, but don't you look fine!" he managed, his voice low with suppressed emotion.

"Mr. Cole," the duchess cut in imperiously, "I believe 'tis proper to congratulate *him* rather than her!"

"Eh?" He eyed the diminutive dowager with a look that bordered on dislike for a moment and thundered, "Dash it, Your Grace! No need t' tell him—he knows I like him! Gave him my greatest treasure, didn't I?" Then, conscious of her affronted expression, he attempted to mollify her. "Aye, but I wish him well—congratulate him too, I suppose. Damme, Leah's a viscountess now, ain't she?" he chortled. "Calls for some sherry t' toast 'em! Crome! Crome!"

The butler and housekeeper, who'd both been watching surreptitiously as Leah wed into the Quality, hurried forward. Leah caught the old woman's furtive brush at tears and enveloped her in a quick embrace. "I will miss you," she whispered.

"Here, now, miss . . . madam, 'tis not fitting," the elderly housekeeper whispered.

"Lady Lyndon, may I be the first to felicitate you?" Hugh Rivington murmured at Leah's shoulder. "All London will envy Tony for stealing the march on 'em."

Turning around, Leah faced Tony's friends and extended her hands, only to have both carried up to be kissed at the same time in an unusual display of gallantry by Rivington and Renfield. "Hugh's right, m'dear—ain't a buck in London as won't go into mourning when he sees you," Gil promised.

"Thank you."

"Oh, Lady Lyndon!" Mrs. Buckhaven clasped her own hands together soulfully as she approached Leah. "I cannot yet credit that dear Tony is wed! Now he will cease raking about and—"

"Bucky!"

"Well, surely he will not—"

"Bucky! I am certain Leah will discover Tony's faults soon enough without having you enumerating 'em for her," the duchess reproved her sharply. "Aye, I wish you well also, my dear," she told Leah. "And don't be thinking you have to name the first gel Hester for me, 'cause you don't, you know—hate the name! Besides, a gel can't carry on the Barsett line."

"Well, I—"

"Leah will take whatever Divine Providence gives us, won't you, my dear?" Tony came up behind her and squeezed her shoulder with one hand while reaching around her with a glass of sherry in the other. "To Lady Lyndon—may the years bring you happiness, my dear," he murmured softly. "Here, let me get one of my own and we will drink to it."

"I am in agreement with Her Grace," Cole announced to anyone within hearing. "No need to name any boys Jeptha—don't know where I got such a name and don't want to pass it on. Humph! Seems to me that Lyndon's got enough names to choose from on his own, anyway."

"Lady Lyndon . . ." Tony lifted his glass to touch the rim of hers.

Lady Lyndon. Lord Lyndon's lady. It sounded foreign to her ears and yet it was fact—Leah Cole was gone forever, replaced by the Viscountess Lyndon. She was Leah Barsett now. Slowly she lifted her glass to her lips and took a sip.

" 'Tis quite good, really." The duchess managed to unbend over her glass enough to smile thinly at Mr. Cole.

"Ain't it? Got it from a smuggler off the coast—said it was from Boney's own stock. Didn't believe him, of course," he snorted, "but it could've been."

"Yes, well, perhaps we should repair to the dining room. Monsieur Lebeau is quite the temperamental cook, and—"

"What Leah's tryin' to say is he's a demned Frenchie! Never know what he feeds us by the name of it, but it's palatable enough! Aye, we'd best eat if you are to make the Dover packet before nightfall.'' Jeptha Cole patted his pocket and beamed at his new son-in-law before reaching to draw out a sheaf of papers. ''Know you don't want m'money, my lord, but thought you might like to have these for a wedding present.''

Everyone turned to watch Tony remove the string that bound the papers together. As he examined them, Gil peered around his shoulder. ''What are they?'' he asked curiously.

Tony turned over the first one carefully and refolded it. ''My thanks, sir—my heartfelt thanks.''

''But what—?''

''Stock certificates?'' Hugh queried.

''No, not quite—'tis an interest in a merchant vessel and bills of lading for her first cargo.''

''Shipping!'' the duchess choked in horror. ''Mr. Cole''—she rounded on the still-beaming man—''Barsetts do not engage in trade!''

''Eh? Beggin' Yer Grace's pardon, but there's fortunes to be made in shipping!'' Cole retorted.

''Not in my family!''

''Aunt Hester, 'tis but an interest,'' Tony reasoned with the old woman. '' 'Tis no different from investing in the funds.''

''Aye, and less chancy, if you was to ask me,'' Cole added.

''Aunt Hester . . .'' Hugh attempted to smooth things between Old Cole and the Old Tartar. ''It ain't like Tony was to sail on it, after all. He merely buys abroad, brings goods to England, and sells them at a profit at Garraway's. He don't even have to go there to do it—can send a man of business if he wishes.''

''Less chancy than faro,'' Gil offered helpfully. ''Done all the time.''

''By whom?'' the dowager demanded awfully.

''By the Cits.'' All eyes swung to Leah as she faced the old woman, her color heightened ominously. ''In case you have not noted it, whilst the nobility has sat clucking their tongues and doing nothing, we Cits have been earning fortunes that are the envy of Golden Ball,'' she answered, biting off each word. "And one day it will be the Cits who live on the estates of the lords who have mortgaged their lands and houses at the gaming tables."

A shocked silence descended over the wedding party like a pall as the oldest Barsett faced the newest. "Yes, well"—the dowager collected herself and her surroundings—"that is not to say that I opposed all trade, my dear. 'Tis that I would leave such things to those who do them well."

"I mean to turn a profit, Aunt Hester," Tony announced calmly. "There are fortunes to be made, and I intend to make mine. Now, if the toasts are finished, I suggest we proceed to dine." Taking out his watch and flicking open the cover, he observed the time. "If we are to board for the crossing this evening, we'd best be on the road by three o'clock, I think."

"Know your mind, don't you?" the dowager addressed Leah. "And you ain't afraid to speak it neither. Daresay there's truth to what you say, but I am an old woman and things change slowly for me. Come give an interfering relation a kiss before we sup."

Leah's anger faded at the duchess's attempt to make amends. Leaning down, she brushed her lips dutifully across the wrinkled cheek and wished fervently that she could indeed know her own mind.

Parked around the corner from the Cole residence was a particularly elegant equipage, complete with a bang-up team of bays, four sweet-goers. To his chagrin, the Earl of Rotherfield discovered he was too late—the careful abduction he'd planned was thwarted by an error in the announcement. Instead of an evening wedding, it had been a morning one.

19

The well-sprung carriage barreled down the road, its swaying motion lulling the tired viscount, who now napped across from Leah. Outside, the rain had ended and the clouds had dissipated, leaving the countryside bathed in the rosiness of early dusk. It was a pretty scene, and one totally at variance with the emotions that warred in Leah's breast.

At first she'd tried to read, but the gentle swaying had threatened to make her sick. Then she'd taken careful inventory of the inside of the carriage, admiring the shining wooden and brass trim, the ornate Italian coach lamps, the lush blue velvet of the upholstery, the thick woolen rug at her feet—everything.

Finally, having exhausted her surroundings, she turned her attention to Lyndon himself. Unlike her, he seemed so utterly unaffected by the change in their circumstances that he slept. As she studied him openly, he shifted his weight to cradle his head against the side of the carriage. After removing his hat and placing it on the seat beside him, he'd combed his blond hair with his fingers, and the unconscious effect was devastating. Idly she wondered if the stories told of the *ton* were true—that gentlemen and their valets struggled for hours to achieve just such charming disarray. In Anthony Barsett's case, his hair fell in short waves, curling boyishly across his forehead and over his ears. In sleep, the strong, well-chiseled planes of his face softened, taking on a boyish innocence at odds with his rakehell reputation.

It was as if her speculative gaze wakened him, for his eyes opened, blinked to focus, and met hers. Straightening in the seat, he smiled ruefully, murmuring, "Your pardon—I must have been more tired than I thought."

" 'Tis scarce flattering, but I did not mind it."

"Did you abandon Caro Lamb's turgid tale?" he asked, noting the book that lay on the seat beside her.

"Well, I cannot think she would have been published had it not been for curiosity. And I do not think she needed three volumes to tell her story," she added with feeling. " 'Tis utter nonsense to suppose that anyone would fall in love with Lord Glenarvon, for a more selfish, tortured, evil man has never been called a hero. I washed my hands of it when one of his many mistresses committed suicide. I think him a dashed loose screw, if you would have the truth of it, and Calantha's passion for him is just plain silly—almost as silly as Caroline Lamb's for Byron."

"Do you not believe 'tis possible to love unwisely?" he asked, the corner of his mouth quivering with amusement at her scathing review of the book that had set society on its ears.

"For a peagoose perhaps," she retorted.

"But not for the practical Leah Cole, I suppose." With an exaggerated sigh he rolled his eyes heavenward to complain, "Alas, but I am given a wife whose heart cannot be touched."

" 'Tis better to have one's heart untouched, sir, than to have it touched too often," she answered primly. But a certain mischief danced in her smoky eyes.

" 'Tis not my heart so much as my purse that the females of my acquaintance have pursued, my dear."

"Perhaps you dangled after the wrong sort."

"One is very like another—except for you, of course."

"What fustian, my lord. 'Tis the same as saying all gentlemen are alike, when 'tis obvious they are not."

"Ah, but we are," he contradicted lightly. "The principal difference between us is merely one of facade."

"What a lowering thought, my lord—you would leave the reformers amongst us with nothing to strive for."

"Four hours a bride and already you would change me." He reached across to cover her hand in her lap, and his fingers played with her wedding ring. " 'Twill be a very long life if we are forever at daggers drawn, you know. We shall both have to change somewhat, Leah."

His voice had grown soft and his blue eyes seemed to communicate silently with her heart.

Keeping her voice light, she answered quickly, "Just because we are to be friends, my lord, does not mean I should be a silly widgeon hanging on your sleeve, does it?"

"As if you could do it!" He leaned closer until his eyes were almost level with hers. " 'Tis so very wearying being an unwanted fortune-hunter, you know. Think how it must look to my friends: 'Poor Tony,' they shall say, 'he has such a hard wife that he's earned every penny of her papa's money.' "

"When in truth they should be saying poor Leah has been sold for a title." Incredibly, she was smiling.

"Does this mean you will pretend some small affection for me?" he asked as his own heart thudded.

"When we are in public, I suppose I must—I am no more proof to false pity than you are," she admitted.

" 'Tis a fair bargain then. And in return, I shall endeavor to be an exemplary husband, Lady Lyndon."

Lady Lyndon. Once again she was reminded that Leah Cole no longer existed. Her eyes dropped to where he still held her fingers in his, but she made no move to pull away as she studied his hand. Unlike so many white, almost limp, and totally effete hands she'd seen amongst those of the *ton,* Tony's was firm, warm, and decidedly masculine.

"I'd almost pay to know your thoughts, Leah."

"What? Oh, I was wondering how much different 'twill be now that I am a viscountess," she invented quickly, striving for a lightness she no longer felt. "How shall I go on, do you think? Shall I look down my nose at the servants just so?" She affected the expression she'd seen on Mrs. Drummond-Burrell the first time she'd met that haughty lady.

He grinned openly now. "I hope you do not—'twill be said you are suffering from indigestion if you do."

The coach rolled to a halt, nearly throwing her into his lap. Righting her, he grasped the pull strap and looked out the window. "We are arrived at the Black Swan, where we shall sup ere we board for passage to Boulogne. And, as you did not eat much at your father's, you must surely be famished."

"I am—and thirsty also."

Jumping down, he turned back to assist her. "A private parlor has been bespoken for us, and I am told the roast beef is particularly excellent here. You'd best enjoy it, as everything from tomorrow morning forward will be decidedly French."

Not trusting her cramped legs, she stepped down rather gingerly to survey their surroundings. "Despite Papa's ships and trade, I have never sailed, my lord—nor have I ever traveled beyond one small trip down the Thames to see the gardens at Hampton Court." Her hand still on his arm, she observed the busy innyard curiously. "Is everyone here going to France?"

"No, 'tis crowded with people coming in from several continental ports as well as those who are leaving for Calais, Boulogne, and the Dutch coastal cities. Someday when we have more time, I should like to take you on the complete tour—Holland, Belgium, France, Spain, Portugal, Italy—all of it. But we have to hurry now if we are to make it aboard the packet to France."

As busy as the place was, it did not take long for the innkeeper to have all in readiness. New covers were laid, sparkling silver and cut glassware produced, and a fire lighted against the chill of a spring evening in the small rear parlor. And all the while the room was being prepared, the innkeeper hovered about them obsequiously.

"There are obvious advantages to a viscount's company," she murmured as soon as they were out of hearing. "Do they always treat you thus?"

"Actually, no. I was about to say the same for your company, my dear. But then perhaps my man told them 'twas our wedding supper and they are merely being romantic about it."

"Oh." She took a sip from her glass and choked. "What in heaven's name is this?"

"Madeira." Swirling it, he took a small sip and nodded. "Yes, 'tis definitely Madeira. If you would prefer it, I will order ratafia for you, but this is quite good really. The thing to remember about Madeira, my dear, is that it is rather strong."

"I am not overly fond of ratafia either, my lord." Raising the glass again, she sipped deeply to slake her thirst. "And no doubt 'tis possible to acquire a liking for this."

"Then . . ." Lifting his glass to clink against hers, he toasted her again. "To Lady Lyndon—may she learn to call me Tony ere I am in my grave."

" 'Tony' seems so informal for a viscount, do you not think?" she responded. "Perhaps 'Anthony . . .' " Her voice trailed off as she paused to finish her wine, and then she cocked her head to consider him. "I mean, for one named Anthony Edward Charles Robert Barsett, 'Tony' is almost too common."

"If you are not careful, you will puff me up with my own consequence, my dear, and I shall begin addressing you as 'Leah Frances.' " He smiled engagingly as he refilled her glass.

"You would not dare—I think 'Frances' sounds as though it belongs to a man."

They were interrupted by a serving girl bringing a tray laden with a platter of beef, a joint of mutton, bowls of peas and potatoes, crusty rolls, Cornish butter, clotted cream and preserves, and a trifle. Even before she withdrew, Tony began cutting the roast and laying slices across Leah's plate, urging her to eat and drink up.

"You'll find the Madeira complements the beef most excellently," he promised. "The more you have of one, the better the other tastes." Taking care to fill her glass yet again, he turned his attention to his own plate.

Warmed by the food, the fire, and the wine, Leah relaxed as the meal progressed, and found herself actually enjoying his company. In between mouthfuls, he managed to regale her with some of his more moderate misadventures as a young man traveling abroad during Boney's wars. "I went at England's expense, of course, and I cannot say the accommodations were all I would have liked, for the ground had little to recommend it."

"You fought as a soldier?"

"Alas, but who did not? But lest you think I managed anything heroic, let me assure you that I had the distinction of reaching most of the battle sites *afterward,*" he added modestly. "My only battle of note was Talavera in Spain, and it was more of a defense than an action, but I was only nineteen and thought it quite exciting at the time."

"You know Wellington then?" she asked, fascinated. Drinking deeply of her fourth glass of Madeira, she leaned forward to rest her elbows on the table.

"But then he was not even Viscount Wellington—that came after Talavera, in fact."

"What is he like—I mean truly like?"

"Wellington?" He sipped his wine and considered Old Douro for a moment. "Well, I cannot profess to know him intimately, for although I was cavalry, I was not under his direct command, you understand. But even then, he was invincible to us—the gift of a Divine Providence to England. And he was not given to mixing with the troops, preferring to stay aloof, which in the end always makes for a better commander. I think what I liked best about him was his laugh, for he is not a humorless man, and he is not puffed up with his own conceit. But I did not really make his acquaintance until we were both back in England."

"And what happened to you, my lord?" she asked, her voice now slurring softly from the effects of the Madeira.

"I was wounded—though not heroically, I fear." Refilling her glass again, he admitted, "I suffered a broken shoulder from being unseated when my horse went down in the crush of a crowded Spanish street, and I was sent home. I was devastated at the time, for I wanted to fight the enemy with all the zeal of youth, but the accident probably saved my life."

"I am glad."

Her words cut through his reminiscing, making him acutely conscious of her. Keeping his voice light despite the surge of hope, he watched her carefully. "I came back and learned to be a bruising rider to salve my conscience. But enough of me, my dear—a man can go on forever with old tales, and I'd hear of you."

"There's naught to tell, my lord."

"Tony."

"Tony, then." Eyeing her newly emptied glass suspiciously for a moment, she decided, "I'd best have no more of this—it makes me giddy. Anyway . . ."

"We were speaking of you," he prompted.

"Were we? I've forgotten—daresay it wasn't important."

"Viscountesses are always important," he teased her.

"Are they? But then I have never been one before, you know," she whispered conspiratorially. "You shall have to tell me how to go on."

"Well, as a viscountess, you will be expected to preside at any number of routs, balls, and musicales."

"Really?" she drawled with an exaggerated lift of her brow, not noticing that he'd refilled her glass for the fifth time. "And what does a viscount do at these affairs?"

"Oh, in this instance, the viscount shall most probably watch the viscountess."

"Sounds deuced silly to me, but I suppose I shall have to learn the proper way to be watched." Her plate finished and the covers removed, she drained her glass yet again and rested her head on an elbow. "How should I look, do you think? I am a positive failure at simpering, and I despair I will ever learn." For effect, she tried fluttering her lashes, speaking in an exaggerated voice, "How de do? Charmed, my dear—that gown is positively stun-stunning—made from French army jackets, is it not?" Leaning even closer, she whispered again, " 'Tis quite the fashion to admire the French, you know."

He'd been enjoying himself so thoroughly, basking in the pleasure of watching and listening to her, that he'd not paid any attention to how much wine he'd given her. But her speech now told him it was too much.

"My dear, you are foxed."

"Am I?" Straightening with difficulty, she started to shake her head and then decided solemnly, "I think you may have the right of it, Tony—I think I am a trifle dish . . . *dis*guised." The rings around her gray irises appeared even darker than usual as she attempted to focus on him. "Thish . . . *this* is rather strong," she mumbled, lifting her empty glass and letting it fall onto the table, where it rolled to rest against a crumpled napkin.

He rose and moved behind her to assist her up. "Come on, 'tis time we left if we are to board tonight," he coaxed as he lifted her beneath the arms. "There—just stand still while I tend to matters." Reaching for the hat she'd discarded on arrival, he set it over her curls and tied the ribbons in a semblance of a bow under her chin. "You know, I did not think of it, but I'll warrant 'twas your empty stomach," he murmured, helping her from the room. "As soon as I have gotten you into the carriage, I'll come back and pay the shot."

"I . . . I am all right," she managed with an effort, trying to carefully place one foot in front of the other. " 'Tis the floor that wobbles."

Having walked her past the interested looks of fellow travelers, Tony managed to lift her into the carriage and settle her into the seat, where she leaned over to lie sideways. After easing her knees up onto the upholstery, he covered her with a carriage rug. "You are going to have a devil of a head in the morning, Lady Lyndon," he told her softly. "And for that I am truly sorry."

20

Leah awoke early, first conscious of the ache in her head, then of the rolling motion of the ship, and finally of the deep, even breathing beside her. It was the latter that brought her fully to her senses. Holding her pounding forehead, she struggled to sit up despite the weight on her coverlet. She would have relaxed with the realization that Anthony Barsett slept fully clothed on top of the bedclothes had she not chosen at that moment to look down. Gone was her rose dress, replaced with a thin lace-trimmed lawn nightrail that clung immodestly to her breasts and revealed the dark circles underneath.

"Unnnnhhhhh?"

To her horror, Tony Barsett turned in his sleep and clasped a shirt-sleeved arm across her lap, cradling his head against her hip. She clutched a corner of the coverlet to her chin and leaned to wake him.

"My lord . . ."

For answer, he snuggled closer and rubbed his beard-roughened cheek against her thigh in his sleep. His tousled hair was oddly appealing, so much so that she actually had to fight the urge to touch it. Instead, her gaze traveled downward to where his tall body sprawled at an angle, taking all of the length and much of the width of the bed. He looked larger lying there than he did standing, and his wrinkled shirt spanned broad and definitely masculine shoulders. No, Viscount Lyndon was no effete gentleman despite the perfect cut of his clothes. And viewed from above, he had quite long legs, with well-muscled thighs and calves that were defined by the narrow, fitted cut of his trousers above his stockinged feet.

Seeking to disentangle more of the covers before she attempted again to wake him, she eased the knot of bedclothes from beneath his head and moved her leg away from his embrace. He rolled backward and then turned again on his side, resting his cheek this time almost where her hand pulled at the blankets. She could feel the softness of his breath against her skin, and it sent a shiver up her arm.

"My lord."

There was a faint rigidity, as though she'd penetrated his consciousness, and then his breathing struck up its even cadence again. For a moment she considered just rising, but she would be certain to wake him when she was least covered.

"My lord!"

She winced from the loudness of her own voice, and still he did not respond. She was about to give up and get up anyway when she detected the slight flutter of an eyelid. He was shamming now, she was positive. Clutching her coverlet tightly with one hand, she reached quickly with the other, grasped a handful of the thick blond waves, and pulled hard.

He came fully awake with a start. "What the devil . . . ?" he gasped, rubbing his head. "You had no call—"

"Get up and leave this room instantly!"

The answering ire in his blue eyes gave her pause and she shrank back against her pillows, muttering defensively, "Well, you have no business being here."

"I could scarce go anywhere else," he snapped irritably as he sat up and passed a hand over the stubble of his beard. "Unless, of course, you would wish me to jump overboard."

"I do not care precisely *where* you go—just go. But it was all of a piece, was it not—the wine . . . everything? You thought to compromise me," she accused. As her voice rose, the throbbing in her temples sharpened to acute pain and she dropped the coverlet to press the heels of her palms against the sides of her head.

He stared where the cover fell away, and his own anger faded. "Got a devil of a head, don't you?" he sympathized.

"Just go away! Ohhhhhh . . ." Falling back against

her pillows, she closed her eyes against the ache that seemed to reverberate from temple to temple. "I shall never taste that foul stuff again."

Reluctantly he eased off the bed and stood to comb his hair with his fingers. "You are merely dog-bit, my dear, and therefore overset." Turning to pour some water from a pitcher over a washing cloth, he wrung out the excess and proceeded to fold the square. "Here." Leaning over her, he laid it across her forehead.

She clasped the cool cloth to her head and groaned. "I am never ill. I don't . . ."

"Poor Leah. I'd give you a few drops of laudanum if I had any, but I daresay that might upset your stomach."

"Where's Jeanne?"

"Asleep, I should think. You were so tired when we boarded that we could not rouse you, and we did not get you into your nightdress before two o'clock."

"We?" Her color heightened beneath the cloth at the thought that crossed her mind.

"Yes," he answered conversationally as he opened his traveling case and rummaged through the neatly folded articles in search of his flask. "Jeanne and Blair arrived while we dined, so all was in readiness. When I could not wake you sufficiently to walk, I carried you aboard and laid you on that settee, thinking you would rouse later for bed. Finally I could see that your maid was tired herself, so between us we managed to wrestle you into your rail. 'Twas not an easy task either, for you had all the animation of a grain sack. Here . . ." He found the silver bottle and unscrewed the lid to pour the liquid into it. " 'Tisn't Madeira, but 'twill have to suffice."

"You looked at me!" she choked. "How dare you! You compromised me!"

"I did no such thing, Leah. For one thing, one cannot compromise one's wife, and for another, there's not much lascivious leering at an unconscious female in the presence of her maid." Carefully carrying the full lid to the bedside, he leaned over her. "Can you sit, do you think?"

"For what?" she asked suspiciously, still mortified by the thought that he'd seen her unclothed.

"Brandy."

"You were not supposed . . . you *promised* you would not—and I will not be drugged with drink again!"

"Do not be ridiculous, my dear. As you can see if you would open your eyes again, I am clothed except for my coat and my shoes, and so I have been all night. Indeed," he added with a wry grin, "I'd thought to be noble and sleep on the settee myself, but the prospect paled after an hour of trying to fold my body to fit it. And I knew you were in no condition to mind if I shared one side of the bed, after all." Balancing the brandy, he reached the other hand to her. "Come on—'twill ease you."

"How do you know?" she muttered, struggling up while clutching both cover and cloth. "Lud, but I cannot stand this—I am never ill," she complained miserably.

"What you need is a hair of the dog that bit you. 'Tis a saying far older than I, but I am told that it does help. As for myself, I have not given myself a bad head since Oxford—the trick seems to be that one should eat *before* one imbibes drink."

Sitting down beside her, he held the bottle cap to her lips and tipped it when she sipped. She choked as the liquid hit the back of her throat and she was seized by a paroxysm of coughing. Tears came to her eyes while he pounded her back. "Devil of a way to begin a wedding trip, isn't it? But you'll be better in an hour or so and we can debark."

"I shall never recover," she retorted.

"Aye, you will. Lie back down for a few minutes whilst I am gone, and I will send Jeanne to you. 'Tis cramped and I must be shaved also, so you cannot stay abed all day." Rising, he went to replace the top of his flask. "I think I shall breathe the salt air to refresh me, as I have never favored close places." He searched for his shoes and leaned down to slip the polished highlows on. "Try to rest, my dear."

She watched him warily until he reached the door. "Do not think for one moment that I do not know what you attempted, my lord, and I will not share a chamber with you again," she announced flatly.

He paused, his hand on the door latch. "You mistake the matter then, Leah, for the intent was not mine. Your father booked but one room for us."

"Oh." Mollified, she lay back to ease the pounding in her head, hoping it was the effects of the wine that made her somehow disappointed. Either that or there was something totally perverse about a female who wanted to be wanted by a man she did not herself want. Turning over gingerly, she faced the wall and closed her eyes, remembering how he'd looked lying beside her.

"Madame?"

Leah awoke to find Jeanne peering over her shoulder, and for a moment she wondered whom the little maid addressed. And then it sank in. She was Viscountess Lyndon now, a married lady wed to Anthony Barsett. Her head still ached, but with less intensity than before, and she was hungry, a certain indication that she meant to survive.

"Lud, Jeanne, I must have gone back to sleep."

"Well, as we are in Boulogne, madame, Lord Lyndon bade me wake you." Moving briskly to throw open a trunk, she lifted a sea-green walking dress and unwrapped it from the tissues, shaking the folds from its skirt and holding it up speculatively. "This will do, I think."

"Where is . . . where is Lyndon now?" Leah asked.

"Well, he would not disturb you, and so Mr. Blair shaves him in his berth, I believe. He is so very kind," Jeanne ventured appreciatively.

"Who? Blair or Lyndon?"

"Blair? Bah—what a dour person! *Mais non,* 'twas the viscount I meant."

"Did . . . did he undress me last night?" Leah had to know.

"Well . . ." The little maid bustled about, selecting a zona, petticoat, and stockings. "He told me to do it, of course, but you were so . . . so *very* sleepy, madame, that I could not do it. So," she explained with a philosophical shrug, "I asked for assistance."

"I was disguised, Jeanne."

"*Oui,* but he was most helpful. He stood you up, holding you from behind, and I did the rest.'' Her dark eyes met Leah's impishly. ''I did not think it improper—he is your husband, *n'est-ce pas?''*

''I don't know what he is,'' Leah grumbled, and then caught herself. It was, after all, highly improper to discuss one's thoughts with one's maid. Sliding off the bed, she padded to the washstand and wrung out the cloth Lyndon had left on her head. ''I do know one thing, Jeanne: I shall *never* have any Madeira again. The stuff is positively poisonous.''

They were interrupted by several sharp raps on the closed door. ''I can give you ten minutes,'' Tony called through. ''After that, I shall have to come in and dress myself. The captain is quite determined to discharge his passengers before noon.''

''Noon? It cannot be . . . that is, we have not eaten!''

''We'll breakfast onshore and rent a carriage for the journey to Paris,'' he answered.

Afraid that he might enter despite his words, Leah stripped her nightrail and fairly dived into her clothing, muttering, ''Ten minutes—who does he think he is?''

Jeanne pulled the skirt of Leah's gown down over her snowy petticoat and busied herself at setting the toilette to rights. ''I believe he thinks he is your husband, madame.''

21

The accommodations Tony found for them in Paris were exceptional, a hotel in the Rue de Clichy favored by Lady Oxford, where the rooms were spacious and the atmosphere gracious. As news of their arrival spread amongst the English who'd descended on the city in droves ever since the autumn of 1814, invitations arrived for more receptions and assemblies than it was possible to attend during a two-week visit. And if the *ton* had been less than enthusiastic about Leah in London, those members in Paris did not seem to know of it.

The city glittered with gaiety, affording her with amusements she'd only heard of as Tony escorted her to the opera, lavish dinners, and a ball at the British embassy. She gawked at the old Bourbon palace of the Tuileries, the wonderful artworks plundered by Napoleon for the Louvre, Bonaparte's private apartments at St. Cloud; she walked the wide boulevards admiring the emperor's victory monuments, she dined on food prepared by one of Bonaparte's chefs at the Rocher de Cancalle and at the exclusive Beauvilliers until she was ready to seek the English cuisine at the Café des Anglais on, of all places, the Boulevard des Italiens. Within three days of their arrival in the French capital, Lyndon's lady had been pronounced a social success, a Diamond of the First Water, an Original, so much so that Tony teased her that he was merely "the man fortunate enough to have escorted the Incomparable Lady Lyndon to Paris." And it was obvious by both the warmth and tone of his voice that he was inordinately proud of her.

Through it all, Tony Barsett exercised considerable patience and charm, standing in lines, walking block after block as she read the guidebooks to him, listening to her gasp in awe at Marie Antoinette's gardens, and escorting her to the seemingly endless round of parties. During the days and evenings, she was in perfect charity with him, sharing thoughts, laughing and teasing, and genuinely enjoying his company. But when it came time to seek their beds, she bade him good night outside her door, thanking him profusely for the day's pleasures, and offering nothing more.

By the end of the first week, by all outward appearances, they were a perfectly matched pair. And on a particularly pleasant morning, he dropped into a chair opposite hers at the small breakfast table and waited while she poured his coffee.

"Well, my dear, is there any building, statue, or other work of art left that you have an express wish to see?"

"Actually, I'd thought to stay in and let Jeanne try the cucumber paste recommended by the Comtesse d'Aubignon," she answered blithely. " 'Tis said to clarify dull complexions after excessive partygoing, you know, and I do so wish to be in looks for Lady Oxford's little soiree. Unless, of course, I might persuade you to take me to the Palais Royal to the shops."

"The Palais Royal, my dear, is like the Dark Walk at Vauxhall even in daylight, complete with the demimonde advertising their wares rather openly."

"Well, I should still like to see it."

"I think perhaps you should try the cucumber paste."

"Tony!"

"For your dull complexion."

"Tony!"

"No." Reaching for a sweet bun, he looked at her with a particularly wicked gleam in his eyes. "I cannot think you really wish to see other females strutting about in altogether revealing gowns, displaying their bare . . . er, their bodies in the most vulgar manner, wearing more paste jewelry than clothing, and offering themselves to passing men. And if you tell me you wish to shop there, I'll know that for a whisker, Leah."

"I never thought you so mean-spirited," she retorted. "If I were not here, I've not a doubt but what you'd ogle them yourself."

"No. Despite what you appear to think of me, my dear, I am a trifle more fastidious in my liaisons. I do not disappear into bedchambers rented by the hour with just anyone."

Sighing soulfully, she pried her own roll apart and slathered butter on it. "There is nothing quite so staid as a *reformed* rake, I suppose."

"The cucumber paste was all a hum, wasn't it?" He bit off a piece with a currant in it and chewed, watching her. "You really want to see that sort of thing? 'Tis rather sordid, you know."

"Yes."

"Why?"

"Because I have heard that all Paris goes there, that 'tis not just the . . . those women that foreigners go to watch like some great fair."

"The best time to go is at night, Leah, and we are promised to Lady Oxford. But," he added as her face fell, "there is nothing to say we must spend the entire evening with her. You must, of course, never tell your father I took you there."

"Thank you, my lord."

"For someone who claims an inability to flirt, Lady Lyndon, you are mistress of the wheedle."

Dimpling in acknowledgment, she appeared to study the linen tablecloth before her. "I shall choose to take that as a compliment, I think."

"I ought to box your ears for impudence—but I shan't. So now that you have had your way quite easily, what else is it that you wish to do today?"

"Could we walk along the Seine?"

" 'Tis dirty and inhabited by all manner of ruffians—find something else in your guidebook not likely to get us robbed or worse."

"But I thought we could see the open markets and buy bread and cheese and picnic beside the river."

"It stinks," he announced baldly.

"All of it?"

"Leah . . . Leah. Just because you have seen nothing of the world does not mean you can wish to see everything, does it?"

"Yes. Tony, if I am to see France, I should like to see it as the French do, and not spend my time with other English merely speaking of it."

"And will you hang on my arm and not wander off as you did at Notre Dame? I thought I'd lost you forever there."

"I will positively clutch at you," she promised solemnly.

"Until the first time you see something you wish to inspect closely," he muttered dryly. "You know, I ought to be clapped up for even considering it, but all right," he relented. "Only the first time you fail to clutch, we are coming back for the cucumber paste."

It did not take her long to ready herself. Popping the rest of her roll in her mouth with the exuberance of a child, she washed it down with her cup of chocolate and was off in a trice to find her walking shoes. A slow smile spread across his face as he waited for her. She was an Original, all right, and her enthusiasm was infectious. He'd not thought it possible to relive his salad days, but in her company nothing bored him. If only her father's health were good, he'd have taken her on the Grand Tour of Europe and shown her everything.

They departed the hotel arm in arm and walked through the crowded, dirty streets, stopping to peer into shop windows, buying ices in paper cones, a bottle of wine, hot bread, a hunk of cheese, and on arriving on the riverbank, sitting to eat and drink in the shade cast by merchant stalls. The street above them was noisy, dusty, and teeming with people and animals, but Leah did not seem to mind. From time to time she broke off scraps of bread and tossed them at rangy dogs who scavenged behind the stalls.

Wrinkling her nose against the stench of the water, she tucked her knees more decorously on her spread-out shawl and looked around. "I had always wondered why we English so admired the French, even during the war, you know," she admitted. "It cannot be the dirt and poverty, for those are everywhere, and it cannot be the buildings, for London has splendid museums and palaces also."

"And it cannot be the people, for they are a rude lot," Tony cut in, grinning at the way they'd been abused at the cheese stall when Leah refused to pay the first price asked.

"No, but they are civilized—perhaps more so than we," she went on. "We have walked in some crowded and disgusting places, and I have not yet seen a chimney sweep."

"Well, they are about, my dear, else how do they prevent fires?"

"I don't know, but I'll wager they do not send four-year-old children up burning chimneys—'tis only England that does so."

"No, I think you are wrong."

She turned those strange gray eyes of hers to his face. "But we consider ourselves so very civilized, do we not? Yet every day in London and Manchester and the rest of our cities, children are beaten and maimed, starved and forced up chimneys, and if they survive very long, they choke from the soot and get great sores on their bodies that do not heal."

"I have never . . ." He had started to say he'd never employed a young chimney sweep, but then stopped, for he'd never noticed just who went up or down his chimneys.

"You never see them, and neither does anyone else, Tony. Oh, maybe a reformer like Hannah More does, but she is more intent on making them God-fearing than on eliminating the problem itself."

"The law—"

"The House of Lords blocks any useful law!" She caught herself and looked down to brush bread crumbs from the skirt of her muslin walking dress. "Your pardon, my lord—'tis not your fault alone."

"Thank you," he observed sardonically. "I'd begun to think you meant to take me to task for the problem."

"But you could speak out, could you not?"

"I have never attended Lords except when the Regent called Parliament into session last year, and I've never been tempted to speak out there. For one thing, I am neither a Whig nor a Tory, and for another, none of my friends go either."

"But it is your right! I mean, are you not entitled?"

"Yes, but it does no good. I should be laughed out of the place if I rose to speak to a chamber full of old men. The power, my dear, rests in the Commons."

"The Lords have blocked every bill written to restrict the use of children as sweeps."

"I have no wish to sit in Paris discussing the woes of London, Leah," he told her finally. "Especially when there is nothing I can do about the problem."

"But I thought a viscount could—"

"You thought incorrectly then. Come, we'd best get back if we are to try for two places tonight." He picked up a small stone that had come dislodged from the hill behind them and skipped it aimlessly across the water before rising to give her a hand.

They walked back quietly, enjoying the sights of the Paris street on a spring day, seemingly unconscious of the fact that his hand had slipped from her elbow to twine in her fingers. Finally he broke the quiet by asking, "You still think me a frivolous fellow, don't you?"

"No."

"No?"

"Actually, I think you are probably one of the best of your class."

"Now, there's a dubious compliment if I ever heard one, Lady Lyndon."

"Well, I find I am enjoying your company more than I thought possible," she admitted with a grin.

"Which is nothing to the point, since you did not expect to enjoy it at all, my dear. I am learning to listen to what you do not say as well as to what you do."

"Alas, I am found out then."

"You know, Leah, I admit I did not think to wed you when I first . . . well, when I . . ."

"When you offered me *carte blanche*," she finished for him.

" 'Tis nothing I can take pride in, but yes. But you have proven to be a delight to me. I—"

"Damme if it ain't Lyndon! And this must be the latest light-o'-love!"

Tony felt Leah's fingers tense in his, and he was vexed beyond reason as he turned wrathfully to the pleasant-faced young lord who greeted them. "This is my wedding trip, Merville," he growled. "Do you not read the English papers?"

"Read you was engaged, but married? Naw—'Tony Barsett'll never get leg-shackled until they come to carry him off to debtors' prison,' I told Holloway, and she don't look like a . . ."

"Cit?" Leah supplied evenly. "And just what are we supposed to look like?"

"Merville . . ." Tony's voice was silky-soft as he faced the suddenly nonplussed fellow. "You will, of course, apologize to my wife."

"Oh, now, Tony, I say," Merville protested weakly, aware now of the underlying edge in Lyndon's words. "Oh . . . uh, yes. Heh-heh. No offense intended, ma'am—none 't all. Devilish temper he's got, ain't it? Don't know when a man's funning." Bowing quickly, he backed away, mumbling apologies.

"You cannot keep them from talking, my lord." Leah pulled her hand free and started walking back. "I told Papa how it would be."

"Leah . . ." He fell into step beside her, at a loss to recover what Merville's careless words had cost him. His declaration now would seem false and contrived.

22

They were going to be fashionably late, Leah decided as she luxuriated in the steaming bath, soaking limbs still sore from so much walking. The pleasant scent of the French-milled soap clung to her and permeated the air, bringing forth the feeling of being surrounded by lilacs. She stretched her leg up to lather it again just for the lazy pleasure of it.

She'd had a wonderful time in Paris—would hate to leave, in fact. Indeed, Tony had mentioned after her father's last letter that they might extend the trip. Her father. She had to smile at the tone of his brief note—it was as though he were writing to someone else, all filled with "your ladyship" and "my lady." But he was well, he said, and by the sound of his activities, it appeared he told the truth.

Leaning forward to rinse herself, she happened to glance in the cheval mirror beside the screen, and her body went rigid. "How long have you been here?" she demanded of her husband's reflection. "Do not come one step further, my lord," she warned. "I am still bathing."

"Your pardon," he managed in a voice that sounded strange even to him. "I thought that since Blair left me to do my own shirt, perhaps you would assist." His mouth had gone almost too dry for words at the sight of her wet body. "I'll wait for you to finish."

"Get Jeanne," she advised, leaning now to cover herself.

"When last I saw her, she was carrying a hatbox, complaining volubly that something was crushed. And, as Blair is gone to remove a wrinkle from my coat, I can only surmise that they are meeting somewhere over a steam kettle.''

''Blair and Jeanne? Do not be absurd.'' From her cramped position, she could see that he was still watching her in the mirror, and the expression on his face sent a tremor of excitement through her. Trying to keep her own voice calm, she told him, ''You'll have to leave if you expect me to get out of here.''

When he moved from view and she heard the door close, she rose to reach for a towel. Water ran in rivulets down her body as she patted her face first. Then, as she was about to slide the towel lower to dry her breasts, she saw him again.

''Of all the despicable, *despicable,* ungentlemanly, unseemly things!'' she sputtered. ''Get out of here, you lecher, you . . . you unprincipled rake!''

As she clutched the towel to the crevice between her breasts rather than above them, Tony's smile widened and the pulse in his temples beat faster. ''There is nothing wrong with admiring one's wife,'' he answered softly, moving closer.

''You have no right to stand there leering at me! I thought you'd left, else I'd not—''

''The door was ajar, and I closed it. Besides, I have every right, Leah.''

''Get out,'' she repeated evenly despite the thudding of her heart. When he stepped forward rather than back, her own mouth went strangely dry. In desperation she cast about for a weapon. ''Tony, you promised you would not—we would not—Tony, get out of here!''

''You are beautiful, Leah,'' he told her softly, coming still closer.

''Tony, I thought we were friends,'' she tried desperately. Her fingers closed over the wet bar of soap as she stepped back out of the tub away from him.

''I'd cry friends and more with you, love.''

''No.''

He stopped, but by now she was too apprehensive to note anything beyond her own racing heart. Whether from fear of him or herself, she raised the bar of soap and hurled it. The suddenness of her action took him by complete surprise, and before he realized she meant to do it, the wet soap had caught him squarely under the brow.

At first she gave a small crow of triumph, but then as she saw him rub his eye and wince in pain, she worried that she'd actually injured him. Grabbing her wrapper from a hook on the screen, she threw it over her wet body and came forward to examine her handiwork.

"I think you have blacked my eye," he managed with a remarkable degree of forbearance through soap-induced tears.

"You would not leave," she defended herself. "Here . . ." Picking up a wet washing cloth, she handed it to him. "I thought you meant to molest me."

Holding the cloth over his smarting eye, he shook his head.

"Then what was your intent?" she demanded.

"I know 'tis blacked," he muttered.

Feeling irrationally guilty, she reached to touch the lump that was forming at brow level. "Let me see." As he lowered the cloth, she peered upward intently. "Well, it is swelling," she admitted, "but 'tis your own fault, Anthony Barsett. The next time I tell you to go, you'd best listen to me."

Her black-rimmed gray eyes were but inches from his, and the clean smell of soap and water floated upward. Her hair, which had been piled high, escaped from the ribbon that held it, and loose tendrils fell about her temples and clung wetly to her neck, while droplets of water beaded on her silky skin and splotched the fabric of her wrapper. His expression changed from chagrin to deviltry to desire, the emotions crossing his face like a parade marching double-time. Time stood still as anticipation and dread mixed in her breast, leaving her mesmerized by what she saw in his eyes.

His hand, still holding the wet cloth, came up behind her head to pull the end of the ribbon, and as her hair cascaded down, the fingers of his other hand twined in it, imprisoning her. Her breath caught in her throat and her heart beat wildly as his mouth came down on hers. There was no brushing, no teasing, and nothing remotely tentative about his kiss. He dropped the cloth to the floor at their feet and slid his arm around her to mold her body to his, blotting all but the nearness of him from her consciousness. Her lips parted in feeble protest to receive instead his exploring tongue as the kiss deepened, igniting something inside her.

She clung mindlessly to him, aware now only of his masculine strength as the hand that held her cradled first her waist and then her hip. Robbed of reason by his touch, she not only let his hand explore her, she in turn clasped her arms tightly about him. And when at last his mouth left hers to trace kisses down to her throat, she arched her head instinctively to give him access to the sensitive hollow there.

Then she felt his hands leave her hair and her hip to feel for the tie at her waist. Some small voice of reason reasserted itself deep within her mind, protesting that it was wrong, that she did not love him, nor did he love her. As his fingers twined in the silken cord, she caught at them, holding them tightly.

"No!"

The vehemence of her protest startled him with its suddenness. He wanted to think that somehow she was like the others, being coy, saying no when she meant yes, and he tried to disentangle himself from the hands that held his. Yet, despite the fact that her smoky eyes were almost dark with desire and her breasts heaved as she mastered her breath, the moment had passed for her.

"We are wed," he whispered.

"And that makes it right?" Pulling away, she retied her wrapper with her back to him. "Forgive my romantic notions, but . . ." she began, still mortified over her brazen response to him.

"I think I love you, Leah."

"You think you love me—you *think* you love me?" Her temper, already strained beyond bearing, flared dangerously. " 'Tis rich to hear you say it just that way, is it not? 'Tis what you think I would have you say, Tony Barsett!" Her chin jutted upward defiantly. "As this is my chamber, sir, I ask you to leave it."

He exhaled heavily, trying to still the desire that fought

for control of him. "Will you do my studs first so that I may finish dressing?"

"Your studs?" She stared blankly, unable to believe he could be so unaffected by what he'd done.

" 'Tis why I came here," he prompted, his eyes sober now. Holding out his wrists to show his unfastened shirt cuffs, he stepped closer. "I'd not meant to do anything else."

Inadvertently her eyes strayed to where the snowy shirt fell away to expose the curling hairs on his chest, and she knew he'd spoken the truth in that at least. "I . . . uh . . ." Biting her lip to hide her nervousness, she nodded finally. "Then you will leave?"

"Yes."

Keeping her gaze low to avoid meeting his, she reached out almost gingerly to take the studs he'd retrieved from his pocket, and awkwardly attempted to insert one of them in his cuff.

" 'Tis better to use two hands," he advised.

He extended both wrists now, and she pulled the first stud holes together with one hand while maneuvering the pearl-and-silver fastening into them with the other. His palms were warm where she touched them, and once again she was struck by the masculinity of his hands—not that they were large or coarse, but rather that they appeared both clean and strong. Quickly she finished fastening both sleeves.

"I have gotten most of the front, but I have difficulty with the neck—would it be too much to ask you to do it also?"

She held out her palm with a sigh and let him drop the pearl stud into it. Her fingers worked it into place and then buttoned the top one. "You'd best hope that Blair returns to do your cravat, Tony, else I shall strangle you with it. Now, leave me be that I may dress also."

Retreating, he passed Jeanne in the hall. "Been on the back stairs with Blair again, eh?" he teased her.

"Monsieur Blair is belowstairs with your coat, my lord," she answered with a saucy smile. "The wrinkle was, I believe, quite a difficult one."

It was a puzzle to him that he could charm every female of his acquaintance save the one he wanted the most. Once he was in his chamber, he poured himself a small quantity of brandy, swirled it in his glass, and stared into the street below. For a fellow whose reputed conquests were legion, he had certainly bungled this one from the start. Why had he said he thought he loved her? Because he feared she would not love him back? Even now, it sounded almost as ridiculous in his mind as it had to her. He thought he loved her. No, he knew better—he *knew* he loved her. And, accomplished flirt that he was, he could not even tell when it was that desire had turned to something more.

It was *rich,* the jests fate played on one, after all. Tony Barsett, the consummate rake, the last of a long line of 'em, in fact, had been caught by a side-facer, blind-sided by himself, so to speak. He loved a green girl, a Cit whose contempt for his class was exceeded only by her contempt for him.

Down the hall, Leah dressed quickly, trying not to think of what he'd done to her. It was, of course, impossible. Everything about him, from his obvious handsomeness to the warmth of his hands, assailed her senses and made her acutely aware of him. And her treacherous mind refused to cooperate, returning repeatedly to dwell on the feel of his mouth on hers, his freshly shaven cheek against hers, reliving again the sensations brought forth by his hands on her body. There was a traitor within her, a weakness that made her want to yield the citadel.

23

"I have gone to masquerades in a domino, my dear, but I assure you 'tis the first time I have ever had to appear with a patched eye," he murmured in the darkness of their hired carriage. " 'Twill be said I mean to go incognito into the den of iniquity."

"Fiddle. If you are seeking sympathy from me, Tony Barsett, you have misjudged your aim. 'Twas you who would come closer, and you cannot say you were not warned."

"Heartless jade."

"Instead of seeking sympathy, my lord, you ought to be thankful that soap was the only weapon at hand," she reminded him. "Had there been anything else, you'd have more than a blacked eye."

"I was overcome by your beauty," he tried soulfully, "and could not control my baser impulses. I was besotted."

"A Banbury tale if I ever heard one. What you were doing, Tony, was . . ."

"Yes?" he drawled.

"You were bent on seduction, and well you know it."

"And as I recall it, you were not depressing my pretensions either."

That brought her up short. Turning to stare into the dark Parisian street, she offered him the shadow of her profile against the side of the carriage. Her long standing sense of honesty prevailing, she admitted slowly, "No, I did not, I suppose, and I cannot account for my behavior. It was immodest in the extreme."

"No." His voice softened as he reached across to her. " 'Tis the way it should be between us, Leah."

"I behaved like the brazen trollop you thought me when we met," she added, sparing herself not at all.

"Hardly that." His hand closed over hers, stilling it in her lap. "If that were the case, I'd not have this black eye, and you—"

"Stop it! I *let* you kiss me!"

"You did that," he agreed as his fingers soothed and stroked the back of her hand. "But is that so terrible? As I told you then, we are wed, Leah—we can do anything we wish."

"But we agreed! This marriage is a sham!"

"It is whatever we choose to make of it."

She was silent for a long time, so long that he began to think she'd closed the subject and meant to ignore him the rest of the way. He released her hand and leaned back against the leather-covered seat with a sigh. He always vowed to himself to go slowly with her, and he always broke those promises to himself. "But I do not know what I wish to make of it. I cannot even decide if I like you," she answered low as her throat tightened. "I am not of your world, and we have nothing common between us but money."

"I am more in your world than you would think, Leah."

There was another long silence, broken only by the sound of vehicles moving down the darkened streets. "Well, my dear," he observed finally, "I believe we are coming upon the Palais Royal."

"How can you tell? There are no lights anywhere that I can see."

"You are on the wrong side. If you will but look out here," he directed, "you will see they are strung across the building. At night, it is almost the only place in the city that is lighted on the outside."

The driver slowed as traffic merged and other conveyances vied for roadway. Leah stared out in fascination at the huge building that loomed ahead. "Why, 'tis hung like Vauxhall or something."

"Or something. But 'tis nothing like on the inside except for the gardens. The rest is shops and cafés and cheap bedrooms. You must not appear too shocked when you see the demimonde parade themselves about, flirt and drink with unattached men, and go upstairs for pay."

"I thought all Paris came here to shop."

"They do. It's an odd place, unlike anything in London, for you will find all manner of people, respectable and otherwise, rubbing together tolerably under the same roof."

Disgorged by an impatient driver and shouted at by those waiting to pull up, they climbed down and Tony tucked Leah's hand in the crook of his arm. She hesitated, prompting him to lean closer and whisper, "I'd stay near me, were I you."

"I don't—"

"You do not wish to be ogled by every man jack in the place, do you?" he hissed.

"Of course not." As she looked around them, she began to wish they'd stayed at Lady Oxford's party, for there was a crush of all sorts vying to get in. One obviously intoxicated Frenchman leaned so close to her that she could smell stale wine and onions on his breath, and his eyes lingered suggestively on the slight décolletage of her gown. Her fingers tightened on Tony's arm and she moved closer to him.

"I tried to tell you how it would be," he murmured, grinning above her head. "If we manage to see the place without my being forced to duel for your honor, I shall count myself fortunate."

The buck, a slim fellow, measured Tony speculatively and moved on. "Well, you might have said something to him," she complained. "The only other person ever to have looked at me like that was you."

"The French, my dear, still smart from the war, and are only too eager to prove themselves with their swords on any available Englishman. The English, of course, always oblige them, choosing pistols instead, and by morning the streets are littered with the bodies of the hot-headed."

"I thought they welcomed us."

"We afford them amusement, I suppose, for the English *ton* has always aped them. I mean, look at that gown you are wearing now." He glanced down at the expensive peach gauze she wore over a slim petticoat of silk dyed the same color. "You were assured by Cecile that 'twas in the French style, were you not? Napoleon lost the war, but his people are the arbiters of what you wear."

They were walking down the shop-lined corridors, and Leah forgot her earlier apprehension as she was caught up in looking at the glittering lights and the gaily festooned stores. Tony stopped short outside one of them to study the display of jewelry that winked invitingly, reflecting color. His arm slid around her waist and pulled her closer to look, prompting the proprietor to come forward immediately with that universal deference common to jewelers of all nationalities.

"Entrez-vous, monsieur," he invited, waving expansively at cases that lined the walls inside. *"Pour mademoiselle . . . ?"*

"What do you say, my dear?" Tony asked, turning to Leah. "I have not yet bought you a bridal gift."

"No, I—"

"Nonsense." He dismissed her refusal briskly. "It can do no harm to look at his wares."

Once in the small shop, the proprietor, having heard them speak to each other, switched to an imperfect English. "Ze laydee—she is your . . . ?"

"Wife," Tony supplied quickly, knowing that the sort of gifts available differed considerably from gaudy paste to fine gemstones.

"Wife, then." The fellow's dark eyes traveled over Leah's face and hair carefully, and unlike his earlier countryman, he did so respectfully. "Paul Revillon has ze diamonds, but zay do not do madame ze justice—madame weeshes colair, no?"

"Yes," Tony answered for her.

This time, the jeweler studied him to ascertain his approximate wealth and, having duly noted the excellent tailoring of his lordship's dark blue coat, the perfect cravat, and the large pearl studs that fastened what could be seen of his shirt, smiled broadly. "Ah, monsieur, one recognizes ze English Quality—you aire a nobleman pairhaps?" he asked to flatter.

"I am Lyndon."

As though that were instantly recognizable, the fellow bobbed respectfully, urged his lordship to wait for a moment, and disappeared into the back, leaving them in the company of a clerk, who merely hung back and appeared bored. "Your fame seems to have spread," Leah whispered to Tony while they waited.

"No, but he thinks he smells gold."

She moved to look at the glass cases curiously, her attention drawn to a pearl-and-garnet brooch. "You know, I rather favor this one—'twould look nice on my black-trimmed pelisse next winter."

"Purchase it, by all means then, but do not think to deter me from getting you something more substantial." He came up behind her to study the brooch. "Garnets are *not* what I had in mind for you."

Monsieur Revillon returned with a ring of keys and several locked cases, laying them on a countertop. "You weel behold my best, Madame Lyndon," he announced dramatically. Selecting a key, he inserted it in a lock to open the first box. Lifting the lid, he revealed an exquisite sapphire necklace, explaining, "For ze eyes, madame—sapphires will become zose eyes." To Tony he passed his jeweler's glass, offering, "Pairhaps Monsieur Lyndon weeshes to examine zem before Madame sees zem on ze neck?"

Tony lifted the double chain of sapphires with the large diamond-surrounded single pendant from the velvet-lined box and held it to the glowing light. Examining it under the glass, he turned it over several times, inspecting the stones carefully. "It's quite fine," he admitted.

"Zat parteeculaire piece was ze Marchioness de Campignon's before hair unfortunate demise in ze Terror. Revillon bought eet from hair zen, but she deed not escape ze guillotine."

"And you have had it all these years?" Tony murmured skeptically.

"*Mais non.* I sold eet to a Bonapartiste, who pawned eet back to me when hees fortunes changed."

"How much?"

"Ten zousand francs."

"No!"

''Madame does not like eet?'' Revillon turned on her with a decidedly injured air. ''But Madame—''

'' 'Tis too expensive. I would see the others.''

Shrugging expressively, the jeweler opened the remaining cases to show in order an enormous pearl-and-ruby pendant, a glittering emerald-and-diamond necklace, and a very fine amethyst necklace, earrings, and brooch. ''Would Madame weesh to try zem against hair skin pairhaps?''

''No, but I'd like this brooch.'' She pointed to the one she'd liked in the glass case.

''How much for the amethyst set?'' Tony asked, ignoring Leah's gasp.

''For Madame and Monsieur, sees zousand.''

Tony lifted the necklace out and held it up against Leah's neck. '' 'Tis lovely, my dear.'' Turning back to the jeweler, he offered, ''Fourteen thousand for the sapphires and the amethysts.''

''Tony!''

'' 'Tis francs, not pounds, Leah,'' he reminded her. Addressing Revillon, he enumerated his terms. ''I have no wish to be robbed on the way back to the hotel, but if you will deliver them in the morning and bring your glass to ensure they are the same, I will pay you then. And we will take the brooch now.''

''Eet eez but nine hundred francs, mi'lor'.''

''Wrap it, and she will put it in her reticule.''

Outside, she rounded on him. ''Fourteen thousand francs! Are you mad, Tony? And nine hundred for the brooch! 'Tis a fortune!''

''It was a bridal gift, Leah.''

''Bought with my father's money! Papa would—''

''Jeptha Cole did not pay for it—I did. Not one franc expended came from your father,'' he retorted as his jaw twitched where he worked to stifle his anger. ''And let me tell you something else, my dear Leah,'' he bit off precisely, ''nothing else I have spent on you is your father's either. Furthermore, if I wish to squander my own money, 'tis entirely my affair.''

''The settlements—''

''The settlements be damned!'' he exploded, losing

the battle against his temper. "Do you know what settlements I have had? I did not take your papa's money, Leah—I borrowed seven thousand pounds at interest against a cargo of Jamaican rum!"

"I know he offered you a fortune!"

"Offered! Aye, there's the word we need, my dear—he *offered* forty thousand pounds, to be exact! But I do have my pride, despite the insults you have flung my direction." His blue eye blazed with indignation at her accusation. "What I took, however, was twenty thousand pounds settled directly on you and our heirs, and the loan."

She stared, stunned for a moment, unable to quite believe him. "But the rumors—'twas said you were done up . . ."

"And there the word is 'rumor'—because my ship went down, 'twas supposed I'd lost everything. Well, I did not—I lost a large sum, but I was not even near dun territory, my dear. I never have been."

"You let everybody believe it!"

"I did not choose to dignify the stories—there is a difference, you know. What was I supposed to say? 'No, you are mistaken—Tony Barsett's purse is far from let?' And how many would have believed me if I had?"

"But even your aunt Davenham—"

"Now, *there* I plead guilty, for I wanted her to accept you, and I could not depend on her liking you before she's had a chance to know you."

"But *why*?"

"That should be obvious to you," he shot back. "If you cannot forget you are a merchant's daughter, how the devil do you suppose she can?"

"Oh."

They were standing in a busy hallway, and when Leah looked away, she became aware they'd attracted a rather large crowd of curious onlookers, most of whom had no idea what they'd said. One fellow, rather lower-class by appearance, offered Tony advice in an idiomatic French she did not understand. In answer, her husband grasped her arm firmly and pulled her along to the first corner. Behind them, their audience broke into applause.

"What did he say?" she asked curiously.

"He said, madam wife, that I ought to take you upstairs and cease haggling over the price."

"He *what*?"

"And if I were not afraid of the vermin, I'd do it." He released her and started walking rapidly.

She stood rooted for a moment, just long enough for an elderly man to ogle her thoroughly, and then she all but ran after him. "Wait—are you saying you did not take any settlement?"

"I said it."

"Then why did you marry me?" She was having difficulty keeping up with his long strides as her narrow petticoat hampered her steps. "*Will* you wait for me at least?"

He stopped so abruptly that she collided with him. "The reason, Leah Cole, should be obvious," he snapped.

"Well, it isn't," she answered peevishly. "I seem to be particularly obtuse on that head."

"All right, then." The sarcasm in his voice was unmistakable as he added significantly, "There did not appear to be any other way to get you."

"But we agreed . . . that is, 'twas decided that . . ."

"That I would not storm the citadel? Quite frankly, my dear, I had not expected you to be so impervious to my efforts to win you. Clearly I was mistaken." He started to walk again, flinging over his shoulder, "Your wish to remain indifferent has finally penetrated my conceit and will therefore be honored."

"Must you keep running off? I cannot keep up!" she screeched in exasperation. "And I am not indifferent!"

That stopped him. Not daring to believe he'd heard her aright, he turned around. "What did you say?"

A gaudily rouged woman, her full breasts exposed in a spangled gown cut deeply to her waist, stopped and gave Tony an admiring look, telling him that if the pale one did not wish his business, she'd take him. Leah's face flushed as she looked across at her husband. A man did not have the right to appear quite so, she told herself as she took in that tousled blond hair, the handsome face, and his tall, muscular frame. The one eye that met hers was the most brilliantly blue she'd ever seen, and the faint, expectant smile that played about his all-too-sensuous mouth was far too appealing. Even the patch did not detract from his handsomeness.

"I said I am not entirely indifferent to you."

"No, that is not what you said, Leah." His voice, although softer now, carried as much as if he shouted.

"Can I not just apologize for my mistake?" she asked, feeling helpless for the first time in her life.

"No."

"Well, I am not indifferent to you, Tony—is that what you wished to hear?"

"Above everything."

"And . . . and I thank you for the jewelry—'tis lovely."

"You are most welcome then, Lady Lyndon." Offering his arm to her, he gestured toward a café that faced the gardens. "And now that we are civil again, I am told that there is a passable *bouillabaisse,* and excellent *pot-au-feu,* and a highly recommended duck to be had here." The bright blue eye sparkled as he covered her hand where it rested on his arm. "And while we are enjoying our newfound candor, Lady Lyndon, I might as well tell you that I have not the least intention of being the last Barsett in my family."

24

Both unnverved and strangely exhilarated by Tony's earlier revelations, Leah undressed quickly, hurriedly pulled on a new nightrail, and let Jeanne brush out her hair. Wanting to be alone to sort out her very mixed thoughts, she dismissed Jeanne and crawled between the ironed sheets to relive the quarrel at the Palais Royal.

The settlements be damned! I did not take your papa's money . . . I borrowed seven thousand pounds at interest . . . I was not even near dun territory . . . He was not the gazetted fortune-hunter she'd thought him, and that changed the complexion of things greatly. But he *was* a rake. Even now she could remember the way the courtesans at the Palais Royal had looked at him—the open speculation, the admiration, and the regret when he'd ignored their lures. He was handsome, he was decidedly masculine, and he held a definite charm for females.

In truth, it was more than charm. The memory of his devastating kiss flooded her yet again, sending a flush of embarrassment all the way to her toes. She'd clung to him with abandon, letting him plunder her mouth and her senses, acting as reckless as the women they'd seen tonight. It was no wonder he'd dared to think that she was little better than a Cyprian when he'd met her—he knew what she had not even suspected, not until he'd kissed her the second time.

"Leah?" He stood in the doorway with that half-smile, that easy lift to one side of his mouth, and apologized: "Your pardon for not knocking louder, but I did not think you would wish me to raise Jeanne."

Her heart thudded all the way to the mattress and she could not help her sharp intake of breath as she stared at him. He'd discarded his coat and his shoes, and his shirt hung open where Blair had removed his studs. He seemed to fill the whole opening, blocking it as a means of escape. She moistened her lips with her tongue nervously and tried to keep her voice calm.

"What are you doing here?"

"I did not wish Blair to see my eye in its full glory, but it still burns like the very devil. If it would not trouble you excessively, I'd like you to look at it."

She looked down, conscious of the thinness of her nightdress, and colored with embarrassment. It was but an excuse—they both knew why he'd come. Resolutely she nodded and reached for her wrapper.

He closed the door softly and crossed the room. "I'd thought of a cold cloth perhaps."

Tying the wrapper, she turned around. He was but inches from her, so close that she could feel the warmth of his body. "Well, you will have to take off the patch at least. And if he got that for you, I cannot see why you would not let him look at the eye, my lord. You'll have to sit."

"Tony."

She could feel his breath when he spoke. Reaching up to untie the ribbon that held it, he let the scrap of black silk fall to expose an eye swollen nearly shut. She gasped at the sight of it.

"I know," he murmured wryly. "I have not had one of these since I engaged in fisticuffs with a stableboy when I was a child."

"Yes, well, I hope it was equally deserved."

"I hope you mean to offer more sympathy to the children." He leaned back and closed his good eye, not daring to watch her reaction.

Her hands shook with the tension between them as she poured water into the washbasin and wrung out a clean cloth. Coming back, she leaned over him. "You will have to lift the eyelid that I may rinse the eye," she decided. " 'Tis probably burned by the soap."

Using his thumb and forefinger, he complied, revealing an extremely bloodshot orb. "Watch it—even the light pains it." He blinked as she dribbled water that welled and then ran like tears down his cheek.

"Is that better?"
"No, but it makes me think I am doing something for it." He opened his good eye to stare into the swell of her breasts as she leaned over him, and his arm reached to circle her waist. He heard the sudden rush when she sucked in her breath, but she did not pull away. For several seconds he held her, leaning into her, and attempted to still the desire that raged within him. He did not want to give her a total disgust of him.
She stood motionless save for the tremor in her hands and looked down where his head rested against her chest. The flickering light from a brace of candles played off the thick blond waves. For a fleeting moment she wondered if he would think her like any other, like another conquest, and then her hands came up to caress his disordered hair.
Her breasts were full and soft where he pillowed his head, and they smelled of the small lilac sachet she'd worn between them earlier. He pulled her onto his lap, leaning back slightly to cradle her, giving him access to more of her body. As his fingers fumbled with the ties of her wrapper, she caught at his hand.
"Tony . . . I . . ."
"We talk too much," he whispered back just before his lips met hers, playing against them softly until they parted. And once again she was overwhelmed by the warmth and strength of him. His tongue teased, tempted, and gave strange new sensations that were far headier than any wine. When he raised his head to look at her at last, his eye glittered with desire, but his voice was oddly gentle. "I'd not do anything against your will, Leah."
It wasn't fair—he was making her confused heart choose something her body wanted and her mind denied. "I . . . I don't know what I want!" she blurted out.
"Poor Leah." His hand reached out and his fingertips stroked her arm lightly through the fabric of her wrapper and gown, traveling from her shoulder to her wrist, and sending a shiver coursing the opposite way. "I know what I want."
Passing her tongue over suddenly parched lips, she could only stare mutely through widened eyes into his

face. "A devil's bargain, Leah," he whispered. "You let me touch you, and I swear I'll not do anything you do not like." His hand closed over hers and his fingers massaged hers with a lightness that belied the look in his eye. While his expression tantalized her, the softness of his voice reassured her. He nuzzled her hair with his chin and his cheek as she hid her face in his shoulder.

Using his palm, he smoothed her hair over her back and then massaged the stiffness there. Oddly, even though she knew what he meant to do, she'd never felt quite so warm and secure. This time, when he worked the ties at her waist, she did not protest, and the silk wrapper fell away from her thin lawn nightrail. Shifting her weight in his arms, he tipped her back for his kiss, and as his tongue took possession of her mouth, his fingers undid the buttons at the neck of her gown.

Her eyes, which had been closed to savor the sensation of being so near him, flew open in shock as his warm hand discovered her breast, but wordlessly his lips reassured her, tracing soft kisses from the corner of her mouth to an earlobe, as though what he was doing to her was nothing bizarre. He returned to explore her mouth leisurely now, but the hand that closed over her breast massaged it, sending new sensations, new anticipations to her very soul. He was touching her where no one had dared, and she not only did not care, she wanted more.

This time, when his mouth left hers, it nuzzled and nibbled down to the sensitive hollow of her throat, trailing fire and giving shivers of delight at the same time. She arched her head back and moaned low in her throat. His head bent lower and his tongue found her breast, tasting, teasing, sending waves of desire through her.

"A devil's bargain"—the words took on meaning somewhere in the depths of what was left of her rational mind. She didn't care if he were the devil himself as long as he did not stop.

Abruptly he eased her off his lap, standing as he did so. She felt a momentarily loss, a deprivation, and then he was lifting her, carrying her to bed. Somehow her gown managed to slide off in a heap on the floor as he laid her down. He stood over her, his eyes devouring her hungrily, and then he followed her down, caressing her even as he undressed himself.

The fleeting thought that she might wish to stop him was obliterated by the feel of his hands on her bare skin, and after that, nothing mattered beyond her own intense need. Wealth, title, reputation—all the things that had stood between them melted away in the fire of their union.

Later, he lay beside her, stroking her damp hair back from her face, watching her catch her breath, seeing the glow of the candles casting their light on her moist skin. Her hair spilled across the pillow in waves of honey-colored satin. She still swallowed to master her tumultuous emotions, and her lashes lay like smudges against her cheeks. When she dared open her eyes to look at him, they were like ringed smoke, still smoldering from the fire that had been between them.

"Sorry?" he asked soberly, his heart pausing for her answer.

"No," she answered solemnly. And then a slow smile spread across her face and sparkled in her strange eyes. "But I know why 'twas called a 'devil's bargain,' my lord. Anything that feels that good must be exceedingly wicked."

25

It was a full month later that they returned to London. After receiving word that Jeptha Cole's health was steadily improving, Tony extended their trip to include Italy, where they explored the seaside city of Venice, visiting the Doge's Palace and floating down the canals in gondolas. Jeanne complained of the dampness and Blair grumbled abut the lack of plain English fare at the tables, but Leah was oblivious of it all as she basked in the glory of a newfound love. As for the jaded Viscount Lyndon, the accomplished flirt and consummate rake, his wedding trip was the best time of his life.

On their arrival in Dover, Tony had had to hire a third coach in addition to the two that had originally brought him and Leah and Blair and Jeanne there when they'd started. And thus they rolled into Lyndon House with one full carriage of boxes filled with *objets d'art*, French and Venetian fashions, collectors' books, furniture, and gifts for everyone from the dowager and Jeptha Cole to the lowliest tweeny.

As Blair unpacked his master's clothing and sorted it for cleaning, Tony met Leah in the hallway. "If you do not change your mind and take my mother's chambers, I fear this carpet will never last," he teased her wickedly.

"A little walk is good for the body, my lord—and 'tis said to invigorate the mind also," she retorted with a grin. "Besides, I should quite dislike giving up my view of the garden."

"Minx!" His eyes measured the distance from his room to hers, and he shook his head. "I calculate that you mean to make me walk the equivalent of an extra five and one-half miles per year then."

"Five and one-half miles? That has to be a mistake, Tony."

"No. 'Tis about forty feet from here to there, after all, twice a night for three hundred and sixty-five days—"

"Twice a night?"

"When I retire and when I arise—'tis twice, isn't it? Unless, of course, you mean to make the trip half the time—then 'tis but two and three-quarters. Either way, consider the poor rug—it has been in my family since I was in short coats."

"Well, maybe when winter comes and the garden turns . . ." She let her voice trail off, dangling the possibility.

"Jade!"

"You are dressed to go out," she noted suddenly.

"The house is at sixes and sevens with the unpacking, and I cannot abide disorder. Besides, I had thought to go round to my clubs to stifle the rumor that I must surely be dead, my dear."

"Oh."

"And I had thought that perhaps you would wish to take the carriage when 'tis unpacked and pay a call on your father."

"Tony, I do not know anyone here but Jeanne and Blair. I mean, these are your servants, and—"

"You have met them. Just tell Mrs. Fitch what you need and she'll see you have it. And if it requires the ordering of something beyond what is here, I am sure that Max will tend to the matter on the instant." Reaching out to lift her chin with his knuckle, he smiled at her. "What you have, my dear, is a severe case of dependence. The sooner you take to the ordering of the servants yourself, the sooner you will make yourself mistress of this house in fact as well as name."

"But we have just gotten home!"

"Would you like me to join you at your father's for supper?"

"Actually, I would eat here—'tis my first night in this house, Tony."

"All right. I'll be home in time to dine then." He dropped his hand and stepped back. "There are stacks of cards in the tray from those who have been to see us whilst we have been gone. Perhaps you would wish to select some, that you may begin paying morning calls."

"I do not know any of them."

"The sooner you are out and about, the sooner the *ton* will welcome Viscountess Lyndon. Take Aunt Hester with you," he advised.

"But I scarce know her either!"

"She would be happy to go, Leah—all you need do is ask her." Leaning to brush her lips lightly, he whispered, "Believe me, there are no delights at a club that can compare with yours, my love."

After he left, she wandered through the house looking for something useful to do and discovered absolutely nothing. It was not like she was in her father's house, where she'd had the ordering of everything for years. Lyndon's housekeeper, the indomitable Mrs. Fitch, assured her kindly, "Don't worry your head about anything, my lady, for we know how to go on here," and suggested, "you must be overtired from traveling and will be wanting a nap."

Leah stopped in Lyndon's library to admire the large collection of books accumulated by the Barsett family over several hundred years. Many were in canvas slipcovers to protect them, while others were locked in glass-fronted cabinets. Idly she wondered if Tony had read many of them. Moving to his desk, she discovered both the letter tray and the card tray from the hall table. He'd been right: there were a number of cards left during their extended absence, and some of the best-known names amongst the *ton* were there—Sally Jersey, Princess Esterhazy, Mrs. Bagshot, the Cresswell sisters, Lady Renfield, Lady Benbrough—and there were conspicuous gaps also. Certainly there were those who meant to ignore her. Just as she was about to put the cards back in the tray, her eye was caught by a folded paper most notable for the rather heavy scent emanating from it. Curious, she opened it and her heart sank. In a decidedly feminine hand, the writer thanked Tony for the gift of a ruby pendant, stating, "It becomes my dark hair and has afforded me many compliments." Her stomach knotting, it finished with, "When you are returned and your little Cit no longer amuses you, I am here.'' It was signed with a graceful, looping E.

Carefully refolding the perfumed note, Leah was certain now that Tony had lied to her, for the date on the missive was a mere two weeks before. Then, to be judicious, she tried to think when he could have sent the necklace to Elaine Chandler. Certainly not while they were gone, not when she'd been with him almost every minute. Perhaps he'd sent it before they left. Pocketing the note, she was determined to ask him. And she sincerely hoped he had an answer.

In a small but elegant house many blocks away, the Earl of Rotherfield greeted Elaine Chandler with three words. ''They are back,'' he told her before she'd had time to refuse him entry into her house.

''Who?'' She feigned ignorance, knowing full well whom he meant. Stepping aside with ill grace, she followed him into the small drawing room. ''Oh, very well, Marcus—so Lyndon and his ill-bred bride are back! What is that to me now, pray? What can that possibly mean to me—or to you?''

''There is the matter of one thousand pounds,'' he reminded her with deceptive softness. ''I understand that the tradesmen grow impatient.''

''Tradesmen are always impatient,'' she snapped.

''I thought you still wanted Lyndon back.''

''It would be foolish for me to care what happens to anyone, Marcus.''

He gave an uncharacteristic crow of triumph. ''My instincts, as always, are impeccable, my dear.'' He leaned against the mantel and flicked open his snuffbox, taking a pinch. And when he finished sneezing into his delicate lace-edged linen handkerchief, he announced baldly, ''I am here to help you.''

''Really? As you did the last time? As I recall it, you dallied with the Cit whilst I was humiliated. No, Marcus—I want no more of your schemes.''

''You prefer I remove him by, er . . . more convenient means?''

''For God's sake, my lord, they are wed! What do you expect me to do about that?'' she demanded, pacing the open area restlessly. ''She is as lost to you as he is to me!''

''Not quite.''

''What do you want with her, anyway?'' she cried out, not wanting to admit the thought that came to mind. ''Kill him and she will not thank you for it.''

He appeared not to attend her, turning his attention instead to a lovely crystal bowl that graced a table beside the fireplace. ''Another trifle from Carrington?'' he hazarded. ''My dear, the old roué is become far too particular in his attentions. You'll not get Lyndon back with him.''

''I don't want Tony back!''

''Tell that to Carrington, my dear—it will not fadge with Rotherfield.''

''I despise you!'' she spat at him.

''And I am not overfond of you either, Elaine—'tis what makes us such excellent allies, after all. None would suspect us.''

''And just how do you think I am to insinuate myself back into his life even? He gave me short shrift the last time I attempted the task.'' She managed a brittle, bitter little laugh.

''Write to him, pester him—I leave that to you.'' He reached into his coat and drew out a sheaf of banknotes. ''There is one thousand pounds here, Elaine. I suggest you pay your bills with it. And I will expect you to seek out Lyndon as soon as possible.''

''How?''

''I do not care if you have to play Caro Lamb to Anthony Barsett's Byron, my dear—you will do it.'' Executing the briefest of bows, he favored her with that strange, enigmatic look of his. ''Until next we are met, Elaine.''

She watched from behind the lace curtain at her window until his smart black coach and four pulled into the street and disappeared. Turning back to the money he'd left on the table, she picked it up and shrugged. It was one thousand pounds, after all.

Having encountered Tony an hour earlier at White's, the earl gambled on finding Leah at home. And despite the decidedly stiff reception from Lyndon's butler, he was not destined for disappointment. Informed by that disapproving fellow that he would ascertain if Lady Lyndon were receiving, Marcus Halvert scarce had time to take his seat before he had to rise to greet her. His critical eye went first to her waist and then to her face. She was even lovelier than he remembered her as she extended both her hands in greeting.

"Lord Rotherfield—'tis a pleasure to see you," she murmured, trying not to be embarrassed as he drew first one hand and then the other to his lips in a gallant gesture. "Er . . . pray be seated, my lord. We are not yet settled, and Lyndon is at one of his clubs, but—"

"I did not come to see Lyndon, my dear. After your rather precipitate marriage, I feared for your happiness, you know, and am come to see how you fare."

" 'Twould be improper of me to state it even if I were miserable," she reminded him.

"Are you miserable?"

"No."

"My dear Leah, it is of the utmost importance to me, I assure you. I have not forgotten your reluctance to wed Tony Barsett, and I quite understood the reasons."

" 'Tis best to forget that, sir, for I am wed to him, and am reconciled to him now."

He leaned across to where she'd taken a seat and possessed himself of one of her hands. "Tell me you are content, and I shall forget the matter."

"I am as content as may be, my lord."

"I would still stand your friend, Leah." His black eyes penetrated hers while his hand still lay in her lap. "Your friendship means much to me."

His words touched her—he'd asked for no favors and had made no improper advances—he merely offered that which gentlemen seldom offered to females. And despite what Tony had said of his awful reputation, she was flattered. "I thank you, sir," she answered sincerely. "I quite count you a friend also."

"You may have need of one now that Tony is back in London. My word of advice, should you ever need it, is to turn the other way when you suspect his, er . . . indiscretions, my dear, for there will be none to last. If naught else can be said of Lyndon, his eye never remains on the same bit of fluff long."

She stiffened and drew away her hand, and for a moment she thought to give him a sharp set-down for his presumption. But there was no guile in his eyes. "I do not expect the problem, my lord, but I shall try to remember the advice. Would you care to stay to partake of tea?" she added to turn aside the subject.

"Alas, no. I am promised to my man of affairs at four." Rising, he bowed over her hand again. "I did but wish to assure you that you may always turn to me as a friend."

It was a strange visit, one that she could not truly fathom, but she was grateful for the sentiment. Sighing, she reached to pick up the third volume of *Glenarvon*. She was going to have to purchase it before she lost her subscription to Hookham's over it, she supposed. Not that she held much hope for Calantha—Caro Lamb's heroine was so enamored of the dastardly Glenarvon that it made no sense. And if the Lamb woman truly modeled her heroine on herself, then Sir William ought to have clapped her up in an asylum. Resolutely she opened the book and sought her place, using Elaine Chandler's letter for a bookmark.

When Tony returned home to dress for dinner, his servants, beginning with Horton, the butler, and ending with Blair, all took it upon themselves to tell him of Rotherfield's call.

"Not that I am wishful of causing her ladyship any mischief, mind you," Blair sniffed, "but a man of his stamp should not be calling on any lady, and certainly not on Lady Lyndon."

Being in wholehearted agreement with the lot of them, Tony sought his wife in her bedchamber, where she prepared for supper. Jeanne pinned up the thick hair into a twisted knot on Leah's crown, chattering all the while about the Lyndon servants, warning her about this one, poking gentle fun at that one. And of them all, it appeared that only Blair received her approval.

"Leave us, Jeanne."

"But Madame's dress—"

"I'll hook it for her," he offered, gesturing politely toward the door.

From where she sat before the mirror, Leah could tell by his reflection that something was amiss. "Is aught—?" She did not get to ask, because as he shut the door, he exploded.

"I won't have it, Leah—not in my house! Do you hear me?"

Stung and nonplussed, she rose quickly to face him. "Of course I hear you, and so does everyone else, Tony. You will not have what?"

"Rotherfield!"

"What about him?"

"I won't have him in my house!"

"Lower your voice when you speak to me," she retorted coldly. "I know not where you had the story, but I assure you that nothing improper—"

"His being here is improper! I absolutely forbid the association—I forbid it!"

Her own temper rising now, she snapped back, "I have assured Lord Rotherfield he is welcome in my house, Anthony Barsett! You cannot leave me alone in this place and tell me whom I can or cannot receive!"

"This place? What the devil are you speaking of?" he demanded incredulously. " 'This place' is your home!"

"Then as mistress of my home, I extend my welcome to anyone I choose."

"Leah, the man's a rake and a scoundrel—and he's not received by anyone," he attempted to explain in a more rational voice.

"Really? I met him at your aunt Davenham's, as you recall, and if you tell me she is not up to every rig and tow in town, I will laugh in your face."

"That is different, and well you know it. Aunt Hester has the credit to do as she pleases, while you—"

"While I am but a Cit, I suppose."

"No, but you are not yet established, Leah."

"If I were approved to waltz at Almack's, you'd not approve my receiving Rotherfield—admit it!"

"If you received Rotherfield, you'd not be invited to

Almack's in the first place! As a newly wed lady, you must be circumspect."

"As circumspect as you, my lord?" she spat at him. Picking up the perfumed note she'd filched, she threw it at him. "How dare you talk to me of circumspection, when you are still buying jewels for that . . . that *fancy piece!*"

"An extremely vulgar expression for a lady," he chided, leaning down to pick up the paper. "And I have not the least notion whom you mean."

"I should not doubt it—their numbers are probably legion!"

He read the letter quickly and a smile of relief crossed his face. "This is what overset you? My dear—"

"And I am not your dear—not until you explain that!"

" 'Twas my parting gift to an old friend."

"Old friend!" she snorted. "I daresay you are friendlier with her than I ever mean to be with the Earl of Rotherfield! And before you think me the complete fool, look at the date—'twas but two weeks ago!"

"I had Max take care of the matter while we were gone."

"You what?"

"Leah . . . Leah." He came up behind her and attempted to put his arms around her, but she broke away. "Your jealousy is flattering but unwarranted, I promise you. I did not even wish to see Elaine after the way she chose to embarrass you. I had Max select a trifling trinket and send it while we were gone. 'Tis the last you will ever hear of her."

"When you are returned, and your little Cit no longer amuses you, I am here,' " she mimicked. "I am not the fool you think me!"

This time he managed to slide his arms beneath hers and lock them in front of her. As she struggled to escape, he nuzzled her hair. "As I expect my little Cit to amuse me for the rest of my life, I think she will have to find someone else." When she tried to duck away, he dropped light kisses on her neck, and still imprisoning her with one arm, began to caress a breast with his hand. "You know you are devilish desirable when you are overset," he whispered, his own anger dissipated by the nearness of her.

"Stop it!" she muttered angrily, slapping his hand away. "I warn you, Tony, if I so much as hear of your seeing Elaine Chandler again, you will find that Lord Rotherfield runs tame in this house—at my invitation!" She could feel him rub against her back, sending shivers down her spine. And the hand she'd slapped away slid beneath the soft cotton of her underchemise, prompting a sudden sharp intake of breath. "Stop it—I have to dress for dinner. Tony!" she squealed as his lips began tracing soft kisses from her earlobe to her neck.

"There's not a fancy piece alive as could compare with you, Lady Lyndon," he whispered as he felt her resistance dissolve.

26

The subject of Rotherfield did not stay buried for long. As Anthony Barsett became more absorbed with his business ventures, the earl began paying increasing attention to his bride in his absence. And Tony, certain that he'd stamped out the problem by ordering Leah not to receive Rotherfield, was shocked and infuriated to learn otherwise, particularly when he heard of it from his friends one afternoon at White's.

"Can't think why you allow a fellow of his stamp around Lady L.," Gil murmured offhandedly over a pleasand hand of whist.

"Gil," Hugh warned, casting a sidelong look at Lyndon, "he don't like anyone meddlin' in his business."

"What fellow? What the deuce are you speaking of?" Tony demanded suspiciously.

"Well, I would not wish my wife racketing about with him if I had one," Gil retorted peevishly to Hugh. "Ain't at all the thing, you know."

"Gil—"

"Racketing about with whom?" Tony demanded ominously. "Leah is not racketing about with anyone that I know of."

"Daresay you ain't home much then."

"Been to Tattersall's to get a mare for Lady Lyndon?" Hugh asked quickly. "Ought to have one, you know."

"I have not had time for Tattersall's," Tony snapped. "I have spent every day with my father-in-law at Garraway's with the commodities brokers until I scarce know whether 'tis Spanish tobacco or sugar I have bought for speculation. I am beginning to bid in my sleep." His blue eyes turned suspiciously on Gil Renfield. "And I am in no temper to guess whatever 'tis you would tell me on this, my first day amongst company for well over a week. Now, out with it!"

"It ain't nothing, really—just don't think Rotherfield fit to be seen with her, that's all."

"I have made it plain that he is not to be received."

Gil coughed apologetically and squirmed uncomfortably in his chair. "Maybe they just chanced to meet," he offered.

"Oh, if you must play the tattlemonger, play it right!" Hugh interrupted in disgust. "What Gil is attempting to say is that Lady Lyndon was in Hyde Park with Rotherfield yesterday. Daresay she had reason to be, after all." Casting a reproachful look at Renfield, he defended Leah. "Ten to one, it ain't nothing—she don't know how it is with him, you know. Not up to snuff yet as to what ain't done."

"Taking little thing," Gil mumbled, aware now of the wrath in Tony's eyes. "Not a dissembling bone in her body—ain't one of them simperin' females neither. Well, dash it—I like her! Don't want to see her run aground before her sail's set, after all."

"Then you should have told her—not him," Hugh retorted.

"Ain't up to me. She ain't my wife." Turning back to Tony, he was dismayed to discover that the viscount was already in the process of collecting his hat and stick. "I say, Tony, but it ain't—"

"Sometimes, Gil, you are a positive slowtop. Now look what you have done! Your interference will start a row between them, and Tony can be deuced unpleasant when he is on his high ropes."

"No, I ain't—he ought to know! Rotherfield's dangerous and she ain't up to his weight at all, Hugh! Tell you the fellow's a devil bent on seduction, if you want my opinion of 'im—and if Sally Jersey gets wind of it, Lyndon's lady ain't ever going to grace the Assembly Rooms at Almack's."

Tony seethed all the way home, his anger mounting as he considered and discarded a dozen or so scathing comments on Leah's inexcusable behavior. He'd *told* her, *ordered* her to avoid the man—had *forbidden* the association even, and she'd not only received the earl at Lyndon House, she'd actually dared to be seen with him. The iniquity, the utter perfidy of her deliberate disobedience defied all reason and was not to be borne. His sense of ill-usage increased with each block as he thought of the hours, the days he'd spent elbow to elbow with corn merchants and speculators, hazarding more than he could afford in an effort to give her what she was used to having. And all the while, she'd been seeing the Earl of Rotherfield behind his back.

His timing could not have been worse. As his curricle rounded the corner, Marcus Halvert's pulled away from the curb. Throwing his reins to his groom, Tony jumped down and stalked for the house with his whip still in his hand. His temper rising dangerously with each step, he flung open the front door and found her still stripping off her gloves in the foyer.

"Where the devil do you think you have been, Leah?" he raged at her. "Answer me! If you think I mean to be cuckolded by the likes of Rotherfield, you are very mistaken! Answer me—where did you go?" Wrenching her arm, he thrust her before him into his library. "Well?"

Shocked by the utter fury in his eyes, she tried to pull away. "I will answer when you speak civilly," she retorted, rubbing where he held her arm.

"Civilly?" he fairly howled. "How dare you, Leah? How *dare* you? I told you I would not have him in this house! And yet as soon as my back is turned, you not only entertain him here, but you also accompany him publicly! I won't have it, I tell you!" Releasing her, he flung her toward a leather-covered settee. "Why? Are you so lost to propriety that my wishes mean nothing to you?"

"Tony!"

"Do not cry 'Tony' to me! 'Tis all over London that you have been seen with him! I warned you, Leah—I warned you!" He advanced to stand over her, and for one moment she thought he meant to strike her with the whip. Her eyes widened in horror at the unrestrained anger she saw. "Answer me! Do I have to shake out of you where you have been?"

"No," she answered coldly with a calmness she did not feel. "And you have no right to come here and accuse me of baseness." Righting herself to stand in front of him, she met his eyes squarely and jutted her chin defiantly. "You have not even given me the opportunity to defend myself."

"Your want of conduct is the *on-dit* of London!" he shouted. "Are you such a peagoose that you do not know what you have done? 'Twill be said—"

"That the Cit seeks her level?" she cut in, her own anger fueled by the injustice of his attack. "That the Cit does not know how to go on? Do you think I care what that den of witches you call the *ton* thinks of me? I have not won their approval—and I do not care whether they like me or not! I never aspired to be the *lady* you and Papa would have me be!" Brushing past him wrathfully, she flung over her shoulder, "I like Lord Rotherfield—he does not try to make me what I am not!"

"Just one minute, *Lady Lyndon*!" The sarcasm fairly dripping from the address, he caught her from behind and spun her around to face him. "What he makes of you is not a very pretty word, my dear!"

"He is my friend!"

"I am your husband, and I forbid the association!"

"Well, you cannot! If I choose to enjoy his company, 'tis none of your affair! Other ladies of the *ton* engage in far more nefarious associations—and no one accuses then of the least impropriety!"

"None of them encourages Rotherfield to dangle after 'em! You cannot afford the gossip!"

"No? Because of what I am?" she demanded dangerously. "Or because of what people say of him?"

"Yes!"

"Well, I do not agree with either reason, my lord. Lord Rotherfield has been naught but kind and pleasant to me. You have been gone every day for a week, and do I ask you to account for where and with whom? No, I do not!" she answered emphatically. "And if I wish to see the flowers in Hyde Park or watch the balloon ascension from St. George's Field, why should I not go? 'Tis far more entertaining than sitting at home waiting for condescending ladies to call."

"Nonetheless, you will not see him again. I will inform him that he is unwelcome here and that you will not be taken up to go anywhere with him again," he answered stiffly.

"You will not! You have your friends and I have mine! It was agreed from the outset that—"

"That was before . . ."

"Before what? Before you wheedled your way into my bed? You have not the right to—"

"I have every right, madam wife! And if you insist on making a laughingstock of me, I will send you to the country until you are able to learn town manners," he threatened.

"I won't go—and I will not cut Marcus Halvert! Do you hear me?"

"Aye, I hear you! 'Twas a *mésalliance* on my part—I should have known that you would not comport yourself like a lady!"

Her face went white as his words cut into her like a sword. "You knew what I was when you married me," she managed as her throat constricted painfully.

"Leah . . ." He too was stunned by what he'd said to her.

"No." Gathering her dignity about her, she walked from the room.

"Leah! I did not—"

"Pray spare me the apology, my lord."

"Leah, will you listen to me, you little fool! I love you!"

"Tell that to Mrs. Chandler, Tony. My door will be locked tonight, and tomorrow night, and every other night of this miserable *mésalliance!* She, on the other hand, will welcome your attentions."

He stood rooted for a moment as his brain tried to account for what he'd done, and then he ran after her, catching her on the stairs. Just as he reached to touch her shoulder, she turned on him and blazed, "You will have your doxy—and I will have the earl!"

"Play me false and I'll kill him!"

"You could not." Supporting herself with the banister, she began to climb again. "Give my regards to Mrs. Chandler, my lord. I will be certain to convey yours to Rotherfield."

"Very well!" he shouted after her. "But do not come crying to me when you are cut everywhere!"

Flinging himself down the several steps, he grabbed his

hat and jammed it on his head. She looked down from the railing above him, calling out, "Where are you going?"

"To see Elaine!" he yelled.

"Good!"

Slamming the door after him, he called to his astounded groom to put his curricle to. His jaws still working to control the rage he felt, he made up his mind to call on the Chandler woman just to prove he could do it.

Still shaking, Leah watched the carriage house behind the garden from her bedchamber window and saw him leave. Her own fury gone in the face of her loss, she threw herself on her bed and indulged in an impotent bout of tears. Self-pity and a sense of ill-usage overwhelmed her. In the heat of his anger, he'd told her what he really thought of her—she was but a low-class convenience and that was all she could ever be to him.

No one, not even Jeanne, ventured upstairs to her as the servants shook their heads and whispered in small groups, some siding with her and others with his lordship in the matter. Even Mrs. Fitch, who'd considered that Lyndon had married beneath him, thought that perhaps he'd been too harsh with her, while Blair insisted that if a man could not tell his wife how to go on, he was naught but a man-milliner. For was not the husband head of the wife? he demanded of all who would listen. "Fiddle," Jeanne fired back at him. "Only a pig-person would be so gothic, Monsieur Blair." And in a trice, the argument shifted to them.

"Ahem," Horton interrupted with the superiority of one who is uninvolved in the altercation. "Will someone please inform her ladyship that lords Renfield and Rivington are paying a call?"

"Tell them that Lyndon is out," Jeanne snapped, forgetting her awe of the butler.

"I did, but 'tis Lady Leah they would see."

"The poor thing is in no state to receive anyone," Mrs. Fitch reproached him.

"Mais non," Jeanne decided instantly. " 'Twill divert her."

Still lying across the bed, Leah twisted the tear-soaked sheet with her hand. At first she ignored Jeanne's knock, but the little maid called through the door, "There are

Rivington and Renfield to see you, madame. Shall I tell them you are not receiving?''

Tony's friends Gil and Hugh. Leah opened her mouth to tell her to send them away, and then thought better of it. Why should Tony be out amusing himself while she wept bitter tears? Resolutely she slid off the bed and walked to open the door. ''Tell them I will be down directly,'' she ordered, wondering how she could ever repair the damage to her face.

''We will apply cold cloths to your face, madame,'' Jeanne reassured her. ''He must not know you have cried out your eyes, *n'est-ce pas?* Horton will tell him that gentlemen came to call, and he will not know he has hurt you.''

''I do not care what Lyndon thinks,'' Leah maintained stoutly. ''Not a fig.''

''No, and if he goes to see this pig-woman, you will show him that you can serve him the same soup with a different spoon—*non*?'' Jeanne observed with Gallic practicality.

By the time Leah emerged some twenty minutes later, there was little to betray the agitation of her mind. If she appeared in high color and her eyes were perhaps brighter than usual, she nonetheless forced a convincing smile as she extended a hand to each man. ''Gentlemen, so kind of you to call. Alas, Lyndon is away at the present, but perhaps you may find him at one of his clubs later.''

Gil thought he detected a certain tightness about her mouth, as though she controlled herself with an effort, and he felt instantly contrite. ''No, no . . . came to see you, actually, Lady Lyndon. We was in the block and thought you might wish to take a turn in the park—yes, that's it—a turn in the park. Do you good to breathe the air, you know.''

''Gil—''

''Dash it, Hugh! Don't need you t' tell me what to say—been talkin' afore you was born!''

''But not well, old fellow. What Gil means, Lady Leah, is that since 'tis considered unfashionable to sit in your husband's pocket, perhaps you might wish to drive out with us. Got new cattle for my vehicle, you know, and thought to show 'em to you.''

"How very good of both of you. Shall I need my shawl, do you think?"

"Warm out," Gil reassured her.

"You will charm every fellow who sees you," Hugh offered gallantly.

"Spanish coin," Leah teased with a lightness she did not feel. "But I nonetheless thank you for it."

Outside, the sun was shining and the temperature quite pleasant. Hugh's carriage, with its leather hood folded back, afforded an excellent view as they wended their way through the London streets toward Hyde Park. Leah, unconscious of the fetching picture she presented in her sage-green dress and her new high-crowned Parisian hat with feathers that curved along the upturned brim, sat across from the two men. Other vehicles drew up as they came abreast and greetings were exchanged by the curious.

A lone horseman approached on Gil's side and raised his hand in salute. Before Hugh could urge his driver on, Leah leaned to the side of her seat to hail the Earl of Rotherfield. "Marcus!" she called out brightly.

"Lady Lyndon," he acknowledged with a grave inclination of his black head. "Had I known you favored a drive, I should have offered to take you myself."

"Oh, hallo, Marcus," Gil muttered. "Got to move—traffic, you know."

As there were not above five vehicles in the park so early, Rotherfield raised a skeptical eyebrow and a faint smile played at his mouth. "Shocking squeeze," he agreed imperturbably. "Your servant, Renfield—a pleasure speaking with you, Rivington," he added.

Gil waited until they were out of hearing before turning his attention across to Leah. "Been meaning to speak to you of him, Lady Lyndon. Shocking bad *ton* to acknowledge him, my dear—ain't at all the sort of man a female ought to admit to knowing."

"Why?" she asked bluntly. "I find him quite charming."

Hugh choked and them reddened when she fixed him with those strange eyes of hers. "It is not the sort of thing one can tell a lady," he evaded. "Sordid story."

"Gil?"

"Can't say—let it suffice that any female'd be queer in the attic to encourage him."

"Lord Renfield, I assure you that I do not suffer from an excess of sensibility, nor am I easily disgusted. If Lord Rotherfield's crime is so unspeakable, then why is he not clapped up in jail? Or swinging from the Nubbin' Cheat?" she demanded. "He has never been anything but a gentleman to me."

"Well, he ain't," Gil answered dampeningly.

"I find nothing to dislike in his person or his character," she persisted, still trying to discover what had put Rotherfield so far beyond the pale.

"His character?" they chorused almost in unison. "He has none!"

"Well—"

"Ah . . . have you seen Eliza Vestris in *The Beggar's Opera* yet?" Hugh asked hastily. "I have heard 'tis quite her best role."

"What? Oh, I daresay it is." Following Hugh's lead, Gil leaned across to address Leah directly. "Have you heard Vestris? Got a prime voice, I can tell you."

"I have never been to the opera, my lord."

"You ain't? Well, now's the time to go, ain't it, Hugh? Promised to each other anyways, so it don't matter if we add another head to the party."

"Oh, no, I—"

"Bring Tony also," Hugh suggested.

"Ah, I believe Tony is out for the evening, sirs." The reminder of how her husband had left his house lowered her spirits again, and then she forced herself to brighten. "But that is not to say I shall not be delighted."

"Done."

On the way back to Lyndon House, she decided that she had too much pride to let Tony know how badly he'd hurt her. She was going to the opera, holding her head high in the company of two of London's eligible bachelors, and the *ton* could stare at her if they wished.

27

Settled into her well-situated box with a full half-hour to spare before curtain time, the dowager duchess gestured imperiously for her glass, ready to begin quite the most diverting portion of the evening. Squinting hideously to focus on those around them, she began duly noting who was with whom for the edification of Mrs. Buckhaven.

"Ah, I knew it," she announced smugly, "the crimcons have the right of it—there is Millbrook with Mrs. Pennington. Tsk," she clucked disapprovingly. "And Lady Millbrook is but lately risen from childbed." Slowly turning her glass around the crowd, she shook her head. "And there is Jeremy Fyfield with that dancer but lately come from Spain—it did not take her long to discover a patron, did it? Oh, look—'tis Lady Cresswaite with Mr. Ratcliffe—never say he is to be her latest lover. If she does not watch it, her brood will be called the Cresswaite miscellany. And there is Sally Jersey . . . mmmm . . . ought never to wear precisely that shade of puce, do you think?"

"Oh, dear ma'am—her companion leaned forward to compensate for her nearsightedness—"is that not Lord Blakemore . . . or could it be Mr. Thurston? The one in the green coat."

"Where? Oh, good God, 'tis Tony!" The duchess let her glass fall, to dangle from its ribbon, as she gasped in shock. "Bucky, my salts!"

"In the green coat?" Mrs. Buckhaven asked doubtfully. "You must be mistaken, ma'am, for Lyndon would not wear green. I—"

"That wretched boy! Whatever can he be thinking?

The salts, Bucky!'' Hester Havinghurst leaned back in her seat as though she thought to faint.

''Now, now, dear ma'am—it cannot be as bad as all that,'' she murmured soothingly as she discovered the salts container and twisted open the lid. ''Here . . .'' Waving it under her elderly employer's nose with one hand, she attempted to gain possession of the glass with the other, but already the dowager was lifting it again. ''And that awful woman, Bucky!''

''Lady Lyndon? But I thought you—''

''Not Leah, paperskull! That Chandler creature!''

''Well!'' Mrs. Buckhaven sank back, offended.

''Well, I daresay you are not a paperskull, Bucky,'' the dowager offered in apology, ''but I own I am overset. What *can* he be thinking? To appear publicly in her company so soon after he is returned from his wedding trip—oh, whatever will Mr. Cole think?''

''Poor Lady Lyndon—I pray she does not get wind of it,'' Bucky offered more to the point. ''But perhaps you are mistaken.''

''I know my great-nephew when I see him—it is he!'' Hester declared stoutly. Her glass dropped again, to dangle from the ribbon.

Moving more quickly this time to retrieve it, Mrs. Buckhaven managed to gain possession and looked for herself. ''Oh, dear—it *is* Lyndon!''

''I *told* you it was! Well, I shall simply have to take a hand in the matter, Bucky. Leah will not know how to go on if this becomes common knowledge, and there will be no scotching the *on-dit* now, I am sure. Mr. Cole will be mad as fire and will cut him off without a penny—the paperskull!''

''I say—''

''Not you this time! Tony!''

''Oh.'' Taking advantage of having the glass, the companion scanned the crowd for herself, sweeping the boxes curiously to see who was attending to Lord Lyndon's behavior. ''Oh, my,'' she breathed faintly. ''Oh, dear.''

''I wish you would pay attention, Bucky,'' the dowager complained with feeling. ''There is Lyndon whistling a fortune down the wind, and—''

"But 'tis Lady Lyndon!"

"*Leah?* Here? Bucky, give over my glass! Where is she? Perhaps you could go over and gain her attention, say I am ill . . . anything—"

"She has seen him."

"Oh, merciful heavens! Whatever . . . ?"

"She acknowledged him, ma'am—nodded to him as politely as you please, she did. Lud! How he could prefer anyone to her is beyond understanding."

"Give me my glass!"

Reluctantly her companion relinquished it, but not until she took one last look. "Between the two of them, I'd say 'tis Lady Lyndon who is the Incomparable, ma'am."

As Hester again scanned the audience, her worst fears were confirmed. Leah, utterly stunning in a sea-green gauze and exquisite emeralds, sat serenely between lords Renfield and Rivington whilst everyone watched her, some even having the effrontery to point and comment openly.

When she'd seen her husband and the Chandler woman, Leah's heart had plummeted and remained like a heavy knot in her stomach, but she'd not give him the satisfaction of a scene. She was no ill-bred harpy quick to dispute possession of a man. Despite her inner turmoil, she turned to her companions with resolve and ignored the looks of those around her. In sympathy, Gil's hand crept to pat hers as he hissed in a low underbreath, "Sorry for this—wouldn't have had it happen for the world."

Hugh, confirmed bachelor that he was, felt for her also. Lifting his program to shield their faces, he whispered bracingly, "Put her on the run—you are ten times better-looking and at least five years younger. Just smile as though you don't care a fig for it."

Elaine stared across the intervening space, ready to gloat over her triumph, but the sight of her rival turned the taste of victory to ashes in her mouth. The Leah Barsett who'd returned from Paris bore little resemblance to the Leah Cole she'd seen earlier. Her tawny hair was knotted almost severely atop her head, pulled back without so much as a loose strand to frame her face, allowing the perfection of that face to stand alone, starkly setting off a profile as fine as any sculpture. The girl's dress was in the latest Parisian style—cut wide, off the shoulders almost, to expose an expanse of creamy skin above a broad ruffle that obscured her breasts and formed short sleeves. And the necklace, which could only be guessed at from the distance, glittered a deep green at her white throat. For the first time in her memory, Elaine Chandler felt dowdy.

Feeling he had created a social disaster, Gil carried on manfully, setting about to give everyone the impression that he was enthralled with the lovely Lady Lyndon. And Hugh, who had never been in the petticoat line himself, betook it upon himself to appear equally enchanted, hanging on every word uttered by her. And all three of them fervently hoped the curtain would go up quickly.

As for Tony, any perverse enjoyment he'd had in asserting his independence from his equally independent wife was dispelled when he saw her. He'd not really wanted to see Elaine at all, had regretted his hasty decision to accompany her to the opera well before they'd even reached King's Theater, and now it seemed that his world was truly crumbling around him. There was nothing he could think of that would make things right with the wife he truly loved. Jealousy, he was fast discovering, was a dangerous and destructive thing.

Mercifully, the music began in earnest and the lights dimmed as the curtain rose. Eliza Vestris, whom critics insisted "sang like an angel," was in exceptional voice, but none of the principals in the dramatic farce unfolding in the audience noted it. To a person, they dreaded the intermission with its gossipy interbox visitations. Almost before the last note had been sung and the lights came up again, Gil excused himself to have a few choice words with Tony Barsett. Hugh, still nonplussed by the social implications of it all, gallantly offered to procure a glass of lemonade for Leah, leaving her quite briefly in the company of Renfield's footmen after her repeated assurances that she was in far greater need of refreshment than conversation. And Tony manfully determined to see his wife, missing Gil on the way.

Rotherfield himself had observed most of the unfolding

drama from the recesses of his own box, and considered the whole affair could not have been better if he had been allowed to plan it. As Gil and Hugh left, he thought to seek out Leah, only to find Tony there first. Biding his time to console the injured bride, he eased himself into the Bagshot box, sending the eldest daughter's suitors scattering and striking horror in both the girl and her mother, who were certain that the earl's attentions would discourage more eligible bachelors.

"Leah . . ." Tony hesitated in view of his wife's decidedly cold countenance. "Believe me, I would not have had this occur for the world," he said, groping for encouragement and finding none. " 'Twas not my intent to embarrass you. I—"

" 'Tis of no moment, my lord," she assured him frostily. "I quite understand the ways of the *ton* now, I believe. Gentlemen are supposed to engage in liaisons with numerous females of every class, unmarried females are forbidden all but the most superficial and well-chaperoned discourse with gentlemen—and for good reason, I might note—while married *ladies* are free to pursue both married and unmarried gentlemen in the absences of their husbands, who are themselves busy being gentlemen. My mistake, of course, has been one of class—I can quite see that now—and I am prepared to rectify my error." Her gray eyes sparking martially, she nonetheless kept her voice calm and clipped. "As a titled *lady,* I shall of course cast about for a suitable lover."

"You will not. Leah—"

"Alas, but did no one of your impeccable gentlemen friends tell you it is considered quite gauche for either of us to cut up a dust over this state of affairs?" she asked with a decided lift to her eyebrow. "I am prepared to be quite *ladylike* about your lapse, that you may go pursue your Other Interests."

"If you think to make me jealous of Gil or Hugh, you are very wide of the mark, Leah. And as for Elaine, you have given me sufficient provocation that—"

"No," she interrupted coldly. "We are far too civilized as lady and gentleman to engage in a fisticuff of words. If you will pardon me, I find you decidedly *de trop*, Tony."

"Leah . . ." he warned.

"Your friends amongst the *ton* are looking at you, so I think it best that you leave before you afford them further gossip," she told him definitely. "Good night, sir."

That her chill reception indicated an anger every bit as great as his earlier was not lost on him. Bowing stiffly over her hand, he attempted to withdraw gracefully. "I will see you at home, madam."

Outside the box, Hugh approached with two glasses of lemonade. "Hallo, Tony," he greeted Lyndon. "Deuced awkward thing for you to do, what with Lady L. in attendance. Don't think I'd try to speak with her just yet."

"I already have," Tony snapped as he pushed past him.

"Sorry, my dear," Hugh told Leah, handing her one glass. "Shouldn't have left you alone." Looking across to where a middle-aged woman in a plumed turban gestured frantically toward him, he waved back. "My mother," he explained succinctly.

"Should you not speak with her?" Leah asked, eager to be left alone just then. "I assure you that the worst is over—Tony has already been here."

"I saw him." He was somewhat reluctant to leave her, knowing full well his mother meant to read him a peal over Lyndon's lady. "Well, I daresay you are right," he admitted grudgingly. "And Gil should return at any moment."

To the Bagshots, it was a matter of infinite relief when Rotherfield murmured a hasty farewell and left them. "Countess or not, miss, I won't have you throwing your hat over the windmill for him," Mrs. Bagshot told her daughter with unwarranted severity.

"Oh, no, Mama—he positively terrifies me," the girl reassured her with an expressive shudder.

"I should hope so."

"Ah, Lady Lyndon," Rotherfield greeted Leah with a genuine smile. "You are in looks tonight, my dear," he approved.

"Spanish coin, sir."

"Now, why is it that those who possess it deny beauty,

whilst those who lack any claim whatsoever preen and priss in the mistaken notion they have it?'' He took the liberty of sitting beside her, leaning closer to congratulate her. ''Well done, my dear—your behavior in the matter is above reproach. And you are quite the most beautiful woman here, Leah. Elaine is hagged in comparison.''

''Thank you, my lord,'' she said this time. Out of the corner of her eye she could see people craning curiously to observe them, so she deliberately reached to tap Rotherfield playfully with her fan. ''You know, you really must do something about this dreadful reputation of yours, as I keep receiving the direst warnings.''

''All deserved,'' he admitted, grinning openly at her.

Across from them, the dowager duchess was again attempting to gain possession of her glass. ''Bucky, your continuing theft prompts me to think I ought to give you one of your own,'' she remarked peevishly. ''Give it over.''

''Well,'' her companion conceded in disappointment as she handed it back, '' 'twas most diverting. First Lord Lyndon called on her, and they were to all appearances quite civil, and now Lord Rotherfield is paying his addresses, I believe.''

''Where?'' Her eyes found the earl actually grinning at Lyndon's wife, and that disturbed the dowager far more than idle gossip. It had been years since she'd seen him smile openly. ''Well, I shall have to take a hand, I think,'' she announced to Mrs. Buckhaven.

''Now?''

''Of course not now! What would that be to the purpose? I shall call on her tomorrow and tell her how to go on.'' Squinting again through the glass, she shook her head. ''Besides, there is Gilbert Renfield.''

''Hallo, Marcus—you are in my chair,'' Gil told the earl pointedly. ''And you are like to stumble in the dark if you do not leave now.''

''I can find my way.''

''But can you repair the lady's rep?'' Gil countered. ''Got to go—my box, after all.''

Hugh, who had been waiting for Rotherfield to leave, sighed with relief when the earl brushed past him. ''Stupid thing to do, Gil,'' he muttered, shaking his head. ''I mean, what if he'd taken the maggot into his brain to call you out?''

''I wouldn't go. Don't have to, you know—and I'd rather be a living coward than a dead fool.''

''I do not understand either of you,'' Leah told them in disgust. ''But then I like him.''

''Don't know him—that's all, and he don't bear knowin' neither,'' Gil added with a finality that forbore further conversation. ''Curtain's goin' up.''

28

"Madame, 'tis the duchess herself come to call," breathed Jeanne as she threw open the shutters to admit the sunlight.

Having spent a night of considerable agitation that did not bring sleep until well past dawn, Leah stirred reluctantly and blinked several times in an effort to assimilate herself into her surroundings. At first thought, it did not seem possible that anyone would call so early, and particularly not an elderly lady who had spent the previous night at the opera.

"Which duchess?" she asked, still puzzled.

"Lord Lyndon's aunt Davenham."

"Then she has come to see Tony." Leah lay back down and pulled the covers about her. "Tell Blair to wake him."

"Fitch said she asked to see you," Jeanne persisted, bustling about to retrieve Leah's wrapper and lay out a day gown of figured muslin.

"Still, he ought to be wakened."

There was no answer from Jeanne, who pulled open a drawer and studiously searched for a petticoat. Finding one, she laid it across her arm and approached Leah again. "Annie has drawn your bath, madame—do you wish it before you receive the duchess?"

"No, I cannot keep her waiting that long," Leah decided, rising finally and stretching. "What time is it?" She yawned.

"Just past eleven, madame."

"Let me wash my face—I'll bathe later when she is gone."

Slipping out of her nightrail, she stepped into her undergarments and pulled on the blue-flowered muslin dress. "No—there's not time to pin up my hair, Jeanne. I shall just brush it."

When Leah appeared belowstairs in less than fifteen minutes, the small elderly woman moved forward, wobbling on her cane, to greet her. "No, no—do not stand on ceremony with me, my dear. We are, after all, family." Smiling through thin lips, she stood on tiptoe to plant a kiss on Leah's cheek. "You are such a pretty representative of the Barsett name, child."

"Thank you, Your Grace."

" 'Your Grace,' " the old woman scoffed. "Utterly ridiculous formality. You will call me Aunt Hester as Tony does. Humor an old woman and do it. Now, let us sit for a comfortable coze whilst we decide what is to be done."

"Done?"

"About that dreadful woman, of course. Oh, I know you and I are not supposed to know of her, but after last night, 'twould be difficult to claim ignorance, anyway. I could positively choke the life from him, of course, but 'twould serve no useful purpose."

" 'Tis not your—"

"My affair?" the dowager interrupted gently. "Call me an interfering old woman, a meddler even, but humor an eccentric relative, my dear. 'Tis the license that comes with old age, I suppose, for we dare to insinuate ourselves into the lives of our heirs. But enough said on that head—I am here to help you."

"Why?" Leah asked bluntly.

"Because I like you! You ain't one of them milk-and-water misses—cannot abide 'em! And if you and Tony are at daggers drawn, I'll never see the next Barsett."

"I fail to see what can be done," Leah admitted. "He obviously prefers her."

"Utter fustian! A Banbury tale if I was ever to hear one! You've got to bring him to heel, that's all."

"I'd rather grind him into the ground."

"Now, there's the ticket! Knew you was a gel with spirit the first time I saw you! What you got to do is keep him at home, Leah! Now, there's more than one way to do it, of course. You can start giving parties here. He'll be in attendance—shocking bad *ton* not to come to his own affair, after all. Or you can get Gilbert Renfield or young Rivington to dangle attention after you. Tony's hotheaded—won't like it one jot! He ain't the sort to climb over your admirers to get to you, I can tell you."

"Are you suggesting that I flirt with Gil or Hugh?" Leah asked incredulously, despite having toyed with and discarded the same idea.

"Knew you wasn't a slowtop the minute I saw you—told Bucky you'd lead Tony, but she wouldn't have it," the old woman crowed gleefully. "Exactly what I was saying! And with your countenance, it won't be a difficult task!"

"I don't know," Leah mused doubtfully. "For one thing, neither of them would make Tony jealous in the least. I mean, would *you* cast out lures to his best friends? Besides, 'twas his jealousy of Rotherfield that provoked the row."

"Well, Rotherfield will not do at all, of course." The dowager was definite on that. "No, it must be a more eligible man. Tell me, do you know Ponsonby? Almost as handsome as Tony and a shameless flirt. Now, there's a man for you—won't let you get burned either, 'cause he knows how the rules are played out."

"What is wrong with Rotherfield?" Leah asked ominously, prepared for another inexplicable tirade against the earl.

"Well, I always did like him, of course, but I was the only one. Oh, that don't signify anyway," she muttered, her digression at an end. "The thing about Rotherfield is that he don't flirt—ain't a gamesman like that, if you was to get my meaning. No, a gel'd get burned on him—I've knowed a peagoose or two that has."

"I don't understand how—"

"The thing about Marcus Halvert, my dear, is that he'd expect you to pay if you played. Now, more to the point—who's to get? Need one of 'em as is handsome and interested enough to bring Tony to heel—don't suppose you know 'Ball' Hughes either, do you?"

"Golden Ball?"

"Then you do know him! Wealthiest dandy in town, I daresay."

"No, I have not exchanged beyond the merest civility with him and I cannot think he even noted me."

"Humph! He notices every female he meets."

Leah bit her thumbnail tentatively and considered the possibilities. "I am not at all certain that I wish a jealous husband, ma'am—I am not even certain that it should be I who attempt to mend matters between us. I did not go to King's Theater with my fancy piece, you know."

"No, no, of course you did not," the old lady said soothingly. "But there is much that is good in Tony—I should dislike seeing him lose quite the best thing that has ever happened to him."

"But he is stubborn beyond bearing, and—"

"Think on it—'tis all I ask. I admit my meddling is selfish, but there must be more Barsetts to carry the Lyndon title."

Once the duchess had left, Leah sank to a sofa to consider what she ought to do. She wanted her husband's love and his loyalty—one without the other was meaningless to her. And yet she did not see how it was her fault that he had gone to Elaine Chandler, and certainly she'd done nothing to make him display the creature publicly. So he had forbidden her association with Rotherfield—he was unreasonable on that head. Why could she be friends with Gil and Hugh and not the earl? Nothing Marcus Halvert had ever suggested carried the least hint of expected impropriety. Indeed, her heart went out to him as she saw the injustice inflicted by an unforgiving society for what surely must have been youthful indiscretions.

In her mind, she turned over every word of the last argument she'd had with Tony. Well, she conceded with a wry grimace, she *had* challenged him to see the woman. Perhaps she ought to at least try the waters this morning and see if he were properly contrite.

"Mrs. Fitch," she called out to the housekeeper as that woman bustled past the open door, "is Lord Lyndon down yet?"

"I do not believe so, madam."

"He's still abed?"

"Er . . . I do not believe so," the woman answered uncomfortably.

An awful suspicion assailed Leah, leaving her with a sick feeling deep within. "Mrs. Fitch," she asked calmly, "when did my husband get home?"

"Uh . . . well, I daresay you will need to ask Blair about that, my lady."

"Did he come home?" Leah asked ominously.

"Uh . . . no, but that is not to say . . . well, he was used to stay at his clubs, your ladyship, and we do not make much of his absences."

"I see."

"And sometimes he stays with Mr. Renfield."

"That will be all, Mrs. Fitch."

As soon as the housekeeper escaped, Leah went to Tony's library to find something to soothe her—reading always provided an escape. Drawing out the steps, she climbed to reach for a volume of Blake's poetry, one of her favorites, *Songs of Experience,* hoping that somehow his cynical, biting, metaphysical poems might help her feel that she was better off than the general condition.

"My lady?" Horton stepped tentatively to the doorway, his disapproval evident on every line of his face. "Lord Rotherfield is here—shall I tell him you are not receiving?"

"Of course you must not! Tell him . . . Oh, no matter, I shall tell him myself."

She found the earl admiring the moldings on the fireplace surround. His back was toward her even as he greeted her. "I thought perhaps you would wish to see the Menagerie at the Tower—or there is an ascension planned by Mr. Graham if the wind holds. I find myself suffering from a surfeit of boredom today, and . . ." He turned around diffidently, all traces of his famed arrogance gone. "My dear," he murmured at the sight of her, "you appear a trifle hagged." Crossing the room quickly, he demanded, "Was Lydndon unpleasant when you returned home?"

"I did not see him." She looked up into those black eyes of his and thought she read sympathy there. "Do sit down—please."

"Something has overset you. If there is anything I can do to assist you . . ."

She sucked in her breath, screwing her courage to the utmost, and nodded. "Lord Rotherfield," she asked baldly, "would you mind very much if I were to engage in a mild flirtation with you?"

To his credit, he did not so much as blink to betray his surprise. "I should be honored, of course," he responded lightly, and then with a faint quiver at the corners of his mouth, he managed to ask, "But, dear lady, must it be mild?"

"If it offends you—"

"No, no, of course not," he hastened to reassure her. "But have you considered the matter thoroughly, Leah?" he asked with uncharacteristic gentleness. "Do not forget who I am—I am Rotherfield. Perhaps you would be better advised to ask Renfield or Ponsonby—you can be seen everywhere with them."

"No. The choice is yours, of course. You may not wish to be seen with this Cit's daughter, after all, and I should quite understand if that were the case."

"Leah, you have but to ask—I stand ready to do whatever 'tis you wish."

"I wish to make Tony think you are my lover." Her face reddened with embarrassment even as she said it, and she hoped he would not think her some sort of doxy.

"I see."

"But of course I should not expect . . . that is . . ."

"I already knew you were not that sort of female, my dear. My only concern is why you have chosen the least presentable of your acquaintances for the task."

"I wanted a dangerous man, my lord. I think Tony could intimidate anyone else."

29

The amethysts nestled in the hollow of her throat and dipped downward to the décolletage of her lavender silk gown. The dress was simplicity itself, a perfect foil for the beautiful necklace Tony had bought in Paris. While waiting for Jeanne to return from pressing the cashmere shawl she meant to wear, Leah tucked an errant strand into the braid that formed an unusual crown of hair on her head.

Her heart nearly stopped beating when she caught the reflection of Tony in her mirror. For well over two weeks they'd scarce exchanged pleasantries even, each watching silently as the other came and went from the house. Leah duly noted that she should have locked the door after Jeanne. She sat very still, not wanting him to know she'd seen him. Her heart beat rapidly and her whole body tensed as he moved closer. An involuntary shiver went down her back when his warm fingers lifted her necklace at the nape of her neck.

" 'Tis as pretty as I thought it would be on you, my dear."

She jerked away so quickly that she nearly bumped her head on the mirror. "I do not believe I gave you leave to come into my chamber, my lord."

"So you are going to be away from home again tonight," he observed, ignoring her coldness. "How long do you think you can maintain this giddy schedule you give yourself?"

"There is so much to do in one short season that one feels one must make the attempt to appear at everything," she answered with feigned indifference.

"Where is it tonight?"

"Well, I have a card to Lady Childredge's soiree, of

course, but since Marcus positively despises such events, I am going to Vauxhall for a concert and to see the fireworks. I believe there is a female who descends from a wire one hundred feet above ground through a blaze of light, to arrive unscathed at the bottom."

"I did not know you wished to go there."

"Oh, I should not think to trouble you, Tony," she responded airily. "Now that I know precisely how I am to go on, I quite understand that 'tis utterly unfashionable to be seen with one's husband anyway, and as you are so seldom home yourself, I have asked Marcus."

"I see." He'd promised himself that he would avoid a quarrel with her, that he would try to be conciliatory, but she was making it deuced difficult. He looked down on the wound braid of her hair and felt a terrible, painful hunger. "I thought perhaps we might spend an evening at home. You wished once to become a political hostess, as I recall, and I thought it would be possible to discuss a small dinner party for the Whigs—or whomever you might wish to invite."

"I did not think you cared for politics, my lord."

"Well, I do not, but I am prepared to listen for your sake."

"How very kind of you," she murmured. "And shall we invite Mrs. Chandler also?"

"You are not going to let me forget that, are you?"

"No."

"You and Rotherfield are becoming the latest *on-dit*, my dear. Do you not think you are a trifle particular in your attentions?" he asked, despite his resolve to ignore the earl.

She appeared to consider the matter and then shook her head. "No, I do not think so. Last night I went to Covent Garden with Renfield, and Saturday I attended the ballet with Johnny Barrasford. And then 'twas Lord Ponsonby who escorted me to the Dinsmore affair last week. Alas, Marcus is not always able to take me about."

"If you would give me sufficient notice, I would make certain I am free to take you to some of your engagements," he offered stiffly.

"And why should you? No, I could not allow myself

to interfere with your Other Interests." To Leah's utter relief, Jeanne reappeared with the folded shawl. "Alas, but I am late, Tony. Would you be so kind as to drape that over my shoulders just so? And remember, 'tis the fashion to leave it lower on one side." She smiled sweetly, knowing full well he'd much rather strangle her with it. His fingers almost burned her where they touched the bare skin at the back of her neck, but she willed herself to stand perfectly still. "Thank you," she managed politely when he was done.

"Leah—"

"Perhaps tomorrow, Tony, as I am late already. Good evening. I pray you will give my regards to Mrs. Chandler."

He wanted to forbid her going, but since that night at King's Theater, there'd been very little to say. He'd made a cake of himself and a laughingstock of Leah, earning the censure of his great-aunt, whose scathing peal still stung, and the cold disapproval of his friends. It was becoming increasingly difficult to see Jeptha Cole nearly every day and parry questions about Leah. While the old man discouraged her visiting him, saying she was a fine lady and must forget from whence she came, he nonetheless wanted to know secondhand of her every triumph. And, his jealousy of Rotherfield aside, Leah's determined association with the man was making her less and less acceptable amongst the *ton*. Even Sally Jersey had cornered him quite literally on the street and had demanded to know when he meant to put a stop to it. Of course, he'd acted as though he approved of the earl, when in truth, only a complete fool would.

"Did you wish to attend the Childredge affair?" Rotherfield asked her as he handed her up into his *vis á vis*. "I am not averse to putting it to the touch, you know."

"Well . . ."

"It might be possible to do both," he offered. "If the Childredges put on a deuced bore, perhaps we could press on in time to see the fireworks."

"You are not afraid of being cut?" she asked. In the weeks since she had really come to know him, she had achieved an easy friendship that allowed for candor between them.

"I am not afraid of anything," he reassured her. "And I feel quite certain that no one will cut you there."

The way he said it gave her pause, for in the several instances when they'd chosen to appear places other than those charging admission, the reception had been decidedly chill. She'd begun to suspect that the Menagerie, the balloon ascensions, the fireworks, and the drives in the park had been contrived with an eye to avoiding any unpleasantness for her.

"Then let us go to the Childredges', by all means."

"You are pluck to the bone, my dear," he said approvingly.

The reaction of their hostess was almost worth the appearance, Leah decided with a perverse glee. When they were announced, she and Lord Rotherfield made a truly grand entrance, with her sparkling amethysts and her fair skin providing a perfect foil for the earl's austere dress and dark handsomeness. Lady Childredge appeared suddenly faint, as though overcome with acute indigestion, while her lord looked faintly amused by it all. Leah, of course, smiled serenely and made Tony's apologies, saying that she had impressed dear Marcus into service on rather short notice. But when they were out of their hosts' hearing, she could not help giggling. "I think you positively cultivate your sinister reputation, my lord."

"It has to be useful for something," he agreed, tucking her hand in the crook of his arm.

It did not take Leah long to realize that it was as Tony had said—she and Rotherfield were on the *on-dit* of the evening. Aside from waltzes with Ponsonby and Barrasford, most of the men gave her a wide berth, preferring to admire her from afar. The earl, however, was not above flouting convention, and elected to waltz three times and stand up for two country dances with her. Finally a rather elderly gentleman who had been watching them intently from the moment they arrived came forward. Rotherfield did not appear surprised.

"Ah, Marcus, pray present me," the old gentleman asked.

"Leah, I make known to you Lord Milbourne. Milbourne, this fair lady is the Viscountess Lyndon." His black eyes on the old man, Rotherfield murmured, "Perhaps you would wish to dance?"

"Alas, but these old legs cannot move as quickly as the music anymore. But perhaps Lady Lyndon would favor me with a few minutes of her company?"

"Well, I . . ." Leah gaped at both of them, wondering how the Earl of Rotherfield could possibly be on civil terms with a man she'd only heard of, a man whose very name was synonymous with the *ton* itself.

"Do go on, my dear," the earl urged her. "I shall procure a plate and some punch for you." Casting a significant glance at the terrace doors, he nodded to Lord Milbourne. "Perhaps you would wish to be more private out there."

"Marcus, whatever . . . ?"

"At my age, your virtue is quite safe, my dear," the frail old gentleman assured her. "And I have been waiting some twenty years to see you, Leah."

"Oh, I should not think otherwise," Leah hastened to tell him. "Indeed, who has not heard of Milbourne? When the dowager listed those whom I—" She colored as she realized how that must sound. "That is, when she would tell me who must be met, my lord, your name was among the first on the list."

"Alas, but I do not go about as I was once inclined. My poor Anne is confined to her bed and there is little enjoyment without her presence." He'd taken her arm and was propelling her gently toward the doors that had been opened to cool the ballroom. "Sometime you really must tell me how it is that you are so often in Marcus Halvert's company, my dear."

She bristled, wanting to tell him that was none of his affair, but when she looked at him, she saw no censure. "My husband's engagements are numerous, my lord, and I choose not to remain at home," she mumbled, not wanting anyone to know the truth.

The breeze was warm, wafting in over a profusion of flowers, carrying their intermingled fragrances, while the stars in the sky sparkled like diamonds against black velvet. For a time, Lord Milbourne studied her beneath the light of a Chinese lantern, and then finally nodded. "You are very much like my Marianna, I think. Our memories trick us, of course, but I am certain you have the look of her."

Marianna had been her mother's name. "You knew my mother?" she asked in surprise.

"It does me little credit to admit it, child, but I was her parent." His eyes met hers soberly in the faint light and he nodded. "Aye, I am your grandfather—your mother's father."

"But you cannot have been . . . That is, my mother was a Cit, sir!"

"No," He smiled faintly, as though the irony were almost amusing. "Your father was the Cit, Leah."

"But Papa—"

"Ask your father—ask Jeptha Cole, my dear. I am not proud of the story, and I promised him I would not seek to see you. But as I have heard your name oft linked with that of Rotherfield, I asked him to arrange a chance meeting."

She stared in open disbelief, trying to understand how it could be that she had never so much as heard she had any living relatives other than her father. And a man who held one of the most respected names in society was standing across from her telling her they shared the same blood.

"Your grandmother is unwell, Leah, else I'd not have broken my promise. She wants to see you, child."

"My grandmother, sir?" she echoed numbly. "But I . . ."

"I had thought to persuade Marcus to bring you for a visit," he continued, his eyes still searching her face for something, "but then 'twas decided we'd best determine your wishes in the matter."

She had a grandmother she'd never seen. She was relation to one of the finest families in England. Her mother came of a class she'd once despised for being useless.

"I realize this must be quite shocking for you, Leah, and I am not unaware of how you have been received amongst the *ton.* I wished from the very beginning that

I could have persuaded your papa to let us bring you out, but his hatred of me was too great,'' he offered soberly. ''Believe me, I did not wish us to meet as strangers at a party.''

''I see,'' she managed, although she did not see at all.

''Would you indulge an old woman's fondest desire, my dear? Would you visit your grandmother while she can yet know you?''

Curiosity and a strange elation mingled, prompting her to decide. ''Yes, of course—I should like that above all things, sir.''

''I spoke with Marcus earlier today, and if you are willing to forgo the pleasures of Vauxhall this evening, he is amenable to bringing you to Milbourne House.''

''Tonight? 'Tis so . . . Yes, of course.''

Rotherfield was waiting with her shawl when they returned, and the three of them made their farewells to an astonished Lady Childredge. ''My granddaughter has the headache,'' Lord Milbourne explained smoothly, giving reason to their precipitate departure.

''Your granddaughter?'' Clearly taken unaware, that lady could only stare with slackened jaw as she attempted to digest this startling bit of information. ''Leah Cole . . . that is to say, *Lady Lyndon*,'' she amended hastily, ''Lady Lyndon is *your* granddaughter, my lord?''

''Of course she is,'' the old man insisted proudly. ''Blood will tell, do you not think? Only child of m'daughter Marianna.''

''But I thought—''

''Thought she was a Cit, didn't you?'' he acknowledged bluntly. ''Well, she is a Milbourne also.'' And with that cryptic comment, he offered Leah his arm. ''Anne will be so pleased to see you, child,'' he told her. ''She has waited years for this night.''

Rotherfield got the door before the Childredge butler could manage it, and waited for them to pass. Behind them, Leah could hear the buzz of excited gossip as their hostess spread the word, ''Milbourne's granddaughter, if you can but credit that. I vow I was never so surprised in my life.''

30

It was extremely late when Leah arrived home, so late that she let herself in with the key and kicked off her slippers in the lower hall to avoid disturbing the servants. Somewhere in the house a clock struck three. Tiptoeing silently in the near-darkness, she had just groped for the newel post at the bottom of the stairs when the library door opened behind her, sending a slice of light across the foyer and casting a long shadow up the wall beside her. She jumped in fright and her breath caught in her throat.

"Oh, 'tis you," she managed, still trying to control the panic she'd felt. "You gave me a start."

He bowed slightly as his eyes glittered strangely at her in the semidarkness. "Home so soon, my dear?" His speech was softly slurred and there was a slight list to his walk as he came to face her. "Had I been your lover, I'd have spent the whole night with you—and I'd not have sent you home to face an irate husband."

"You are foxed, my lord," she snapped. "And your accusations are offensive." Her hand still on the bottom post, she started to climb the stairs.

"Not so quickly, Leah—I am not done with you." He caught her from behind and pulled her off the bottom step. Grasping her chin with his hand, he forced her to turn and look at him. "For the innocent Cit I wed, you have certainly learned to be the fashionable lady, have you not?" he gibed into her face. "You have even managed to acquire a lover."

"Unhand me, Tony," she ordered coldly, still trying to still the painful beating of her heart.

"But you have forgotten the most important rule, my dear—it is not at all the thing to engage in these little liaisons before you have given your husband his heir." His other hand closed on her shoulder, gripping it tightly.

"I do not have a lover—yet," she informed him, striving to keep her voice level. "Though I shall certainly inform you when I do, so that we may be even on that score, my lord. After all, you were so kind as to arrange a public display of yours."

His fingers still on her chin, he forced her head back to stare into her face. She put her hand on his wrist to break the hold. "Release me, my lord," she tried again. "You are hurting me."

"Release you?"

He gave a derisive half-laugh and pulled her against him despite her protest, while his mouth sought hers hungrily. She tasted the wine and felt the heat of his breath as she tried to push him away. For answer, his hands slid down her back, imprisoning her, forcing her body into the hard contours of his. With an effort, she willed herself to remain motionless even when his tongue traced the edges of her teeth. When at last he left her mouth, it was to trail hot kisses from her earlobe to her throat. An involuntary shiver sliced downward from where the hairs stood up on her neck.

"Leah . . . Leah . . ." he whispered hungrily, "do not deny me what you give him so freely." His hand slipped under the fabric of her dress and kneaded the soft skin against the bones of her shoulder. "Let me love you, Leah."

She wanted to yield, but not like this, not when he'd had too much to drink, not when he believed the worst of her. With an effort, she broke away from him, moving back so violently she almost tripped on the first step of the staircase.

"You mistake the matter, Tony—Marcus is not my lover," she spat at him.

"Do you think me blind, Leah?" he rasped, grasping her wrist painfully and pulling her back to him. "I made you mine—I'll keep you mine."

She'd never seen him like this and it frightened her. "If you do not release me this instant, Tony," she threatened, "I shall scream and bring this house down about your ears."

"You'll have to hurry then," he whispered undeterred against her ear. While one arm held her against him, his other hand began unhooking her gown. His mouth sought hers again, and as the material slackened across her bodice, his hand left her back to find her breast.

"Please, Tony—not this way," she gasped desperately, trying to resist his assault on her reeling sense. "Please."

"Please what?" he murmured against the corners of her lips. "I shall try to be as good as Rotherfield this time." Still nibbling, playing, sampling of her mouth, he slackened his hold enough to finish taking down the bodice of her gown and the thin camisole underneath. "You are beautiful, Leah," he breathed.

She could not let him know how much she wanted him, how much she had missed his touch. His hunger was evident, his desire blazing in his eyes as they raked over her bared breasts. And every inch of her body wanted to slake that desire and feed her own, but she forced herself to meet his gaze. "No, you will have to take me by force," she lied.

"You have no reason—"

"I have every reason."

"Why Rotherfield, Leah?" he rasped thickly, his eyes still glittering.

"Why Elaine Chandler?" she retorted. Wrenching free, she ran up the stairs, pausing only from the safety of the top to pull up her gown. This time, he did not follow her, but flung himself back toward the library, from whence she heard the crash of a bottle or glass against the fireplace.

Unnerved, she managed to undress without waking Jeanne and, turning the key in her bedchamber lock, she retired to agonize over the way things stood between them. Her life was in shambles, a wreckage brought about by jealousy, greed, and distrust, and she had not the means to rebuild it. She'd been married to satisfy her father's ambition for her, when in fact it had not been necessary at all. And the worst of that was that she was not really even a Cit—her own mother came from the very class that she professed to despise. Her Milbourne grandparents could have made her a lady without Viscount Lyndon's title.

In an effort to draw herself out of her self-pity, she considered her newly discovered relations. They were kind, they were obviously *haut ton*, and appeared quite proud of her, making it even more incomprehensible that her father had hidden their existence from her.

She heard Tony's steps on the stairs, heard them come down the hallway to pause outside the door. She sucked in her breath and waited, afraid she had not the will to deny him again. The doorknob rattled as he tried it, and then there was silence for a moment. Finally she could hear him retreat to his own chamber at the other end of the hall. Then, after a time, his door opened and his footsteps sounded again, first on the stairs and then in the hallway below. The door slammed.

Lying back among her pillows, she was certain he'd gone to seek his mistress. Fighting back tears, she wondered if she'd played the game all wrong, if she should have yielded to his desire, for at least then she would have been the one to share his bed. No, she decided resolutely, she had too much pride to share her husband with anyone. It was time she went home.

As for Tony, he drove his curricle recklessly through the streets of London, oblivious of the Charlies who rounded up the more boisterous drunks. The fog had rolled in up the Thames, making the gaslights into hazy yellow dots that faded into the gray mists. An occasional dog, one of those half-wild denizens of the city, reluctantly fled from scavenged garbage before his wheels, only to slink back in his wake. Somewhere in the distance, the watch called five o'clock and the bargemen could already be heard shouting at each other in the fog.

Elaine Chandler's house was dark when he reached it. He reined in and stared for several minutes at the whitewashed brick structure, knowing full well of his welcome there. But he didn't want Elaine. Even before his precipitate marriage to Leah Cole, he'd known that if the fairest Cyprian in the world cast lures at him, he'd decline, and it was still so. There was some justice in his predicament, he supposed, for he'd raked about with hedonistic abandon, deserving every epithet Leah flung his way. His ardor cooled in the chill mists of morning, replaced by the quiet reflection of self-reproach, he clicked his reins and returned home at a much slower pace.

As difficult as it was to accept it, he concluded that she wanted Rotherfield—whether because he'd driven her into the earl's arms with his jealousy, or whether the attraction had always been there, the fact remained the same. His wife wanted Rotherfield, had chosen the notorious earl over him. And Rotherfield certainly wanted her. Given that pass, what was to be done? Maybe he ought to simply apologize for his jealous behavior and hope that somehow he could win her back.

The next morning, she was already gone when he came down. His head ached from the night's wine, his mouth was dry and tasted as though Napoleon's army had marched through it, and his mind was fogged from a lack of sleep. Seeing the footmen lugging heavy trunks down the service stairs, he was befuddled for a moment.

"What the devil . . . ? James, what is this?" he demanded in alarm. As his voice rose, the pain in his head hit like an ax blow from somewhere between his eyes to the base of his skull. Combing his hair distractedly with his hands, Tony tried to assimilate what was happening. "Where's Leah—where is Lady Lyndon?"

John Maxwell coughed apologetically behind him to attract his attention. "I believe she wrote to you, my lord."

A sick knot formed in the pit of Tony's stomach as he followed his secretary into the library. Dropping into the chair by his desk, he leaned his aching head in his hand. "You might as well let me have it, Max." He spoke tiredly.

" 'Tis on the desk, sir."

Tony found it and withdrew a folded sheet from the envelope. The color drained from his face as he began to read:

My lord,

After much consideration of the matter, I have

decided to leave your house. You have accused me of the basest violation of my marriage vows, and I have done the same with you. We were wed for the wrong reasons and I find it repugnant to remain in what can only be called a *mésalliance* at best.

Papa will be overset at first, but his natural affection for me will outweigh his objections. And you must not blame Lord Rotherfield, for the decision is mine alone.

LCB

"That's it—she said nothing else?" Tony asked, too stunned to believe it. Leah had left him over Rotherfield. She was gone from his house.

"Nothing, my lord."

"Well, she cannot do it!" Tony exploded. "The little fool—she will ruin herself!" Heaving himself up despite the ache in his head, he ordered loudly for any who would hear, "Put my curricle to! Blair, my coat!" He was going to face Rotherfield down if it was the last thing he ever did.

Alternating between despair that she'd left him and fury at Rotherfield for encouraging her, Tony took the ribbons himself and careened through the London streets like a madman. How could she possibly have fled to the other man? Whatever could have possessed her? And what if he found her? He could scarce grasp her by the hair and force her to return to him, after all. And he would not want her that way if he could. As he took a corner on two wheels, he considered going to Jeptha Cole and discarded that idea. The old man's health was too precarious —he'd not overset him if it could be helped. No, he had to find Leah and reason with her.

Pushing past Marcus Havert's astonished butler, Tony found the earl still at his breakfast. "Where is she?" he demanded harshly, removing his driving gloves.

Rotherfield finished transferring marmalade onto a piece of toast before looking up. His black eyes betrayed none of the excitement he felt when they met Tony's. "I am afraid you have the advantage of me, Lyndon," he murmured. "Er . . . would you care to join me?"

''No!''

''I collect I am being privileged to see the legendary Barsett temper, my lord,'' the earl observed, unperturbed by the intrusion or by Tony's outburst.

''I did not think you would stoop so low as to ruin a female's reputation!''

''By being seen with her?'' One of Rotherfield's black brows rose skeptically. ''It has been seven years, Lyndon. Full half the *ton* cannot recollect the scandal, and the other half will never accept her anyway.''

''Where is she?'' Tony repeated. ''Dammit, where is she?''

The earl bit off a piece of the toast and masticated it thoroughly before shaking his head. ''Leah? Dear me—has she left you? It does not surprise me, I suppose,'' he decided coolly. ''And I should not tell you if I knew, Lyndon. Suffice it to say that she is not here.''

Tony's right hand came up, striking Rotherfield so hard with the driving glove that it left a red mark across the high cheekbone. For a moment the black eyes flashed malevolently and then they were veiled.

''Name you weapon, Marcus.''

A slow smile of triumph spread across the darkly handsome face. ''A widow is always preferable to a divorcée,'' he murmured with deceptive softness. ''Pistols.''

31

Jeptha Cole's welcoming smile turned to a scowl within minutes of his daughter's arrival. Had she not thrown herself in his arms and burst into tears, he would have been inclined to send her back to Lyndon House without listening to her side of the matter. But she's seldom ever cried, not even when actually injured, so he held his peace and enveloped her in his arms, patting her awkwardly and mumbling soothing platitudes about everyone's having a turnup with a spouse from time to time.

Taking her into his library, he poured her two fingers of brandy and told her to calm herself. "Papa, I have made such a mull of my life," she wailed, gulping the contents of her glass and choking on it. "Aargh!"

"Well, you ain't supposed to drink it like water, Leah! Sniff it—savor it, you know! Havey-cavey business—the thing about Rotherfield. I ain't from the *ton*, my dear, and even I know he ain't at all the thing! Man's a deuced devil, they say, and he ain't received!"

"But Tony was seeing Mrs. Chandler!" she tried to explain.

"That don't signify!" Then, seeing that she was about to begin crying anew, he tried a different tack. "Daresay it's my fault, after all—I rushed you into the marriage before you was to know what you was about. But damme, I like young Lyndon—and I was afeared of what Rotherfield meant to do. I didn't want any brats coming in the side door 'cause you didn't know how to go on."

"Papa!"

"Well, I didn't think you was a peagoose, but it's been known to happen, and then Lyndon allowed as how the earl was too particular in his attentions—well, I couldn't take the chance. Afraid Lyndon'd get away—and I wanted you to be a viscountess, you know. Knew Rotherfield was rich as Croesus himself—stood to reason he had something else in mind.'' He raised his gaze to his dead wife's portrait. ''Promised her.'' Looking back at Leah, he nodded. ''You understand, don't you?''

''No, Papa, I have never understood it.''

''Got to sit—m'leg's painin' me,'' he explained, taking a seat close to the window. ''Don't eat what you'd want me to since you been gone. Sit down.''

Instead of taking the chair he'd indicated, she slid to the floor to lean her head against his leg as she had done when she was a small child. ''Why did you never tell me about her?'' she wondered as she dabbed at her eyes with her handkerchief.

'' 'Cause I miss her too much to speak of her—talk to her instead.'' He shifted uncomfortably in his chair and looked down at her. ''You are the image of her, you know—cherish you for it.''

''But what was she like?'' she persisted.

''Well, she was a proud and willful girl, much like you really. Now, this may surprise you—don't know if I ought to tell you of it—but she was Quality. Met her by accident.'' His eyes took on the faraway look of one remembering across time. ''Back, then, her papa was heavily in debt and needed the blunt badly to come about, so's he was wantin' to sell Marianna to a wealthy gentleman some twenty years older'n she was.'' He shifted in his chair, seeking greater comfort, and continued, ''The end of it was that she ran away from 'em. Met her in the posting house then. Oh, but she was a pretty thing—only seventeen and frightened by the bucks that was ogling her. Not that she was a dieaway miss, mind you, but some of 'em was coming too strong.''

''You met Mama in a posting house?''

''Aye. She was runnin' to her granny's—now, there was an old Tartar for ye. I offered to take her there, and I guess she thought I looked less a menace than the rest of 'em. Anyways, the old woman wouldn't have her—was goin' to send her back to Milbourne, you know. Well, the end of the matter was we went to Gretna—got married over the anvil."

"You *eloped*?" somehow she could not imagine her father as a dashing romantic figure.

"I know what you are a-thinkin', missy!" he retorted. "Jeptha Cole didn't always look like this, I can tell you! She thought me quite handsome, she did—and I was."

"And what did Lord Milbourne do?" she asked, returning to his story.

"Disowned her! Said I wasn't fit to put on his boots—cast her out. Anyways, we came to London and set up housekeepin' out beyond Smithfield Market—not too fashionable for a girl like Marianna, but she never complained of it. Learned to do for herself and me too. We was poor as beggars, Leah. My parents were nobodies—my father was naught but a chandler in Liverpool ere he died. Aye, missy, I was a come-down for your mother—nothin' like she had a right to expect."

His eyes traveled to the portrait above them. "I miss her—Lud knows I miss her, Leah."

"Papa . . ." Her hand sought his and held it.

"Oh, it's all right." He patted her head affectionately and looked down through misted eyes. "I'll see her again, you know. But I wanted to make it up to her for takin' me, don't you see? When we was just married, I came here and worked for a founderer for fifteen shillings a day—and hard work that was. But as hard as things was on me, they were harder on her. She wasn't made for bearing—narrower in the backside than you—and we lost three babes before you. You was the only one to come into this world breathin'. "

"Oh, Papa."

"Ain't done yet." It was as if the years of pent-up memories would not be stilled now. "What broke her heart was Milbourne. 'Twasn't enough that he disowned her. He wouldn't let any of 'em—her mother or sisters even—come near her. Said if she wanted to be a Cit, she could live like one. She never had the things she was used to after we was wed. I wanted to give 'em back to her, but I couldn't.

"Then there was a fellow named Asa Pierson—foreigner,

you know—wanted to go into shipping here. Well, he had the money, and he liked me—we went into it not knowing what we was doin' even, but I learned the business. Bought anything and sold it at a profit—weevily meal, rum, sugar, salvage rice."

"And you prospered."

"And we prospered—damme if we didn't. Worked six and one-half days a week to do it, but we did. Best thing I ever did for your mother was when I was able to build her this house before she died."

"No."

"No?"

"No, Papa—the best thing you ever did for her was marry her. Everyone should have as romantic a tale to tell."

"But it didn't end right." He sighed and was silent for a time. "At least she knew she had you, puss—knew you breathed. Begged me to care for you even. As if I wouldn't—you were all I had left of her."

Tears streamed down Leah's face, tears for the mother she'd never known. Her hand tightened on her father's and she leaned closer to his leg.

"But that wasn't the end of it. You always get the chance to misuse them that misuses you if you wait long enough. The year after Marianna died, Milbourne turned to me for money, said he wanted to rear his motherless grandbaby, give you everything if I was to frank the business. Told him where he could go, I did—told him I'd make you a lady myself. But I guess you ain't happy, so's—"

"But there was no need! Papa, I am not ashamed to be your daughter—and Mama was not ashamed to be your wife! What is there to a title, anyway?"

"I gave him the money." His mouth twisted into a bitter smile. "I had my revenge for her—he crawled to me for the money and I gave it. He had to seek out the son-in-law he despised. And in return for it, I made him promise not to see you."

"I have seen him, Papa," she cut in quietly. "And my grandmother also. I saw them last night."

He sat very still.

"Lady Milbourne is very ill—she wished to see me. She said I reminded her of Mama."

"Daresay she could have made you a finer lady than I," he answered heavily.

"No. She said you had done better with me than she did with three daughters, Papa."

"She did?" He brightened visibly. "Well, daresay Marianna had to get her breeding somewhere—must've been her." Patting her head again, he shook his head. "My mistake was doing like Milbourne, I suppose—making you take a fellow you didn't want."

"I am sorry to have ruined your plans."

"Fiddle. Ain't a day gone by since you was born that I ain't been proud of you. Only thing I ain't got is a grandson."

"Viscount Lyndon, sir!" Crome announced self-importantly from the doorway.

"Tony! Here?" Leah looked at her father in consternation, as though she ought to flee.

"There, there." Jeptha Cole patted his daughter's hand. "Don't have to go home with him if you don't want."

"Sir . . . Leah."

In spite of her anger, in spite of her hurt, in spite of everything he'd said to her, Leah's heart lurched and her senses reeled at the sight of him. Pulling up by the arm of her father's chair, she turned away from her husband to keep him from seeing the hope in her face. She had left him, after all, and she had her pride.

"What are you doing here?" she asked shakily.

"Like you, I have come for a visit." The blue eyes that met hers were alive with mischief and more. "I wanted to be here when you shared your interesting condition with you father, my dear," he told her with a reasonably straight face.

"My *what*?"

"Or perhaps you did not wish to tell him because it is early days yet," he suggested helpfully.

"Tony, what are—?"

"Then *that* explains it!" Her father's face took on such an expression of pure joy that Leah could only stare. "I *knew* it was a queer start, my lord! Marianna was like that—could always tell by the way she was blue-deviled at first. Well, if that don't beat the Dutch!"

"Tony!"

"My own blood Quality! Now, if you was to name a girl Marianna, I'd do right by her, you understand," Cole told Tony. " 'Course, if it's a boy, I daresay you'd want a family name—and there ain't one as I'd have on this side of the blanket."

Leah stared across the room at Tony, not knowing whether to laugh or scream with vexation. "You will have to pardon us, Papa, but I am wishful of speaking with my husband."

"When do you expect it? I mean, it ain't but a while since you was wed—wouldn't want talk, you know."

"There will be no gossip about that, Papa," she reassured him. "Tony—"

"Take him to the garden." her father suggested. " 'Tis private—and a pretty place t' settle a dust-up. 'Course there's a breeze," he added doubtfully. "Don't know if you ought—"

"The garden will be fine. Tony, would you care to take a turn about Papa's garden?" she asked sweetly.

She waited only until she was sure they were alone before she rounded on him. "Of all the mean-spirited, the idiotish, the . . ." She groped helplessly for something to convey her opinion of what he'd done and, finding none, sputtered, "I left you, Tony! You cannot go about raising false hopes when you know very well—"

"No, I don't know. It *is* possible, you know, and I am prepared to attend to the matter with relish—abandon even," he offered with a grin.

"How could you? You know he will be disappointed beyond bearing!"

"Actually, I thought that would overset him less than hearing you'd left me for Rotherfield."

"I did not leave you for Marcus!" she hissed, furious at being outfaced. "I left you over that Chandler woman! And because you are overbearing and . . . because we do not deal well together!"

"I thought we dealt extremely well together—of course,

I should like to deal with you more often," he added wickedly.

"Tony, 'tis hopeless."

"Tell that to your father."

"And 'tis monstrous unfair to use that against me!" she burst out.

"I have to use what I have. You see, Leah, I do not want to lose you. I may have been all those things you have flung at me, and I am not proud of them, but since I have met you, I am a *reformed* rake, gamester, and whatever else 'tis that you call me."

"A libertine."

"A reformed libertine then."

"A dissolute libertine."

"A reformed dissolute libertine." He stepped closer and attempted to draw her into his arms. "And I am prepared to let you continue reforming me—within reason, of course. I am even prepared to become a Whig for you."

"This is ridiculous!"

"I am to give my maiden speech in Lords."

"When?"

"As soon as I finish writing it," he announced smugly.

"Now I know that's a hum, Tony Barsett," she retorted, backing away. "You do not have a speech—and you never will."

"Max started writing it last week, but I find I need to work on it myself. Max, idealist that he is, expects me to attempt redressing all the ills of the world at once, you know."

"A Banbury tale," she scoffed, realizing she'd backed herself into a stone wall.

"Well, he has given me opinions on everything from Catholic emancipation to chimney sweeps, my love. I shall hold forth at length on workhouses, poorhouses, child labor, street urchins—"

"Stop it!"

"Perhaps you would wish to help me edit it," he suggested, leaning into her.

"Tony, I need time. This is not fair—"

"What isn't?"

"Everything!" she exploded. "You cannot follow me here—I left you! You cannot tell my father I am increasing when I am not! You cannot be at daggers drawn with me over Rotherfield when I like him! You cannot—"

Reluctantly he backed off, disappointing her. "All right. Do you wish me to go in there and tell your father it was all a hum? Do you wish me to sit at home without you? If Marcus is naught but a friend to you, I can accept that, I suppose."

"I don't know what I want! Please Tony—"

"All right. Perhaps 'tis best to think everything out," he sighed. "If you wish, I will tell him now." He turned to leave.

"Where are you going?"

"Home."

"Don't tell him yet." She raised her hands and then dropped them helplessly. "I shall tell him it was a mistake later."

When he reached the garden gate, he stopped with his back to her. "I do love you, you know."

She wanted to run after him—he'd said almost everything she ever wanted to hear from him. He'd promised her everything. But he hadn't mentioned Elaine Chandler. She stood rooted to the ground until long after she'd heard the gate shut.

32

Gil and Hugh stared at Tony as though he'd lost his mind. The first to recover sufficiently to speak, Gil gasped, "You wish us to do *what*?"

"Second for me."

"That's what I thought you said."

"You actually challenged Rotherfield?" Hugh asked finally. "I hope he chose swords."

"He chose pistols."

"The man's a crack shot! A marksman! Devil take it, Tony, but why'd you do a cork-brained thing like challenging Rotherfield?" Gil shook his head in disbelief. "You'd have been better off if he'd chosen rapiers."

"I am an excellent shot also."

His friends looked at each other and shook their heads. "But it ain't the same thing—shootin' a man's different from shooting game," Hugh complained.

"Well, now, Lyndon has a good eye, come to think of it." Gil allowed. "But can you kill a man?" he asked. "Hugh's right—and Rotherfield's as cold as they come. It don't make any difference to him that you're going to bleed."

"I don't know. In the war, I killed several people, but I didn't know any of them." Tony appeared to consider the matter and shook his head. "I can fire first and delope."

"And he can fire the second ball into your heart."

"Come to think of it, Tony is a crack shot. Thing is to get the first ball off," Hugh decided.

"I ain't going—don't like blood—never did. Much as I dislike Marcus Halvert, I ain't one to watch someone stuff a handkerchief in a ball hole—even on him." Gil shuddered visibly. "And if 'twas Tony, I know I'd be sick."

"I have already named you."

"Apologize to him."

"Leave him be, Gil—you do not know why Tony challenged him."

"Got a good idea. And if she was my wife, I'd take her to Lyndon Park and stay with her. She don't know how to go on, and someone needs to teach her."

"Leave Leah out of this," Tony growled.

"Dash it, but I like her! I mean, if it'd been Ponsonby or somebody like that, he'd have played the game right. But no—'tis Rotherfield!"

"Day after tomorrow, eh?" Hugh cut in on Gil's tirade. "I don't like it, but you can count on me—Gil too, for that matter. Thing is, if he gets you, what'er we supposed to tell Lady L. ? And if you get him, you'll have to flee the country. Don't see how you can win either way."

"You better hope I win." Tony favored Gil with a wry grin. "Otherwise, I shall leave it to you to make my speech in Lords for me."

"You going to speak out on Liverpool's taxes?"

"No—chimney sweeps."

"Chimney sweeps?" they chorused in unison. "Whatever for?"

"That, my friend, is precisely why I am doing it—positively no one cares a jot and 'tis time someone does something about the problem." Rising from his chair, Tony reached for his hat and set it at a truly wicked angle. "Good day, gentlemen. I am afraid I have to get my affairs in order."

Gil eyed Tony's empty glass curiously, even going so far as to sniff it. "Sherry—that's all." Waiting until he was certain that the viscount had left the club altogether, he leaned across the table to Hugh. "You don't think he's dicked in the nob, do you? I mean, he's been queer as Dick's hatband lately."

"If your wife chose Marcus Halvert for her cisisbeo, you'd be ready for Bedlam yourself," Hugh observed dryly.

"Ain't got a wife—and don't want one," Gil retorted.
"You know, Tony just might take Rotherfield. If I was a gamester . . . But I am not," Hugh decided regretfully. "No, the thing to do is go to Lady Lyndon—ten to one, she can put an end to the nonsense."

"I dunno. Say, did you hear it? 'Tis all over London that she ain't a Cit at all."

"Of course she is a Cit! She's Old King Cole's daughter, ain't she?"

"No, no—that ain't it, Hugh. She's Milbourne's granddaughter—had it from Bagshot, who had it from Lady Childredge. Seems the old lord's youngest daughter ran off with Cole when she was still in the schoolroom."

"You don't say! Well, it don't make any difference—I liked Lady L. anyway." Hugh Rivington rose and stretched. "No time to waste, old fellow."

The intent proved easier than the execution. The two men left White's in Gil's curricle, called at Lyndon House to discover that Lady Lyndon was not in and was not expected in, and drew up at *point non plus.* As a last resort, Gil suggested they try Tony's father-in-law in hopes that the old gent was fond enough of him to try to stop it. As Gil explained it, if all else failed, a Cit could go to the Charlies and swear out a complaint, whereas that would be an ungentlemanly thing to do.

To their astonishment, they found Leah Barsett instead. Speaking privately with her in Cole's library, Gil floundered about, seeking to tell her without precisely coming out and saying it, which would be a violation of the acceptable. By the time he was finished, she was thoroughly mystified.

"Forgive me, but I don't—"

"Pardon his roundaboutation, Lady Lyndon," Hugh interrupted her in disgust. "The plain fact of the matter is that Lyndon is to fight a duel, and we thought—"

"A duel! With *whom*?" For a moment she thought her world had turned on its end. "You cannot be serious!"

"Dead serious." Gil nodded. "That is, deuced serious."

"She knew what you meant the first time," Hugh

snapped. "And Lyndon has challenged Rotherfield, so there is no drawing off from it."

"*Rotherfield*? But why?" The color that had drained from her face returned in a rush. "Oh."

"Thought you ought to know of it—day after tomorrow at dawn out by Smithfield. Er . . . I trust you will not mention this matter to Lyndon? Don't want to be called out myself for telling you," Hugh explained.

"No, of course not. I appreciate knowing of it."

"Thought you might be able to stop it, you know," Gil threw in.

"Got to run—promised to m'mother for a musicale tonight. Daresay 'twill be a screeching bore, but the old girl's a widow. Come on, Gil—she cannot do anything if we are about, after all."

Leah sat and pondered the problem, wondering how she'd brought herself and Tony to such a pass. It did not seem possible that she could love him as much as she did and still be forever at daggers drawn with him. But then she'd never quite been able to discover why it was she loved him. Neither his handsomeness nor his reputation actually had much to do with it in the final discovery. Maybe she liked what every other female liked about him. Or maybe it was that precarious balance between boyish good humor and volatile temper that gave one a sense of security and danger at the same time. She didn't know, but if she did not attempt to intervene, she just might be a widow and never again know what it was to wake up next to him.

Impulsively she slipped from her father's house and persuaded one of the grooms to take her to Rotherfield's mansion in Mayfair. Bribing him to wait, she climbed the steps of the house and vigorously applied the knocker.

"Here, now . . ." his butler complained as he opened the door. And seeing her, he nearly closed it again.

"Please, is the earl at home?"

"Not to unattended females," the fellow replied stiffly.

She licked her lips, suddenly afraid he might not see her. "Pray tell him that Leah requests an interview, sir."

"Leah?" The butler looked at her again. "Just Leah?"

She did not want to risk any further gossip that might overset Tony. "Just Leah."

As fortune would have it, Rotherfield emerged from a side door and gave a start when he saw her. "Leah!"

Favoring the man who still held the door with a look of triumph, she stepped past him. Rotherfield, who now stood watching her with a faint lift of an eyebrow, nodded curtly to the butler, dismissing him.

"Er . . . you find me surprised, my dear. I would offer you some ratafia, but I have none." He opened the door to a front saloon and stood back to let her pass. Closing it after them, he turned to face her. "Is aught amiss, Leah?"

"Yes. Marcus, I have come to you because you are my friend," she began.

"Won't you sit down?"

"No—I have to think."

"And you cannot think seated," he murmured.

"No." She paced before the empty fireplace, twisting her handkerchief nervously in her hands. "We are friends, are we not?" she asked soberly.

"Of a certainty."

"Then will you mind very much not killing my husband?"

He gave a start at the directness of her appeal. "I had the distinct impression from Lyndon that you had left him."

"Well, I have, but that is nothing to the point."

"I see."

"Then you understand more than I do, my lord, for nothing is quite plain to me anymore." She caught herself and took a deep breath. "We quarreled, you see, over you."

"I collected he did not challenge me for any other reason, my dear."

"It was because I would not give up my friendship with you. You see, Marcus, I quite like you," she attempted to explain. "I still do—I always will—but . . ." She was suddenly aware that he was watching her in a way that had nothing to do with friendship. And to her horror, he was moving closer. "But what I wish to say, my lord, is that . . . that if I must choose between being friends with you and losing Tony . . ."

There was a hunger in his black eyes that almost frightened her, but she held her ground. Looking up at him with pounding heart, she found it almost impossible to finish. She'd brought herself and him and Tony to this pass with her foolish jealousy. His eyes burned as he sought something, some answer in hers.

"You are choosing Tony," he decided.

"I don't want to! Why cannot I have both?" she cried, echoing the age-old dream of women who think they can be friends with men. "You are important to me! I care that you are received! I . . . I like your company! I treasure the time we have spent together, Marcus."

"Then . . . ?" Hope flared briefly in the black eyes.

"But I love Anthony Barsett, Marcus—I love him dearly. And if he is lost to me, I do not think I can love another in quite the same way."

"I want more than friendship, Leah," he told her harshly. Moving closer, he lifted her chin, imprisoning it with long, strong fingers, holding it until he hurt her. And then his mouth came down on hers savagely, passionately, as though he could bend her to the greater will. And when he released her and stepped back, she wiped her bruised lips with the back of her hand.

"I'm sorry, my lord—truly sorry."

"So am I. I had thought to make you countess to this unworthy earl, my dear—at whatever the cost." A sad, ironic smile twisted his sensuous mouth as he looked at her. "But, alas, I could not abide loving someone who yearned for another—my pride could not stand it."

"I wish I loved you."

"Why did you leave Lyndon?"

"It doesn't matter—I'd not discuss it."

"If it was because of Elaine Chandler, the fault was mine."

"Yours?" Her eyes widened in disbelief. "How in the world could you think the fault yours? 'Twas not you who took her to King's Theater . . . 'twas not you who stayed the night with her . . . and 'twas not you who flaunted her in my face, my lord,'' she blurted out, giving voice to her hurt.

''I paid her a thousand pounds to do it.''

''You?''

''Sometimes when one wants something too much, one does not act wisely. Anthony Barsett's little affair with Elaine was over from the beginning.'' He turned away to avoid her. ''Elaine is marrying Lord Carrington, she tells me, because she wearies of being spurned. 'Tis I who should be begging your pardon, Leah.''

''You paid her to throw herself at Tony's head?''

''Yes. Now, you'd best leave before I tire of being noble, my dear.''

''Oh, Marcus.'' She came up beside him and stood on tiptoe to kiss his cheek. ''I have always known you were a better person than is thought.''

''You don't hate me?''

''Hate you? Of course I do not hate you! You are quite my dearest friend—you have given me back Tony! And you have given me my grandparents—though I am not precisely certain what to do with them,'' she admitted.

''You are most welcome,'' he muttered dryly.

''You aren't going to meet him—Tony, I mean?'' she remembered suddenly.

''If you wish it, I will delope.''

''And let him kill you? Do not be ridiculous, my lord? Just don't meet him.''

''Unless he withdraws the challenge, 'tis a matter of honor between us.''

''Unless he withdraws the challenge? Oh, he will—he *will*, I promise you! And you will cry friends with me, will you not?'' she pleaded earnestly. ''I shall miss the balloon ascensions and the drives and—''

''So should I, my dear.'' He turned around and opened his arms. ''Friends.'' And as his arms closed around her, he wondered if he would ever find another like her.

33

It was dark when Jeptha Cole's coach drew up at Lyndon House, where there was a dearth of lights. For a moment, Leah worried that he might not be home, but then noted the faint glow from his library windows. Leaning over, she kissed her father's cheek.

"D'ye want me to go in and beard him with you?" he asked gently.

"No."

"Well, I am glad for you, my dear—knew it was a good thing from the beginning. And now, with the babe and all . . . well, you'll see. Boy's got a good head, Leah. Paid me back down to the last farthing already. Damme if I don't mean to teach him m'business so's the grandson can have it."

"Papa—"

"It ain't going to be like this forever, puss," he continued, ignoring her eagerness to see her husband. "Time's coming when money'll tell as much as Quality, you know, and then my grandson'll have it all. Or the granddaughter—I guess I ain't too picky in the matter, when all's said and done. You been a joy to me—stands to reason a girl'd suit Lyndon fine, 'cept for the name, of course. But you go on—out with you."

"Thank you, Papa. I love you."

"I know you do—just like Marianna, a few thorns with the rose."

She found the house dark for the most part, the way it would be when neither she nor Tony was at home, with the servants withdrawing to their own rooms on the third floor. Letting herself in quietly, she walked carefully to where the light came through a slit beneath his library door. She half-expected him to be drinking or to have fallen asleep over a bottle. Indeed, in her mind she'd pictured every possible scene from all the lurid novels she'd read.

Instead, he was writing at his desk and did not look up when she eased the door open. For a time she stood there diffidently, watching him and waiting for him to notice her. But his pen continued to scratch across the paper rapidly, stopping only for a quick dip in the inkstand. She felt suddenly very self-conscious and unassured.

"Tony?"

A look of genuine surprise crossed his face, followed by a grin almost as wide as his jaw. His blue eyes sparkled, lit not only by the reflection of the candles but also from within. "Do not tell me—you are come home to finish this duel of hearts between us," he guessed. "You cannot leave me to my painful peace."

"Yes." Relief brought an answering smile to her face and lit her smoky eyes.

"And the battle is rejoined." His chair nearly overturned as he arose eagerly, boyishly.

"Well, I hope 'tis not always to be a battle," she offered.

"What—no citadel to be stormed?" he teased, crossing the room in easy strides.

"The defense is minimal, sir." She took a half-step back just before he reached her. "But before I capitulate entirely, I have something to say."

He stopped and nodded, the smile still on his face. "Say it now then, for the siege is about to begin."

"About Lord Rotherfield . . ." She hesitated, aware that his smile had vanished, and then forced herself to explain quickly. "Tony, I know you do not understand it, but he is a particular friend of mine. He is. And just because I love you does not mean I will give him the cut. I still mean to go about with him from time to time, but I hope you will understand that I do not love him. I never did."

The sound of insistent banging on the front knocker interrupted her. Coming from outside, they could hear the shouts of Gil and Hugh as they attempted to raise the servants. Tony padded in his stockinged feet to let them in. The two of them looked from Tony to Leah, and Gil grinned. "Glad to see you at home, Lady L!"

"Listen, you two, as much as I like you, you are decidedly *de trop*. I was just about to show my wife my speech."

"Now I know that for a hum," Gil protested.

"Won't be staying," Hugh explained. "About that little matter we discussed concerning day after tomorrow . . ." He looked up into Tony's frown. "Oh, it don't matter—she knows of it. Anyway, got to thinking—deuced silly to fight a duel when it was all a mistake, you know. Anyway, the short of the matter is that I sent a note of apology to the earl."

"You sent Rotherfield an apology? Why? The quarrel was not of your making, you know."

Hugh coughed apologetically and stepped back a safe distance. "Well, I did not say *I* was sorry actually—said you were."

"You *what*?"

"And I signed your name," he added in haste, still backing away. "Well," he continued defensively, "stands to reason he don't know your script, don't it? And I am like Gil in this—don't want to plug holes in either of you."

Behind them, Gil appeared to be having some sort of fit, going off into paroxysms of coughing that threatened to strangle him. Hugh turned around and snapped. "Now what the devil's the matter with *you*?"

"Sent him a note also," Gil choked between coughs. Catching his breath, he realized that all three of them were staring at him with expressions that ranged from incredulous to downright irate. "Well, dash it, Hugh! How was I to know you'd done it?" he demanded with a decidedly injured air. "If you'd a *told* me what you was doing, you'd a saved me the trouble."

About to deliver a scathing set-down to those who would meddle in his affairs, Tony suddenly noted that Leah had succumbed to a nearly hysterical fit of giggles. "I suppose you think 'tis amusing, but I—" He rounded on her wrathfully.

" 'Tis worse!" Leah burst out, gasping. "*I* sent him

a letter also, assuring him 'twas but a mistake, and I signed your name to it! Oh, *Tony*!'' Overcome again, she succumbed to whoops of laughter.

The ridiculousness of the situation came home to him then and his anger dissolved as he joined them, laughing to the point of tears. ''I shall look like the veriest cake,'' he groaned when he finally wiped his streaming eyes. Sliding his arm around Leah's still-shaking shoulders, he confessed, '' 'Tis as well that Marcus does not gossip in the clubs, love, for I have written him also—four apologies in all, in four different scripts. Poor Marcus—I doubt he will know what to think.''

''You were not going to meet him then?'' she managed to say as she mastered her breath. ''Oh, Tony!''

Hugh perceived that she was going to throw her arms around her husband in front of them in an unseemly display of affection. Hastily jamming Gil's hat on his head, he turned him toward the door. ''No harm's done then, I daresay—just did not wish to lose a friend, Tony. Your servant, Lady Leah. G'night. C'mon, Gilbert—we are *de trop,* I think.''

''I was afraid you would be so angry with me,'' Leah admitted, her face against her husband's shoulder as she heard the door close.

''Angry? How can I be angry? *I* had already decided that climbing boys were more important than quarreling with a man certain to put a hole in me. Besides, it is comforting to know that there are at least three people who value my skin,'' Tony told her. ''And now, my love—did you wish to see my speech?''

''I had not finished mine when we were interrupted,'' she reminded him.

''Well, as I recall, you were being apologetic and humble.'' he prompted her with a devilish gleam in his blue eyes.

''Yes—and 'tis said that confession does make one feel better, does it not? Besides, I *have* thought a great deal about what you said earlier today.'' She wavered under the warmth of his gaze. ''I—I don't want to reform you—truly I don't. I like you the way you are—no, no, that is not precisely right—I *love* you the way you are. There. I have said it. You may storm the citadel whenever you wish,'' she finished quickly.

''Alas, but you are too late.''

''Too late? But I—'' for a moment, her face mirrored her consternation, and then she perceived he was funning with her. ''Tony!''

He nodded toward the desk. ''In the morning, my dear, you may begin editing my speech.''

''I do not believe you.'' Brushing past him, she went to look. Two separate sets of papers rested on the desk. A quick glance revealed that one of them was indeed a speech on limiting the ages and working conditions of climbing boys. The other was a handwritten draft of a will.

He followed her gaze and saw her wince at the sight of the latter. ''I know,'' he consoled her, squeezing her shoulder. ''It sobered me also—made me think that there are more important matters that need attending between us ere I am ready to cock up my toes.'' His eyes twinkled as they met hers and he nodded. ''But you will have to edit my speeches, you know, else Max will have me a positively rabid Whig.''

''Morning will be quite soon enough, my lord,'' she answered saucily. ''Right now, I am more intent on making Papa happy.'' Her ringed grey eyes met his and she could not resist adding, ''Little Anthony Charles Edward Robert—or Marianna, as the case may be—is already in a fair way to being a rich merchant in Papa's mind, you know. I think we should attend to that matter first, do you not?''

''That is Anthony Edward Charles Robert, my love,'' he reminded her as he began removing pins from her hair. ''And I am committed to making him fact.''

Her arms circled his neck and she leaned back to savor the love and desire mirrored in his handsome face. ''At least we have four names with which to begin—and Marianna, of course,'' she whispered seductively.

For answer, he bent his head to hers, brushing her lips with tantalizing tenderness at first, while his hands twined in her loosened hair. And, as his kiss deepened, she answered it wholeheartedly, responding with an eagerness that matched his, savoring the strong, warm, masculine feel of him, knowing he was the grand passion of her life. There would be battles between them, verbal duels, skirmishes to be won and lost, she knew, but just now there were no words for what she felt for him.

When he raised his head at last and looked deep into her smoky eyes, his own smouldered with the intensity of his desire for her. Wordlessly, he swung her up into his arms and carried her from the room, not bothering to snuff the brace of candles that flickered behind them.